PRAISE FOR G[...]

Goh Sin Tub has reveale[...]
life through his inimitabl[...]
but are powerful in their sincerity [...]
and inspire. The Angel of Changi and Other Stories [...]
Mary Seah's spirit and altruism cannot but inspire us and give us hope
for the strength and goodness of human nature. Sin Tub always insists
that his is a small man's perspective and experience. But what he tells
are nevertheless immense in their contribution to the knowledge of
ourselves, our country and our fellowmen.

ABDULLAH TARMUGI, SPEAKER OF PARLIAMENT

I was deeply touched by Sin Tub's accounts of "ordinary" Singaporeans
as they struggled to make a living and bring up their families with
love and dignity in a bygone age. Sin Tub's book made me appreciate
just how much his generation gave us. This is truly our history brought
to life.

DR VIVIAN BALAKRISHNAN, MINISTER FOR COMMUNITY DEVELOPMENT,
YOUTH AND SPORTS; SENIOR MINISTER OF STATE FOR TRADE AND INDUSTRY

The stories brought warmth to my heart and tears to my eyes. They are
about life, about spirit, about family, about friendship... So important,
yet so often taken for granted.

CHAN SOO SEN, MINISTER OF STATE FOR EDUCATION

Storytellers have existed from our beginnings when mankind first
started to form human communities. They give a society its voice and
its memories. And through recording the past, they give it coherence
and confidence for the future. All communities must have their own
storytellers. Singapore has Goh Sin Tub and he is a very good one.

HIS EXCELLENCY, GARY QUINLAN, AUSTRALIAN HIGH COMMISSIONER
TO SINGAPORE

In reading Sin Tub's stories, one cannot help but like both the stories
and the author. The stories take us back in time and space to witness
events and meet interesting people. The author brings everything to life
with warmth, nostalgia, insight and perspective.

DR LIU THAI KER, CHAIRMAN, NATIONAL ARTS COUNCIL

THE
ANGEL
of Changi
& other short stories

GOH SIN TUB

Angsana Books

Published by  Angsana Books

Angsana Books is an imprint of

FLAME OF THE FOREST PUBLISHING Pte Ltd
Blk 5 Ang Mo Kio Industrial Park 2A
#07-22/23, AMK Tech II, Singapore 567760
Tel: (65) 6484 8887, Fax: (65) 6484 2208
mail@flameoftheforest.com

FLAME OF THE FOREST PUBLISHING
95085 North Bank Rogue Road A/B
Gold Beach, Oregon 97444-9543 USA
Tel: (541) 247 2924, Fax: (541) 247 0373
info@flameoftheforest.com

www.flameoftheforest.com

Printed in Singapore

ISBN 981-3056-90-8

This book is humbly dedicated to

M. P. S.

who has been
my inspiration and guiding light

My Husband, The Author

Sin Tub was a family man, a devoted husband, father and grandfather. Despite his varied and demanding career spanning over five decades, he always made time for family and friends.

He was also a very compassionate man, serving the community by being involved in numerous charities.

It was always his ambition to establish himself as a writer and he set about doing this when he retired from banking in 1986. I'm glad that he achieved this personal goal before he passed away in November last year.

His writings are a real treasure trove of memories for me. Whenever I read one of his stories, I can remember the enthusiasm and the hard work he put into it. He was very passionate about Singapore having been in the civil service before independence, and in the formative years. Those were exciting times and my husband felt it was his mission to capture for posterity the aspirations of those times.

He always felt as in everything he did, that Singapore could be more than just an economic success. It could also become something more meaningful; a special caring community. This is what drove him to write so many books. In all his stories, there are some lessons or values that he hoped current and future generations of Singaporeans would appreciate.

Sylvia Goh
July 2005

FOREWORD

It gives me great pleasure to write this foreword.

Mr Goh Sin Tub was one of Singapore's most gifted and admired citizens. In a long and productive career, he had distinguished himself as a teacher, social worker, civil servant, banker, property developer and writer. During the past 20 years, he had published 20 books of poetry, fiction and short stories.

It has been said by a wise man that one of the things which binds a people as a nation is their shared memories of the past and their shared aspirations for the future. Memories of the past are therefore important to the life of a nation. Many of Goh Sin Tub's stories embody such memories, about people, events, places, etc. Mr Goh was an accomplished storyteller. I have always enjoyed reading his stories. I like the fact that many of his stories are positive and uplifting.

There are many wonderful stories in this new volume. For example, the story about Mary Seah, the Angel of Changi. I had not heard of her before. I was inspired by the heroism of this brave Singaporean and very proud of the fact that Australia has conferred on her its highest award, the Order of Australia.

Mr Goh Sin Tub passed away recently. This volume will therefore be published posthumously. I want to thank Mr Goh for his contributions to our history and heritage. I am proud to have known him.

Tommy Koh
Chairman
National Heritage Board
July 2005

CONTENTS

ENCOUNTERS

DISCOVERIES

FAMILY GEMS

Unforgettable Vignettes

We Live And Learn

ENCOUNTERS

THE ANGEL OF CHANGI

NOT many Singaporeans have heard of her. She was called "The Angel of Changi". The Australian POWs in Singapore during the last War affectionately christened her with that name. Indeed Australians know more about this heroine of World War II than her own fellow Singaporeans, myself included till I discovered her recently.

Six whole decades had to pass after the Japanese Occupation of Singapore before I found the Angel: Mrs Mary Seah. And then only by accident, a chance mention in a conversation with her son Seah Kim Bee, a soft-spoken and modest man whom I knew from way back in the years of the Occupation.

We were exchanging nostalgic memories at a recent reunion of a few surviving Occupation buddies when the subject unexpectedly turned to our families. And Kim Bee casually mentioned, "You know, my late mum's a heroine to Australians. They have actually named her 'The Angel of Changi' in their newspapers. And the Australian government has even recognised her with a prestigious award: The Order of Australia."

I was intrigued. Kim Bee had never mentioned his mum to me before. I plied him with questions and dug out the story of "My mum, the Angel of Changi…"

MRS MARY SEAH was an accidental heroine. She never saw herself assuming that role to captured soldiers. When war broke out, she was a woman young and good-looking in her late 30s, a nurse, and a single mother separated from her husband and raising nine children in straitened circumstances made worse by the war (in that respect, already very much a heroine!). A committed Christian, she cared deeply for others, and she raised her children that way.

Her third son, Kim Tee, enlisted in the local volunteer force to fight for Singapore. Well-built for his age (16 years), he was able to get past the registration staff and enrolled despite the minimum age requirement of 18 years.

When General Tomoyuki Yamashita's Japanese soldiers invaded Malaya in December 1941, sweeping swiftly down the Peninsula, Kim Tee went on active duty at the front, serving in logistics, delivering food supplies to the front-line forces. Mary and her fifth child, my friend Kim Bee, who was only 13 then, helped him in those hazardous convoys of supplies to the troops fighting north of Singapore. Kim Tee was well-liked by his Australian comrades-in-arms. But his underage status was soon uncovered and, even though the fighting had already started, his concerned Australian friends were adamant that he was far too young to be in such grave danger of life and limb, and saw to it that he was immediately sent back home.

Unfortunately his name remained on the service records — and the Japanese uncovered that when they occupied Singapore.

So they came for the boy at the family home. They required him (and other local volunteers) to report for registration at the YMCA at Bras Basah Road. There, after waiting long hours for transport, those not packed into the trucks that came were told to go home and report again another day. Kim Tee was twice released that way. Then on the third and last occasion he was accommodated on a truck, though others got off.

He was never seen again.

The volunteers who were herded into the trucks were not sent to POW camps. Instead they were taken to the beaches of Changi.

There they were shot dead.

Mary Seah did not know that then. She kept on hoping that her son might be detained with other POWs in the camps set up by the Japanese. After all, as she heard, the Australian and other allied soldiers were kept in such camps. So why not the local soldiers too?

News reached her ears in 1942 that Kim Tee could be in the camp in the Sennett Estate area. Food was already in short supply and Mary worried whether the many prisoners there were getting enough to eat.

She wanted to go to the camp to look for her son — or at least, to help those brave comrades with whom her son had fought side by side in the war.

She hesitated. She was under no illusions. It would be dangerous. She had heard stories about atrocities committed by the invaders: Shootings and assaults. As a young woman, there was also the very real terror of rape.

Should she go?

A devout Anglican, that night she prayed to God for courage and guidance. She opened her Bible and the words of Psalm 23 gave her strength:

"Yea, though I walk through the valley of the shadow of death,
I will fear no evil;
For You are with me…"

The next day Mary packed some food and got Kim Bee to go with her. He took her on his bicycle from Sophia Road, where they lived then, to the Sennett Camp seven kilometres away. She sat on the handlebar tightly holding on to her packed food with one hand and the bicycle handlebar with the other, while young Kim Bee sweated on the pedals and the bicycle wobbled all the way to the camp.

At the camp entrance they found fierce-looking Japanese guards in front of the barricades with barbed wire. Mary and her son approached them. Before they could even get near enough to request to be allowed in, the guards yelled at them in Japanese and signalled them to scram.

Instant failure!

They left the entrance but started to walk around the perimeter of the camp. They found it enclosed by an earth bund, forbidding-looking though only about one-and-a-half metres high. Above the bund was a hostile fence stringed with barbed wires.

Mary got her son to climb up the bund to take a look. "See if your brother is in there. Throw the food over to the prisoners!"

Kim Bee climbed up. He did not find his brother there. What he saw was a mass of POWs. And all in their birthday suits! It was four in the afternoon and the POWs had returned from work duties outside the camp and finished their baths and washed their clothes. With only one set of clothes to use, they now wore nothing.

They were excited to see Kim Bee on the top of the bund holding the packages in his hands. They beckoned to him to throw down to them whatever he had — the cooked food and fruits he had brought. Without hesitation he did so and they rushed forward to grab them. And then the boy climbed down, back to the safety of the road outside.

Only then was Kim Bee aware that behind him some local people had been shouting to him to get off the bund. They told him why. Other people had climbed up the bund to have a look before and they had been shot at by the guards, and some had been killed! Kim Bee turned pale. And he saw his Mum's face — it was even paler.

That was the first visit Mary made to the Aussies and other POWs in the camp — she was their angel-to-be. It was a beginning, inauspicious and insignificant though it was.

Others would have given up, but not Mary. She thought over what had happened. She prayed for guidance: *How could she get in through the entrance to find out if her son was in there — or at least to see what help she could give to the prisoners? How was she to enter that doorway?*

"Knock and it will be opened to you…" The words of the Bible came readily to her as she read through the good book.

So Mary, inspired with faith and hope, went again to the

camp. This time she did get in, past the Japanese sentry at the entrance without being chased away. What happened was a miracle. As she was trying to communicate with the sentry, the door of the guard office opened — and out stepped a Japanese officer, someone who spoke English. To Mary it was as though she had knocked on that door and it had opened to her! She boldly asked the officer for permission to go into the camp to sell or give away her vegetables and fruits to the prisoners.

And Mary noticed something about the officer. He was not well. His voice was hoarse and he was sweating although the day was not hot. Her nursing instincts surfaced. She revealed her profession and offered him some medicine she had brought along in case her son had needed it. The officer's attitude towards her changed instantly. Concern was rare, especially from the local people for the Japanese — and he appreciated it all the more as he was feeling low.

The officer gave her permission to go in, though escorted by a guard.

Nervously she walked in. The prisoners crowded round her. She sold to those who had money — which she needed to buy more supplies. She gave freely to those without money. Mary was not doing what she did for gain. After the war, surviving prisoners would refer to her as visiting them "disguised as a hawker".

On the way out after that visit, the guard reported to the officer what he had witnessed. Mary saw a gentler look in the officer's eyes.

He told Mary candidly that feeding the prisoners was a chore the Japanese might willingly share with any trustworthy person willing to help out. He authorised her to organise daily supply of some items of perishables to the prisoners. He even promised to try to meet payment for them in part, though he made it clear his funds were limited. She should not expect to make any profit at all — more likely she would have to beg from others to help out. Mary nodded.

Yes, the door had been opened to her.

Mary and her family then organised themselves for their POW supply operation, small though it was. They secured transport: An old tricycle. They sourced for bananas, pineapples and vegetables from Malaya that arrived daily at the wholesale shops in Rochor Road not far from their home in Sophia Road. And resourceful young Kim Bee made friends with the wholesalers, providing them free manual labour over and above the meagre subsidy they got from the Japanese camp officer to pay for supplies.

For five days every week the boy would pedal his loaded tricycle, with his mum on it as well, all the way from Sophia Road to Sennett Camp. The guards at the entrance would randomly bayonet the packed baskets of perishables in search of forbidden items that might be concealed — anything other than the fruits and vegetables allowed.

After that check they would be allowed in, at first always closely escorted by a guard but later under more relaxed surveillance. Some of the guards were more sympathetic by nature and these became friendly with her — especially as she was a dedicated nurse and would help them with much-needed advice when they were ill. But some remained hostile, especially those few who tried to touch and otherwise take advantage of her and got soundly rebuffed.

Mary always asked if anyone had news of her missing son. And always the poor mother would be disappointed. But her mission of searching for her missing son had translated into a mission of mercy to help her son's erstwhile comrades-in-arms. It no longer mattered that her son was not among the prisoners — at least she could help her son's comrades.

And her help began to go beyond supplying food. Soon the POWs were begging her to smuggle in medicines, something prohibited by the Japanese. She agreed to run the risk. But how was she to get such special supplies?

"Whom shall I ask?" She prayed for the answer.

A name came to mind. She boldly went to ask him: A doctor she knew, one Dr Lim Han Hoe. She knew the man's reputation as a compassionate doctor. But would he be willing to risk his life supplying medicine for her to smuggle to the prisoners? And would he tell on her? In those anxious times good people had been known to turn bad. The doctor listened to her. To Mary's relief, he responded positively to her request on behalf of the POWs. He would not accept any payment at all and he continued to keep her supplied with medicine the POWs needed.

Then the POWs went further. They asked their angel for more.

They needed parts for their secret radio sets. And technical books for the set-up know-how. They explained why radio reception was so vital to the POWs. The overseas broadcasts kept them informed on the progress of the war. The Allies were already winning. Soon it would all be over. Receiving such heartening news gave a great boost to the prisoners' morale. For many it supplied the will to survive.

But it was a thing of high risk for Mary to get involved in. The Japanese were ruthless with those caught with short-wave sets. Those possessing or listening to prohibited broadcasts, or abetting by providing parts, faced possible execution.

Still the brave woman agreed to help her POW friends. And miraculously, somehow or other, she was always able to find whatever parts or manuals they needed. And somehow make delivery without getting caught.

Where did the prisoners conceal their radio sets? They showed Mary a secret radio hidden in an oil drum. The top part was a planter for a tomato plant. The bottom was empty — except for the concealed radio. They also showed her how they hid essential radio parts inside the false leg of an amputated soldier.

They trusted her. They knew she would never betray them, no matter what.

That trust was to be put to the test.

The Japanese guards had begun to suspect that somehow the POWs were receiving radio news. Perhaps the increasing cheerfulness of the prisoners gave them away as the Allies were beginning to win significant battles at land and sea and in the skies, no matter what false propaganda the Japanese came up with in their news releases.

The Japanese searched the camp many times but they could never find radios or anything connected to them. *How were the prisoners getting their radio parts? Who was helping them?*

Some guards (those who did not like her) suspected the plucky woman who seemed the POWs' only link to the outside world.

So those guards detained her.

They slapped and punched and kicked her mercilessly, accusing her point blank as though they had evidence. Some POWs said that she was even bayoneted, though she never mentioned anything about that to her family.

The guards also alleged that some prisoner had already squealed on her. She did not believe them. They threatened to chop off her head if she did not cooperate and reveal how the prisoners got their radio parts and where they hid their radios.

They could not get anything out of her.

So they made her stand in the sweltering sun and the drenching rain out on the driveway of a building they occupied near the camp — the St Andrew's School building in Woodsville. They thought the anxiety of uncertainty and the agony of torture would surely break the woman down.

For days they kept up their torment. But brave as a martyr, she remained silent, praying all the while, giving away nothing — and no one. Faith gave her indomitable strength as the words of the Bible sustained her:

> *"The Lord is my light and my salvation;*
> *Whom shall I fear?*
> *The Lord is the strength of my life:*
> *Of whom shall I be afraid?"*

The prisoners heard about what the guards were doing to Mary. They went in a delegation to the more sympathetic guards. They got them to speak up for her. Those tormenting her were at first unrelenting, but some had begun to waver after the woman remained tight-lipped despite a week of punishing treatment.

Perhaps, it was true: The woman hawker knew nothing about secret radios in the camp?

Then providence came to her rescue. (Or was that engineered by some guards with connections?) News came of an impending inspection by a team headed by a General coming to check on camp control — and on the guards in charge.

There would be questions asked about perceived lapses in control, and who knows what might come out of all that? A quick decision was made to sweep all potential evidence of faults under the carpet — and Mary found herself suddenly released and told to go back home!

Before she left, she boldly asked her tormentors, "Can I come back to carry on my business here?" That gave weight to her stance of innocence — why else would she want to come back? The guards who detained her concluded they might have been barking up the wrong tree. They agreed she could return later.

So Mary resumed her help for the POWs who, by now, worshipped her as their invincible heroine.

THEN came the transfer of the POWs to Changi Prison — most of them were moved off, though some were left in the old camp.

Before their transfer out of Sennett Camp the Australians begged Mary to come and visit them. She promised them she would try although she was worried. She knew Changi would be more strictly guarded — and therefore more dangerous for her if the POWs needed her to smuggle in any forbidden items.

She got a letter of introduction from the Japanese officer-in-charge at Sennett Camp and, armed with that, she went to see her friends inside the Changi prison.

Fortunately, Changi was better supplied with food and medicine. And the prisoners did not seem to need more transmitter parts — or perhaps they were aware of the greater risk and decided they could not endanger their angel of mercy.

Mary made her visits to Changi alone. She did not want to put her children at peril. And she continued to visit her Changi POWs right up to the end of the war.

Her visits meant a lot to the POWs, and after the war many of them remembered her and wrote about her (both in public testimony in the media as well as in private letters): How she brought good cheer to them when they sorely needed a friend — and more than a friend, an angel!

A few days after the end of the war, Mary and her family were pleasantly surprised to be at the receiving end of a POW visit.

A prisoner, one Mr E A Parker, upon liberation by the Allied forces, actually walked all the way from Changi Prison to Mary's family home (then shifted to Tronoh Road in the city) to thank her personally and to bring her his gift: His very first ration of provisions and chocolates from the Red Cross, precious things indeed, and hard to come by in those first days of liberation!

And the plaudits just continued to roll in:

"Hundreds of Australian and British troops remember Mrs Seah as 'The Angel of Changi' who endured fearlessly as she was slapped, bayoneted and exposed for long periods to the searing sun by suspicious Japanese guards…" (*The Australian,* Wednesday, February 22, 1961).

"Many Australians are indebted to her…" (Dr E E Dunlop, President of the Prisoners of War and Relations' Association).

"Wherever we are gathered in reunions of today,
Synonymous with courage is the name of Mary Seah,
For in that hell of Changi with its depth of misery,
She kept alive the gentle spark that spells humanity…"

(from a poem by Ruby Penna of Victoria Park published in *Countrywoman* magazine).

Mary became so highly regarded by the ex-POW community in Australia that they invited her as the Guest of Honour at the National POW celebrations of the 50th anniversary of Victory in the Pacific (VP) Day on August 15, 1995.

With such persistent accolades, the laurels heaped on Mary had to be endorsed by the Australian Government itself. So on Australia Day, 1996, Mary Seah was conferred the prestigious Order of Australia.

MARY SEAH passed away on February 28, 2000. The Australians have saluted their Angel of Changi — recording her beloved name into their history books and their national roll of honour as revered heroine, even though a foreigner.

Singapore has precious few war heroes and heroines enshrined into legends. Mrs Mary Seah, humble nurse and homemaker, but our very own Angel of Changi, deserves like remembrance in her own country. So far she has received scant mention, a spot here and there — truly spotty recognition.

Come 2005, we celebrate the Diamond Jubilee of VP Day. That could be the time to accord her a place in our national memory. Let us all then hold up, for overdue honour by Singaporeans, Mary Seah: Mother, nurse — and Singapore heroine!

Mrs Mary Seah, The Angel of Changi, with her five sons (standing, from left) Andrew, Kim Khoo and Kim Bee; and (seated, from left) Kim Tuan and Joseph. Picture taken in the early 60s.

Mrs Mary Seah with her extended family: Her five sons (standing, from left) Andrew, Kim Khoo, Kim Bee, Kim Tuan and Joseph, and son-in-law (standing, second from left); two daughters Rosie and Winnie (middle row, from left); four daughters-in-law (seated, front row); and eight grandchildren. Photograph taken in the early 60s.

Mrs Mary Seah (front row, fifth from left) with her younger sister Stella (on her left) and extended family. Photograph taken in the late 70s.

The Angel of Changi, Mrs Mary Seah Snr A M, after the investiture of the Order of Australia award at the 1996 Australia Day Honours function with her youngest daughter Rosie (left) and granddaughters Anna and Pamela (right).

THE GAKKO

THOSE of us who survived it came through the time with recollections of the strangest episode of our lives, weird and intense, even though brief — an existence literally under aliens from another world, three-and-half years of Occupation by the Enemy.

Yet Goh and his fellow students of similar vintage who enrolled at the Gakko were fortunate compared with other Singapore people then.

The Gakko (school) was set up by the Japanese Military Administration to be a special place, a kind of "hothouse" for the new youth. Its mission was to teach young Singapore people Nippon-go (the Japanese language). And its full name was long enough to be a Nippon-go lesson in itself: Syonan Gunseikanbu Kokugo Gakko (Syonan Military Administration National Language School).

Those selected found themselves special wards of an extraordinary band of Japanese people. These were the *sensei* (teachers) cadre conscripted into the Imperial Army from schools in Japan to serve overseas with conferred honorary officer ranking that ranged from captain to colonel. These *sensei* were sensitive persons compared to their compatriots, though we students still found there were barriers to be crossed — learning to understand *them* and getting them to understand *us*.

The *sensei* (Torii, Nito, Abe, Watanabe, Uemura, Matsuda, Sugihara, Hayashi and others) soon proved themselves worlds apart from those savage soldiers who first swept in and tyrannised our conquered country, a lost people.

Goh had been at the school some weeks earlier studying under Nito-Sensei, but he had fallen ill and had to absent himself; and so, on his return he had to join a new intake.

He wondered about his new teacher.

Would he be like Nito-Sensei? Would he relax after a while and transform into someone who would likewise show us sympathy, perhaps also to the extent of passing on his food ration coupons and clothes and shoes to some of us? Or would this sensei keep that rock-like hardness, that indoctrinated Japanese trait of acceptance of hardship, rigid obedience to superiors, the hallmark of a war-readied generation raised on that austere code they called "Nihon-seishin" (the Zeitgeist of Japan that allowed no compassion)? If or when tested, what would prevail with this new teacher? Personal conscience and compassion or only that Yamato-damashii (Spirit of Old Japan)?

That first day of Hiro-Sensei at the Gakko was to prove unforgettable for the students. It was the new intake's first ceremonial assembly in the school yard. All who lined up there, except for Goh, had joined the Gakko only a day earlier.

They were standing *yasume* (at ease) when they heard the school prefect suddenly yell out, *"Ki o tsuke!"* The class jumped to attention as ordered. A Japanese officer in uniform, complete with samurai sword in leather scabbard, mounted the platform and executed an elaborate right-angle bow (which compliment the class obediently returned — that being one of the lessons of staying alive that they had quickly imbibed: Always bow to the Japanese, stiffly all the way down, nothing short of 90 degrees).

"Hiro-Sensei *desu*," the new teacher introduced himself solemnly.

Hiro-Sensei was not tall, at most 1.6 metres. He was broad of body, built like a boxer. His head was clean-shaven giving him a Buddhist monk aura. His shiny face was unsmiling even though it did not look threatening. His small eyes looked unblinking at everyone, neither friendly nor unfriendly, though a glint in them warned Goh: *The man is strict even if probably fair.*

Goh was soon to be provided with one word in Nippon-go to sum up Hiro-Sensei, an ideal of character that the teacher himself stressed repeatedly to his class. From Day One, Hiro-

Sensei himself presented that word to his class:

Man-majime!

Majime meant earnestness, and *man-majime* was literally complete earnestness. That was the epitome of character to Hiro-Sensei. It meant, to the best of the students' grasp, the zenith of honesty and integrity, dignity, dedication, steadfastness, in full control no matter how provoked — and all that expressed with dignity of mien and deliberation of movement.

"First we raise *Hinomaru* (flag), then we sing *Kimigayo* (National Anthem), then we bow in direction of *Tenno-heika* (Emperor), and then we shout three cheers: '*Tenno-heika banzai!*' (Long live the Emperor!)," Hiro-Sensei ordered in Japanese, considerately adding English subtitles since the students were new.

Hinomaru was raised, *Kimigayo* was sung, *Tenno-heika* was duly bowed to, then came the last act: The *banzai* hurrah. That should have been rendered smartly and with vigour, both hands raised and lowered for each round, voice loud and face grave, all in solemn synchrony.

Unfortunately, there was a joker out in front of the assembly that day. That stupid fellow, Siow, after his first shout truly and properly rendered, could not resist doing the then in-thing, a joke privately shared among local folks, a mispronunciation in Hokkien, which he deliberately delayed so as to be out of synchrony:

"Tenno-heika pang-sai!"

Which translated nicely, or rather not nicely, into "The Emperor is shitting!"

That naturally had a few students in giggles and the rest in barely contained spasms of mirth amid their general shocked silence.

And any remnant of control burst into open guffaws when, for the third hurrah, loud and clear, the joker repeated the Hokkien version.

Hiro-Sensei was no fool. He did not understand Hokkien, but he understood ridicule.

Goh could read what the teacher must have been thinking: *This moment is a moment of high earnestness. That impudent young-ster is mocking the most sacred cheer. The Emperor has been insulted The fellow must be taught a lesson — and instantly too, otherwise there will be no more discipline!*

Hiro-Sensei did not lose his cool. The next thing the class knew, agile and a sudden samurai, the deceptively heavy-look-ing teacher had leapt off the stage! He was now in front of Siow — in confrontation stance.

And his right hand on the hilt of his sword.

It was touch and go — or looked like it. Would he go the whole hog? Unsheathe his blade? Slash the boy down like a pig?

As the scene froze, everyone waited with bated breath.

Hiro-Sensei let that suspense sink in.

Then his hand moved away from his sword. He was not going that way.

He opened his big hands and walked towards Siow.

What? He's going to embrace that benighted lad?

Instead he waded into the youth and slapped him left and right, hard and deliberate, calling out *"Bakayaro!* (Fool!)*"* with each blow.

But despite his anger, his face stayed solemn — and unmoving.

And he did not throw Siow out of school.

He made him climb up on stage and bow to everyone to whom he owed apology: To Hiro-Sensei, to the other students and, of course, to *Tenno-heika* — three times with due solem-nity.

The incident was the cue for Hiro-Sensei's discourses on his expectations of high seriousness: The landmark introduc-tion to further glimmerings of that mystique of *man-majime*.

Over the next few weeks and months, Goh and his classmates began to discover what made Hiro-Sensei tick.

They did not understand him completely, only better, through his lessons that taught Nippon-go while introducing Nippon *bunka* (Japanese culture), and through moving songs that had stirred young Japanese minds — and were now, strange to say, stirring the hearts of us, the Singapore students at the Gakko.

Some of Sensei's pronouncements called for impossible faith and remained an enigma, such as the claim (bare-faced but not pressed) that the Japanese Emperor was a god, nothing less, and a direct descendant from Amaterasu-Oomikamisama, that legendary ancestor goddess of the Japanese race.

Other teachings sank in readily: The decadence of the West. The iniquity of colonial rule. The arrogance of white supremacy claims. Asia must be for Asians. Indeed Asia was destined to be the new day as sure as sunrise: *Hikari wa toho yori* (Light shines from the East)…

Above all things, the keyword, *man-majime*, spelt stern purpose and uncompromising dedication. The seriousness of life left no place for ignorance or innocence, nor for pleasure or frivolity!

HIRO-SENSEI'S savage chastisement of Siow shocked everyone at first. Surely what the boy did was only high jinks. The new teacher had come to them, looking polite and placid, yet he could suddenly turn physical and inflict an assault on the teenager so fierce that it sent him sprawling on the ground. And all that while Hiro-Sensei kept his uncanny control, his face expressionless and enigmatic — in *man-majime* mode…

Siow was not let off after that first day.

He was required to see Sensei after school daily for the next few days. *Was he being whacked repeatedly, at least verbally? Or just being made to stay back in penance class?*

The day after his thrashing, Siow bravely showed up in

class, though he carried a hang-dog look on his normally cheeky face. Goh and some others made it a point to chat with him, more to show peer sympathy. Not a single word was said about the *banzai* incident, neither in funny Hokkien nor in *majime* Nippon-go.

But a few days later Siow was holding his head high again, though he was no more his old perky self. That frivolous Siow was gone for good.

Hiro-Sensei seemed to be warming towards him. In class he asked Siow to read passages from the textbook and even got him to lead the rest in going over songs already learned. Whatever they were, those sessions with Sensei were changing the boy.

Before long Siow was appointed class monitor, the one given the honour of shouting aloud the *"Ki o tsuke!"* order as Sensei walked in, and leading the *"Sayonara, Sensei!"* salutation at close of class — duties the boy took dead seriously and performed with lively aplomb.

Cheeky Siow had come full circle, becoming Sensei's full convert — the first of the students to embrace *man-majime!*

AS OCCUPATION stretched from months into years, things became tougher for Singapore people.

Food was now in dire short supply. Rice was so precious people ate only watered down gruel, and that with tough leaves and roots, or even only sauce or salt.

To aggravate matters, destitute immigrants swarmed in from neighbouring islands — to beg or steal.

And soon they were collapsing as starving vagrants in the streets of Singapore. Crimes, especially petty thefts, were a daily happening.

And now and then, in the alleys and drains, Singapore people would come upon inert bodies of those strangers, bloated and stinking to high heaven, flies buzzing all over them...

One day one such beggar was caught red-handed by Hiro-Sensei and some students. He was trying to steal an old bicycle one of the students had left in the yard. The man, his dark face pale with fear, fell on his knees and begged to be let off. He said he was starving. That was why he had to steal.

Sensei was unmoved. He sent for the police, the *mata-mata* (or local police constables) under the Japanese regime. They came and for openers instantly administered on the weak fellow that mandatory barrage of resounding slaps, Japanese-style.

The poor man just let himself be hit till he crumpled, a whimpering bundle on the ground.

"Poor fellow! Hungry beggars like him are dying in our streets," Goh heard the owner of the old bicycle voice his pity aloud to Hiro-Sensei. Perhaps hoping that Sensei might tell the police to let the fellow off.

Even the police seemed to seek a reason to let him off. "You did not actually see him take your bicycle, did you?" the police asked the owner. The youth decided to shake his head.

"Did anyone see him steal?" the police now asked generally. Everyone kept quiet — except Hiro-Sensei.

"I have to tell the truth. People must not tell lies, whatever the reason… Yes, I saw him stealing it," he said.

The police took the thief away.

"What will they do to him, Sensei?" Goh asked.

"They may execute him. They have authority to do that. They can't allow stealing to go unpunished, can they? As it is, there's too much crime. If he's lucky, they may just dump him back on one of the islands," Hiro-Sensei said.

Goh saw his expressionless face and wondered.

No feelings at all, Sensei?

"Criminals must be punished. Black is black and white is white," Hiro-Sensei repeated his point, this time with a frown on his white face. It was a tough moment, indeed — for *man-majime* had been tested.

35

GOH did well in Hiro-Sensei's class and moved up to a higher class. Sensei somehow got the principal, Takayama-Sensei, to approve appointing Goh as a teaching assistant even though it was not strictly right as he had not yet graduated. The principal was a tough nut to crack, another *man-majime* kind of guy. So Hiro-Sensei must have been very persuasive on Goh's behalf.

Sensei felt it necessary to justify to Goh what he did. *It was because Goh earned the appointment as his best student.* But Goh knew better: Sensei did it to help him earn money to tide over the increasingly hard times.

Goh treasured the appointment for another reason. It brought him into the Gakko's inner circle. He was now Sensei's colleague, addressed as Goh-Sensei by teachers and students alike. And he could talk with his Japanese mentors more often and at (more or less) equal level.

Those exchanges were to open new doors…

ONE evening Goh was alone with Hiro-Sensei after school. Sensei opened up to him. He told him a story and ended it with a song. He had a soft but gravel-like voice that suited the story he told. And Goh sensed the confiding of a personal sorrow deep inside Sensei's heart.

It revealed something Goh had never thought about — that victory was not necessarily a triumph, it could come bitter as defeat. The story told the feelings of a Japanese soldier entering the just-conquered town of Singapore at dawn on February 15, 1942. He bore in his arms the treasured remains of his fallen comrade, a close friend who had gone through the hell of war with him. The story details were bare: He went on to bury his buddy on a hill, beneath a flying *Hinomaru* flag… it was Sensei's feelings that infused depth into that narration.

And then Sensei sang.

And the song transported the two of them into the surreal

atmosphere of that scene on a Singapore hill…

Goh felt Sensei's inconsolable anguish even before he started to explain the words — and, at the very end, reveal the meaning it held for him:

"Ichiban nori o yarunda to
Rikinde shinda senyu no
Ikotsu o daite ima hairu
Singaporu no machi no asa…"

Goh knew enough Nippon-go to understand the import of the dirge even as Sensei's voice cracked while reciting the verses in a toneless chant. He saw that Sensei's eyes were filled with tears — the first time ever that the man in Sensei allowed his feelings to show through his *man-majime* face.

Goh's eyes reddened too as Sensei quietly went on to share meaning — and soul. The despair of loss. The utter waste. And yet, at the end of it all, that endorsement of undying devotion to duty and to cause — onward with the war… *Bushido* (the way of the warrior)!

Hiro-Sensei concluded: "That song was written soon after the battle for Singapore…"

And then, in a whisper, he added, "It is about my own brother…"

He did not clarify which one was his brother — the soldier grieving over his comrade's ashes or the one killed in battle. Goh did not ask. It did not seem right to ask. Also it did not seem to matter. What mattered was *Bushido* was upheld — with *man-majime*…

Yes, that sadness of bitter victory came through, full force, to Goh. As his pulse quickened and his face reddened, he felt that rush of spirit. Yes, he too felt *Nippon-seishin* (spirit of Japan).

And yet, was he not of the other side, the conquered people, the enemy, the ones terrorised and battered and many even killed by those very invading Japanese soldiers: The ones Sensei sang about as heroes?

Should he, on his part, reveal to Sensei the atrocities committed by those soldier-savages under General Yamashita? Those Japanese over-ran Singapore town and immediately set about to tyrannise and kill the conquered civilians. For Japanese people like Sensei, those heinous things must have been glossed over — they could not have known about that inhumane cruel first wave!

Goh now wrestled with his own *man-majime* — commitment to truth and high seriousness, no matter what consequences...

Goh decided to do what he had to do. Duty. *Man-majime*.

In a soft voice, he spoke to Sensei about the *Sook Ching*. That heinous Operation Sweep Clean unleashed in the first days of the Japanese conquest of Singapore town. That massacre which the Singapore people dared to speak about only in secret. The thousands of victims haphazardly accused of being anti-Japanese and taken away in trucks never to be seen again. (After the war the estimate rose beyond thousands to tens of thousands.)

Goh had no song with which to end his story. His heroes remained unsung.

Hiro-Sensei listened in silence. His head bowed down low, his broad shoulders now drooped to a slouch of shame.

And Goh saw that Sensei's eyes were tear-filled once more.

This time the tears were not for *Bushido*...

IN THE days that followed Goh and Sensei entered each other's world again and again with new candour, as never before — and yet always without criticism or rancour between them.

Goh spoke about the tragic aftermath of the *Sook Ching* — the further toll on families of the missing. The anxiety of the bereaved. False hopes cruelly raised and brutal victimisation by swindlers who came with lies about survivors needing help and money. And, in the end, the total despair...

On his part, on other occasions, Sensei still spoke about the heroism and sacrifices of the Japanese soldiers, warriors now aware of prospect of defeat yet fighting on...

And then he spoke about the *Kamikaze* (the storm of the gods). Suicide bombers who dived headlong into enemy battleships in those desperate last battles against superior forces.

Man-majime to the end.

He was proud of them.

And so too was Goh.

A unique bond was forged between them. Facts were facts — not to be denied or argued. *Seishin* (spirit) was *seishin*, not to be denied either. No futile judgment to be passed. Only the judgment of grieving face and grave spirit...

THEFT occurred again at the Gakko.

Things were stolen from the teachers' room. It could be one of the students, or an outsider — or perhaps even the caretaker himself.

Goh's chief suspect was the caretaker. He had an honest face but Goh no longer trusted anyone on face value.

Han was small-built, a bony scarecrow of a man. He was already working as caretaker at the building before the Japanese commandeered it for use as the Gakko. So he was hired as caretaker. His wages were low, but he was a bachelor and did not need much to live on — at first. As life became grimmer and his starving relatives ate through their savings and now came to live with him and depend on his earnings, he looked even more gaunt.

At first only small items went missing. Then more valuable things, many of them teachers' personal belongings left at school.

Takayama-Sensei gave orders that no mercy should be shown to the thief when caught. Man or woman or child, the fellow was to be beaten up and handed over to the police.

Then one night Goh and Hiro-Sensei caught Han red-handed in the teachers' room.

The two were the only ones around. Goh returned from the toilet, only minutes before Sensei came back from meeting a friend nearby.

As Goh walked in he caught Han opening a teacher's drawer to take out something. On seeing Goh he dropped the item back at once and closed the drawer.

Looking guilty and frightened, Han held on to Goh's hands, crying repeatedly, "Please don't report me!"

At that moment, they heard Sensei behind them asking what the matter was.

"I've caught our thief. I saw Han going through a drawer. He's now begging to be let off…" Goh told Sensei.

Han went on his knees to Sensei. He claimed he did not take anything. He begged for mercy, pleading for his relatives dependent on him.

He wept as he said his only brother was one of those who had disappeared in the Sook Ching. His family had become destitute and turned to him for food…

Goh now regretted accusing him before Sensei.

He recalled what had happened to the bicycle thief. And how Sensei had been unrelenting.

But Sensei had already rung up the principal. Takayama-Sensei lived close by and he came over at once. He asked what happened?

"Before we call the police, tell me what did Han steal? Who saw him? The police will want the facts — and witnesses."

Han looked pleadingly at Goh.

Goh decided on what to say — and what not to. "I found Han here in this room — the teachers' room. But now that I think about it, I did not actually see him take anything. I could have jumped to the wrong conclusion. He could have been only dusting and cleaning the place…"

Han took the cue. He said yes, yes, he was only dusting

and cleaning the room.

Takayama-Sensei looked disgusted. He turned to the one person he could trust to be *man-majime*, to tell the whole truth, regardless of feelings or consequences.

"Hiro-Sensei, you saw him steal, right?"

Sensei did not hesitate.

He said no.

He could say that truthfully. He did not personally see Han steal.

"But, Hiro-Sensei, you do suspect him of stealing?"

Sensei hesitated again. Then he said no again. He said he had relied on what Goh said. As Goh was not sure now, he too could not be sure.

He did not add a word more — neither fact nor opinion. Those sharings had imparted to both teacher and student variations of perceptions… *man-majime* — was this time softened with a touch of feeling.

Goh looked at Takayama-Sensei's face. He looked disgusted. Goh could read his mind. *Hiro had become weak. Majime — but not man.*

But to Goh, Hiro was now exactly that:

Man.

And Hero!

RECLINING WOMAN OF CHINATOWN

WHEN we were children, Mother would often stack us up on to a rickshaw that would lug us with her from the peace and quiet of Emerald Hill, the Singapore "countryside" where we lived, to spend a day with her parents and siblings in bustling Chinatown, "the town" as she glowingly called it in those long-ago days.

We children seldom reflected any bit of her glow. We preferred the greenery of our trees with their birds and butterflies and year-round fruits, the playing fields on which we played our endless games, the clear running water of those monsoon drains where we could scoop up rainbow guppies with our bare hands, the joy of life under the clear blue skies of those days.

Apart from Grandma's spoiling us with food and stories, we found our Chinatown sojourns hot, humid and ho hum. We never shared Mother's palpable excitement as our sweaty rickshaw-puller heaved us into that hubbub of human babble that was Chulia Street, Synagogue Street, Market Street, Cross Street, Telok Ayer Street and Japan Street (renamed Boon Tat Street after the Japanese war).

Grandma and Grandpa lived in Japan Street, amid that bedlam of teeming humanity. With their other children and grandchildren, they shared the living-cum-dining area, kitchen-cum-toilet and two low-partition cubicles alongside a dark corridor-cum-storage room, in the second level of a congested shop house in that street, once upon a time notorious for its brothels that offered cheap Japanese girls. (That was long before the war. The colonial authorities had since then clamped down on them and converted the street to regular residential use.)

The ground floor of Grandma's house was a noisy coffee-shop separated by a filthy five-foot path and a dirty drain from roadside food stalls that peddled noodles and other cooked food in frenetic competition with exuberant itinerant hawkers who came and went all through the day and early night.

Law and order (or at least, order) within that hurly-burly of conflicting interests was maintained by a self-appointed corp of dedicated enforcers who assured order within their "territory", exacting levies as and when they dictated for their strong-arm services rendered (or not rendered). These were, of course, the Tong people, the boon and the bane of almost every Chinatown.

As soon as we arrived at our destination we children would scamper up the dark and dingy side staircase that took us from the five-foot way direct to the second level (and the third level too if we wanted to go up further). We would always be heartily hailed by everyone on the premises. And we too would greet everyone — robustly too, as pre-instructed by Mother with promise of corporal punishment later if our voices were not high-decibel enough for her.

Once within Grandma's domain, we would be fed repeatedly till it was time to go home. Grandma was a compulsive feeder of kids, very Chinese in that respect: Greasy but yummy noodles fried with clams, eggs and generous helpings of lard, brought up piping hot from the stalls downstairs… soups of pig's brain or liver or kidney with fatty slivers of pork, personally cooked by Grandma… plus globs of thick coconut milk poured lovingly over honey-sweet stews of beans and yam as dessert. Such profligate spoiling with delicacies did in part make up for the poor ambience of the surrounds…

But what I personally enjoyed most, more than the eating, was the time in the evening that Grandma, the chores of the day done, would spend with us children. She would gather us around her bed as she reclined on it to tell us stories of her life.

That serene image of her lying there, head propped up by hand or pillow, was to remain in my mind, a cherished memory of dear Chinatown Grandma, long since dead and gone — if only my impressionistic picture of Grandma. The actual words to describe her would only come gradually, gain definition slowly till they came out expressly, years later, like the opening words of a cryptic Chinese poem or Japanese haiku, starkly simple yet striking. From a world away, almost alien and unexpected, would come the pithy haunting words:

"Reclining Woman
   Grand Mother of Chinatown

Mother beloved…"

As I approached my teenage years and became bolder in my questions, I found Grandma still forthright and frank, always ready to give me answers. She was a woman in advance of her time — I asked about the birds and the bees, and she replied with candour, without vague or evasive talk.

"Grandma, how did Mother come to us?" I recall asking words to that effect.

In simple words she took me through marriage, copulation, conception — and on to childbirth.

"Grandma, you gave birth standing up? Or did they cut your stomach and take Mother out?" I asked.

From her reclining position she used her hands to show how a baby would be born the natural way: Another image of Reclining Woman carved into my memory bank…

"You gave birth to Mother at home, right here in Japan Street?"

"No, not here," Grandma corrected me. "Your Mother was born in Synagogue Street nearby. We were staying there at the time."

I thought about the row of shop houses in that short Synagogue Street, which our rickshaw would pass sometimes, plain and unattractive compared with Japan Street which at least had its own buzz. I pictured Grandma there: A reclining woman of Chinatown giving birth to Mother in one of those ugly shop houses…

After that, entering adolescence, I would think of Chinatown women in general reclining to be copulated, and in due course reclining to give birth in all those crowded cubicles of Chinatown… all those thousands of reclining women of Chinatown.

THAT was in my childhood in the 1930s.

Four decades later in the 1970s, reclining women of Chinatown all but forgotten, I returned to Chinatown in the prime of my life: A middle-aged top executive, CEO of the OCBC Centre Private Limited, tasked with putting up one of Singapore's first high-rise buildings, the 52-storey bank head office on a site flanked by Chulia Street and Synagogue Street.

OCBC (The Overseas Chinese Banking Corporation) was the most successful public Chinese business entity in the country, an icon of local financial strength. The bank wanted to make a statement in the city — rising up from its old-fashioned low-rise image amid a cluster of dilapidated shop houses to become a state-of-the-art skyscraper that all in Chinatown and the rest of the land would have to look up to.

Work on the foundation began. And one day I stood at the site watching our contractors demolish some recently-acquired shop houses in Synagogue Street — that row of shop houses, one of them the house in which Grandma gave birth to my mother.

And I suddenly remembered a reclining woman of Chinatown… a deeply sad, but passing, moment. That momentary pang in my heart, I told myself those reclining women were part of history, a past to be forgotten. Old memories must give way to new, like old houses of Chinatown smashed down to make way for skyscrapers.

Que sera sera — what will be, will be!

Three years later, my skyscraper, all 52 stories of it practically completed, I moved on, signing on an assignment to put up a hotel and department store edifice in Orchard Road. I left behind a prime space at the corner of the Chulia Street frontage with Synagogue Street reserved for a prestigious artwork — a world-class sculpture that our American architect, I M Pei, undertook to source for us in a world-wide search, something that would make an appropriate statement on that spot in Chinatown.

Pei did not know it but powerful forces would lead him on to an almost mystic choice.

I CAME back to the now fully completed OCBC Centre to view the sculpture Pei had selected and installed.

I was overawed.

The sculptor was the world-famous Henry Moore of the US. He produced a huge figure, abstract yet concrete enough to show what it was and what it was doing.

But how did the sculptor know exactly what to do? *Perhaps time and distance do not count when a genius is inspired by forces beyond the ken of men.*

Moore's magnificent work, commissioned at a US$1 million, is a landmark piece of art, absolutely apt in its Chinatown location. It is a tribute, a milestone monument to mark the crossover from old Singapore of Chinatown shop houses to modern Singapore of skyscrapers. It depicts a woman in that old time location captured in a masterpiece in modern art idiom:

Pei told us it was called Moore's Reclining Woman.

To me it is more — more than just Moore.

It is Reclining Woman of Chinatown, immortalised in her domain. She who symbolises all women of her time, cast in masterly expression of everlasting female beauty. The functional high-rise that is the OCBC Centre may soar up sky-high beside her, masculine, solid as a rock, ambitious, concretely successful — but she, supremely low-rise in relaxed sprawl on her plaza pavement, engages the passing world at human eye level, telling her own unspoken story:

My Grand Mother. And all our mothers from the Singapore of our past…

MADAM OH'S AWFUL OFFENCE

IT CAME as a shock to me — that rumour making the rounds at the office: Our motherly Madam Oh Su Chen had run foul of the law. She had received a summons from the police!

"Impossible!" I yelped, "That good woman committing an offence? Someone must be telling a fib about her. Where did that news come from?"

"She herself told one of our staff," my informant replied.

As usual with rumours, there was soon a whole spectrum of versions. Some said it was a serious traffic offence! She might even have her licence taken away? I found that hard to believe. She was such a careful driver, excessively cautious if anything. I have watched her taking ages to pull out from a side street into a main road. Someone speculated that she had run over someone.

And there were even wilder rumours — assault and battery, subversive activities, and other such-like incredible speculations.

Our Madam Oh? Never! I threw my mind back to her first day at our office…

MADAM OH SU CHEN came with status. She was a VIP, Chairperson of the ruling party's woman's section, no less. Something you would never guess from the easy way she mixed about with all who came to her.

When we civil servants were told that Madam Oh, a party bigwig, would be posted to us, assigned to our Department by the PAP, the newly-elected people in office, we felt uneasy. Were we about to be hit by a lightning bolt out of the blue? Few of us had met her before. We only knew her from press photographs. She looked big and menacing. Apart from the fact that she had been a Chinese schoolteacher, we knew next to nothing about her.

So, from now on we will have Big Brother, or rather Big Sister, watching us? This meant having to look over our shoulders all the while? And endlessly answering her on complaints from dissatisfied customers — people who did not get everything they wanted from us civil servants?

But the day Madam Oh arrived in person, our anxieties evaporated. She arrived unobtrusively, no fanfare, no airs, dressed in plain samfoo, casual and friendly, and ready to fit into our culture. She told us that she was proud to join our ranks. We in the Social Welfare Department had a superb reputation among the proletariat, she said. And she hoped we would teach her and help her fit into our welfare work.

She asked for a small partitioned space, just like those allocated to our hands-on officers. And she got down to business at once, humbly seeking our help, learning the ropes fast. In no time she was lunching with our little groups as we went to the nearby hawker stalls and coffee shops — a trusted member of our gang.

Soon it seemed to us that everyone among our new clientele at the Social Welfare Department wished to see her first: This energetic woman who had been posted to join us as a liaison officer when the PAP first became the Government of Singapore.

She would listen to them, counsel them, or quickly arrange for them to see other personnel in the Social Welfare Department.

Everyone sang her praises. For she was one of those rare women, naturally humble, humorous and hearty. And utterly down-to-earth — as heartland and Hokkien-rooted as they come, vibrant with her unique vim despite her close to six decades of age.

As word got around that Madam Oh was to be found in our Department, a lot of new business came to us. She soon became so busy, some of us had to join her to give her a hand to cope with clients. And soon other PAP women leaders (Chan Choy Siong, Ho Puay Choo, Fung Yin Ching, Sahorah Ahmat) could be seen coming to her office to help her out too — and so we got to know well the women stalwarts of the PAP. We found out that these PAP women had one distinctive trait: Their honest commitment to helping ordinary people. Like Madam Oh, they were dedicated and hard working — and high in integrity. So they were an inspiration to all of us in Welfare, required as we were by profession and mission to be committed and diligent. And law-abiding too.

SO HOW did that rumour arise — about our Madam Oh breaking the law, committing an offence?

I went to her for the truth.

She was frank. She confirmed it straightaway. Yes, she did have a brush with the law — and she did get a ticket from the police!

Speaking in Hokkien, she explained with red face and much embarrassment what had happened:

"I was driving along the main road at my normal cautious speed, watching out for other vehicles and careful not to knock down pedestrians. As usual I was giving way to every-one whenever I could, exercising my normal concern for safety and of course ignoring all the impatient honking by the drivers behind me..."

Yes I could see all that in my mind's eye. I had rode in her car before.

"Then all of a sudden a police motorbike came up next to me. I waved a friendly hand at him. He did not look friendly — his face was stern. He signalled to me to pull over at the roadside. I did so at once, wondering what I had done wrong. Did I fail to signal at a turning? Or did I pass a red light? Or worse, knock down someone or something without noticing it?

"With a stern face, the officer handed me a ticket. 'Madam,

I'm sorry, I have to give you this. You have committed an offence!' he told me. 'Impossible! What offence have I committed? I've not been speeding or anything like that at all. In fact I've been going slow all the way — really, really slow,' I protested. 'I know,' he told me."

And then the police officer revealed to Madam Oh her awful offence:

She had been driving too slow on a busy road — the first person I have ever known cited for such an offence, and perhaps the only one in the entire annals of offences on our roads!

THE FINGER-MAN OF THE TONG

SINGAPORE by the early 20th Century had been under British rule for close to a century, but daily life in Chinatown still remained unchanged — under rule by the Tongs.

These were the underground societies that came with the early immigrants, branches of that great Chinese Secret Society in the mother-country, the Tien Ti Hui or Heaven-and-Earth Society. That Society was established way back in the 17th Century to overthrow the Manchu Dynasty, but through the years their political purpose had waned and they had turned to crime.

In Singapore they assumed a different role. They became the providers of counselling and help, and the keepers of order in a lawless ghetto, largely because they alone had the will and the strong-arm means to enforce whatever needed to be laid down as law. So, accepted by the Chinese immigrants, especially the clueless *sinkheh* (or new arrivals), the Tongs ruled the roost in Chinatown, though often not just and fair.

Men in Chinatown were loosely linked to the Tongs, most

of them as passive tribute-payers. In return they got protection. But disagreements often surfaced between them and the Tongs (and sometimes amongst themselves), and there were fights and bloodshed, made worse as power inevitably began to corrupt some leaders.

The colonial Government's philosophy then was to distance itself from the fray. However, whenever things went too far, the police would flex their muscle and rope in Tong people, though usually only the small fry, jailing them or even deporting them back to China.

As a child, the first generation born here, Siong knew that his family elders were in with the 18 Tong, that powerful Hokkien gang whose "turf" was the Telok Ayer Street area where their family lived. In fact his father, a seaman by occupation, enjoyed some status within his Tong, though only at about middle-hierarchy level.

So Siong was shocked when his father was unexpectedly arrested by the police, speedily tried and found guilty. The adults did not tell him much, though the boy understood that the charge was serious. The offence warranted deportation back to Amoy. Whatever it was, smuggling or possession of counterfeit plates or running a gambling joint — the boy heard all manner of stories but could only guess at the truth.

But there could have been more to it. Siong heard whispers. And he began to suspect the old man was framed. Or, more likely that he had been made to take the fall for the sake of the others in the gangs. There was also talk that someone in his own gang had pointed a finger at him. Someone with access to the police had given his name to them!

It was not till Siong was in his teens that his Uncle told him what the adults knew but had been sworn to keep secret.

This was the story: The Cantonese gang, which operated mainly in the Sago Lane area, had been encroaching aggressively into Hokkien territory — and there had been counter-intrusions and reprisals. There were bloody clashes, usually during funerals and other processions.

The Chinese Protectorate (the Government agency for Chinese affairs) stepped in again and again to arbitrate and settle the disputes. Each time the gangs would give "face" to the Protector of Chinese, a British civil servant who spoke the Chinese dialects and kept rapport with the community leaders, and after the customary compensation with apologies (and the mandatory two red candles wrapped in red cloth ceremoniously presented to the aggrieved party), things would settle down for a while — until the next round of disputes.

Then the gangs went too far. The Tong war spilled over into the hitherto sacrosanct Raffles Place, the domain of the white man and his offices. The Governor of the Straits Settlements, of which Singapore was then part, blew his top. He gave the police a stern directive: Teach the gangs a lesson — arrest one or more of the gangs' leaders. Charge them with some crime or other, serious enough to warrant banishment. Get evidence that would stick. Go for a swift trial and conviction. And make sure that there would be no riot or other reaction from the gangs following the police action.

The police knew exactly what to do.

They had already a set-up in place. They had developed rapport, even unofficial cooperation, with the more amenable leaders in the gangs. These also functioned as invaluable liaisons. And at times they also served as unofficial police agents within the gangs.

The police got these trusted moderate leaders to explain the Governor's wishes to their gangs. The gangs would have to decide and nominate which of their top people, at least middle-rung level leaders, to take the fall.

How and who? Details were left to those liaison men. All the police wanted was at least one scapegoat from each side: Men the police could charge — and successfully convict. In

other words, the whipping boys should come complete with their own whips — either confessions of guilt, or alternatively, the Tongs could supply the evidence of guilt, true or manufactured. All this was in aid of putting up a show of police force, and thereby also end the gang war — and initiate the desired return of peace for all.

"The Governor wants tough action. He says heads have to roll!" the police chief said.

"Heads have to roll?" the agents turned pale, recalling bad old days in the motherland when the Manchu mandarins used to behead their predecessors caught in old China.

"Don't worry," the police chief laughed, "that's only the way we say we must find people to punish. But we won't do anything truly nasty to them."

The agents still looked dubious. After all each had one foot solidly planted in his own gang's camp as well. Indeed the principal purpose of their liaison with the police, countenanced by their Tong brothers, was to help their gangs, not harm them.

The chief understood their concern. He assured them, "We only want a show of imperial power and might. We want at least two people, one from each gang, people we can convict for Tong crimes, that's all. We'll treat them right — the ones pointed out by you. We'll try them, find them guilty and banish them back to China. They'll get free passage home, all expenses paid..." the chief assured them.

"Still the Chinese authorities will punish them on arrival, perhaps even chop off their heads!" the agents remained worried.

"No, I promise you, they won't — because the Chinese authorities won't be told. As far as they are concerned, the people named by you will be folks returning home to their farms," the chief promised them. "Actually it won't be a bad deal for them. We'll even give them money — seed money to resume their farming life..."

The arrangement did not look bad, although deportation would mean separation from family in Singapore and that might make it hard to pick the scapegoats wanted.

That was how Siong's father came to be fingered as one of the two from the Tongs. The liaison man in his Tong gave his name to the police — and provided the evidence too. Who that finger-man was, Siong did not know.

Did his father know?

That was entirely possible. Someone in the Tong had to be sacrificed. His gang could have decided he was expendable. But it was more likely that he was persuaded by the liaison man and nobly accepted the need to sacrifice himself for the sake of his comrades in the Tong — and for peace as required by the police.

After Siong's father was deported, the Tong helped Siong's mother. They gave Cheng money regularly for her family's living expenses including her sons' schooling, although with her large brood she needed to go out to work as well.

Cheng missed her husband sorely and began to resent that finger within the Tong that had pointed him out to the police to take the fall, never mind whether her man himself went along with the sacrifice or not.

Then a new regime under a new *Tua Koh* (Eldest Brother) took over the tong leadership, and her husband's close friends in the tong arranged for her to see the man.

Tua Koh listened to the poor woman, obviously still grieving even after all the years of separation from her husband, yet in dignified control before the powerful man.

"That man, that Tong liaison man or police agent, whoever he is, deserves to be punished for sacrificing my husband, pointing his finger at him instead of someone else: Someone lower down in the Tong, a more expendable fellow, without a large family here. Especially one of those many others who later proved themselves traitors or ineffective Tong men — one of them could have been fingered. That police agent clearly made a mistake singling out my husband. He should be punished!" Cheng stated her case.

Her husband's friends supported her. *Tua Koh* was sympathetic. A new police liaison had in fact taken over from that old one who had retired with the rest of the old leadership. *Tua Koh* promised her he would do something.

Days later, *Tua Koh* and his henchmen came to see Cheng in her home in Pasir Panjang. She and her family had moved to that remote countryside place where they could plant food and rear pigs and chicken — and the atmosphere was more healthy for her children than in Chinatown.

Tua Koh took out a small black lacquer box. He said, "We summoned our former liaison man with the police. He confessed. He himself had been feeling guilty. He said he did what he had to do then. He claimed it was for the sake of settling the ugly situation without further spilling of blood. And there was the threat of police action against all of us as well. But he now himself admits it was his error of judgment to point his finger at your husband instead of someone else.

"He volunteered himself to be punished — in a way that will prove to you his sincere regret. We prescribed the punishment. He agreed to it. We bring the proof of it to you. Here it is, what we did to him — the personal price he had to pay. At his request, he wants us to present it to you. He expresses his sorrow through us. He hopes you will accept this — and allow him to come, reveal himself to you, say sorry to you in person…"

Tua Koh took out from the box something wrapped in cloth. He uncovered what was inside. At first Cheng could not make out what the thing was. Neither could Siong who was present. The dark cylindrical shape looked ugly and dirty, a loathsome old thing, almost obscene looking.

"He fingered wrongly. He hurt you grievously," *Tua Koh* said in his quiet manner. "Here is that pointing finger of his. Will you accept it in atonement? And will you let him come to apologise to you in person?"

Cheng recovered from her shock. She looked closely at the thing. It was indeed a man's index finger. Whose was it? She did not know. She could not know. She did not want to know.

What to do? What to say? She did not know what to say. She did not need to know what to say.

She knew what to do.

She picked up the thing between the tips of her thumb and index finger. Followed by her wondering visitors and Siong, she walked out with it, holding it away from herself, to the outside of the house. She stopped at the pen where she kept her farm animals. She threw the thing to the pigs. They ate it up. She spoke no words. No words were needed. The Tong men left.

The finger-man's finger was gone. His identity remained unknown to Cheng and Siong — by their choice.

A FEW years on…. It was Siong's wedding day.

Fortune had shone on him. He had been match made to a pretty girl, a lovable young thing, the daughter of a merchant whose business in Chinatown was up and coming. The match-maker was untypically a man, not a woman. Furthermore, a dignified greying man of standing and means. He had appeared out of the blue. He arranged that wonderful match for him, a poor boy from a family with limited means.

After the wedding came the tea ceremony.

After serving tea to their families, Siong and his bride knelt before the matchmaker to serve him the customary cup. Siong held his cup up respectfully with both hands. The man received it with both hands as also customary.

Siong, for the first time, caught sight of the man's right hand:

His index finger was missing.

The Twilight Of Western Gods

"YOUNG man, you look absolutely ghastly — a bloody disaster! For God's sake, straighten that stupid neckpiece of yours! Don't you people even know how to wear a tie properly?"

That was no pompous headmaster bearing down on a timid boy. It was a colonial master, nothing less! My first encounter with one. An expatriate Establishment Officer of the Civil Service, stretched tall to full stature of divine authority, putting down an upstart native, one daring to step into the ranks of the heaven-born, the gods come from the West.

Before that obese presence of overbearing majesty in his equally obese-looking office, the silly grin on my face did nothing for me. I stood there, suddenly reduced to microbe, wishing I was happily back in my home in the Peranakan precincts of Emerald Hill, instead of flopping about here, a fish out of water, on the alien turf of The Colonial Secretary's Office in Empress Place.

That was December 3, 1951, my first day in the Civil Service. The prestigious Singapore Administrative Service, into which I was one of two local people selected, was created barely a year before that.

That morning I had slung on my best tie, carelessly knotted it on, the way we young colonial subjects put on our *yu cha kuay* (or Chinese dough fritter, as we bumpkins irreverently called that piece of neckwear back in college).

My critic, Mr Hawke, was not exactly a natty dresser himself. And he was not even my boss-to-be. But that did not stop him from doing his bossy bit on me.

On reflection I realised what that show was all about. It was to put me in my place, make clear from Day One how matters stood between the established British rulers and the new Singapore public servants, reluctantly recruited because of the ineluctable dictate of Whitehall, London, culled and sedulously pruned down from the thin crops of local university graduates.

I was to be posted to the Colonial Secretary's Office. Mr Hawke grimaced as he passed on that information, clearly nauseated by the very idea. He could not even bring himself to provide me with more details.

I could not have received a less promising reception to my new career.

"And, for God's sake, tuck in your shirt!" Mr Hawke bawled out a parting shot as I turned to exit through his open door. His hawk eye had spotted yet another heinous lapse of decorous dressing. I instinctively felt about my waist to see where my shirt had come untucked. I swear every bit was well and truly tucked in. But I wasn't about to argue the point...

His secretary, a native like me, but one well-tutored into boot-licking, heard that exhortation. She tittered dutifully as it was no doubt expected of her.

I knew better than to look back at her. I knew what a running dog looked like. Or, more correctly, a bitch.

THAT was a milestone memory. Shrapnel from a different world, a different lifetime, more than half a century ago.

I had been selected by the newly constituted Public Service Commission for that rare honour: The first of the handful chosen to join the top echelon, the exalted ranks of the colonial mandarins who still ruled the roost during those end days of Empire. I suppose, in grassroots anti-colonial circles, that selection qualified me to be labelled a running dog (though perhaps, it might be a mite more precise to call me a colonial dog runner — but more on that trail later).

My official designation was more sedate: *Assistant Colonial Secretary*. That job label might well evoke fantasies of grandiose power as the Honourable Colonial Secretary was the *de facto* CEO of the colony. His superior, HE (His Excellency) the

Governor, was mostly preoccupied with pomp and pageantry — doing his oodles of full-dress ceremonials, plumed hat and all, that the British masters loved, especially in the colonies where it was felt the natives needed to be duly awed with spectacle.

However I soon learnt my ABCs. I was only the Assistant Colonial Secretary "C", a below-the-line truly humble third in alphabetical ranking. Actually it was even worse, for I was four other worthies removed from the august Colonial Secretary in office hierarchy — after the US or Under Secretary (another real powerhouse with daily access to HE), the Principal Assistant Secretary (a busy, busy general factotum), and two other Assistant Secretaries "A" and "B" (both local officers who, unlike me, had real jobs).

Then came me — with a long schedule of duties full of sound and flurry (no misprint, not fury), signifying nothing! Indeed some of my real duties came to me fully pre-processed and effectively decided from below me — by Assistant Secretary "D", a long-service trusted Eurasian officer, who (I suspected) filtered my work before it came to me. For significantly, that worthy had access to Government House, to that great man, HE himself.

That Assistant Secretary "D" was clearly a trusted officer compared to me. He was a good man who had no doubt earned what he enjoyed. To the whites he was at least a half-white — even though, colour apart, work-wise he did deserve trust. I began to sense that he must have been assigned to watch my back, which he was doing with eagle eyes, putting up things for me to sign (as if my signing them counted for anything!). And it was entirely possible he was also directed to report on my performance to the US who seemed remarkably well-informed about things I did — or failed to do.

As I came to suspect, the posting of local officers to that control room was actually a sop to instructions from Whitehall. The upper echelons were then dominated by whites recruited under the MCS (Malayan Civil Service) scheme. Whitehall had launched the SAS (Singapore Administrative Service), and three local officers were duly recruited in the first year of the new scheme, two in the second (myself being one), and one in the third.

The colonial powers on the spot not only dragged their feet, taking in recruits. They also saw to it that duties given to the newcomers were innocuous enough.

But unfortunately for them, the momentum towards self-determination had begun, and before long the SAS became real enough.

BACK to my duties as Assistant Secretary "C":

Among my more meaningful tasks was an administrative procedure euphemistically called *Naturalisation*.

That was a true misnomer, that legal process by which people were unnaturally transformed from aliens into British subjects. The assignment looked good on my schedule of duties. That was probably for Whitehall consumption. Actually I only performed the mundane clearing house duty of a clerk checking application forms to make sure they were properly filled in for the various departments to process after which I collated their reports. Even then it was the Assistant Secretary D who carried to HE the applications I checked (and no doubt double-checked them before he passed them on).

I suspect there were occasions when he was able to uncover sins of omission, if never commission, by me. He did not take issue with me — that would not have been the done thing, he being junior in alphabetical ranking to me. I would find myself hauled up by the much-harassed US. My transgressions would then be pointed out to me by that worthy as he sweated profusely under his whirring ceiling fan. A few were oversights or minor errors of judgment on my part, but most of my sins did not seem to me all that horrendous.

For example I inadvertently omitted to include one unimportant original testimonial in Chinese with the translation thereof. And once (believe it or not) when one sheet of paper accidentally got folded at one corner! Stuff like that, hardly heinous enough to hound a senior civil servant about. Still, perhaps it was the opportunity that counted — to make an upstart feel a nincompoop.

"We demand a peerless standard of performance from our top level civil servants! Unless you can meet this yardstick, we will have to let you go after your probation period," the US would warn as he wiped his forehead with a trembling hand. Those were the days before the invention of air-conditioning relieved excess heat under the collar. Those were also the days when expatriate civil servants had been known to cool down and ease the burden of colonial domination with plentiful guzzling on the quiet with consequential copious sweating in public. (Though, apart from his plentiful perspiration, our US never gave me cause to suspect him as one of those guzzlers.)

There was, however, one meaningful job under my schedule. That was the disbursement of periodic payments to the Singapore descendants of Sultan Hussein, the Sultan of Johor, who had lorded it over Singapore before Raffles bought the place over from him dirt-cheap. This was a sad duty — handing out dole to once-upon-a-time royalty, and listening to poignant tales of woe from the progeny of princes now reduced to the pitiful penury of paupers. At times I knew I was being conned by exaggerations of exigencies, fibs told without much finesse. But still I would accept what they told me. Perhaps mine was a foolish heart, but it was a modest salaam within my dispensation to pay to past royalty.

One duty grandiosely listed in my schedule was *Private Secretary to HE*. At first I was utterly enchanted by what that could mean. I was speedily disenchanted. I learned from hand-over notes left by my predecessor (an expatriate officer) that the job merely meant running errands for the wife of HE.

And the main task was taking out her plump sausage dogs for their daily jog. Fortunately this dog-runner job on my duty list was never activated during my tenancy and I remained PS to HE only in name.

I learned through the grapevine (admittedly not always reliable) the reason why I was let off. It seemed that Her Lady-ship was aghast to discover that a Chinese had been appointed to those designated duties of PS to HE.

"A Chinese?" she was rumoured to have uttered with understandable unease, "those people eat dogs, don't they?"

They told me she tried to have a civil service reshuffle done so as not to risk a potential canine carnivore as PS to HE. Apparently the powers that be decided they could not risk Whitehall umbrage to accommodate her wishes. So she did the next best thing. She leashed in some other poor soul to run her dogs. Which was why I never even really became an official colonial dog-runner!

WHEN the time came to evaluate my performance, the result was a foregone conclusion, something pre-ordained from Day One. I was naturally found wanting. Perhaps the fact that I was getting chummy with the civil service trade unionists could have had something to do with it too — I will never know for sure.

They had enough ammo to fire on me, but not to fire me on. So I was penalised — perhaps in the hope that I would resign and leave the service. I was to have gone off to Oxford University for training in public administration, an important step to my career prospects. My trip was postponed *sine die*. Actually they went on to forget my training entirely.

My colleague, the only other local SAS officer (an Eurasian Singaporean) recruited the same year with me, was in slightly better blood with the expatriate masters. He went on to Oxford. Whitehall would not have been happy with the full cohort of two SAS recruits shot down — a 50 per cent survival was a good enough show.

And the next cohort recruited to the SAS whittled down to only one recruit. He, too, was an Eurasian Singaporean. He was an excellent recruit, unchallengeably an outstanding success as a civil servant by any standards.

Both these Eurasian recruits proved themselves to be invaluable assets to the civil service, as our local political leaders who took over from the colonial masters were to discover…

IN MY disappointment over the way things had worked out, or rather not worked out for me, I considered throwing in the towel.

I sought advice from my colleagues, the few other local civil servants. They were unanimous in their counsel: *Stick it out! The days of the Western gods are numbered. We local civil servants will take over. Just stand ready.*

"Ask for a transfer to the social services — Labour or Welfare or Education," Lee Siow Mong, the Assistant Secretary "B", wisely suggested. He knew they had a more friendly expatriate crowd in social services.

I took that advice. I was transferred to become an Assistant Commissioner for Labour. In my new department, I did indeed find a different breed of expatriates. Perhaps people naturally become more human, having to deal hands-on with human problems. I made many good friends in my new office, expatriate as well as local.

And I learned a lot from the trade unionists. I wised up to the political realities of Singapore. And I got to know our local political leaders from the different parties: The Progressive Party, the Labour Front, and then the PAP…

Backed and tutored by KM Byrne, then an outstanding and fearless local senior civil servant (later on to become a PAP Minister), I returned to the Establishment Office of the Colonial Secretary's Office, this time as opposition — as unionist, leading civil service union delegations to demand better terms on behalf of the junior grades.

And I joined our local leaders in their planning and campaigning for the early retirement of our expatriate civil servants and their replacement by local officers. There was no blood let. Instead, all was carried out in a civilised and orderly manner.

We had arrived.

No one had call to demean the local civil servants any more. We were fast transforming ourselves into a force to be reckoned with.

Yes, our dog days were fast running out. The sun was setting on Empire. It was the twilight of Western gods.

A GREAT (OR GOOFY) LEAP FORWARD

AT 42, in the full bloom of my mid-career, an ardent headhunting search agency wooed me and made me an offer I could not refuse. So I forsook the security of my superscale civil service job for the hurly-burly of the private sector. I said good-bye to my iron rice bowl, farewell to prospects of the zoom up to Permanent Secretary heights, not to mention handsome pension and lifelong medical benefits: A great (or goofy?) leap forward!

My initial posting, no doubt an acid test of my potential, was as personal assistant to the Number One honcho of the corporation: Tan Sri Tan Chin Tuan, the Chairman of OCBC, the bank I joined.

That straight-off control room posting was daunting, even to a self-proven performer in his fearless 40s.

To start with, there was my boss' countenance. His piercing eyes and square jaw jutting out solid as a rock, seemed to augur a bulldog disposition. And his high-integrity stature and no-nonsense reputation in the working world preceded him to awe all who step within range.

I wondered how I would fare functioning under such scrutiny.

But I discovered on my very first day with him that, on close-up, the image was softened by the reality.

"Mr Sin Tub," the great man actually got up and came forward to warmly shake my humble cold hand, addressing me in that peculiar mix of courtesy and intimacy which I soon discovered was the culture of the company. "Welcome to OCBC!" he said.

And he spent that morning briefing me personally, firmly refusing to be side-tracked by phone calls and papers placed before him by his secretaries.

His voice was remarkably soft and even, and he paused to listen attentively whenever I opened my mouth to respond.

I went home that day feeling affirmed in my career switch — more than that, I sensed I had been welcomed into family.

And more!

His head was largely bald. My late beloved father too had a shiningly bald pate. His warm demeanour, in sharp contrast to those penetrating eyes and that aggressive jaw, was reassuring — that was also like my father's stern look but kindly disposition. Yes, from Day One, Mr Chin Tuan reminded me of a father missed since sudden demise not many years earlier…

In the months and years that followed, sitting "at his feet" through discussions with his managers and consultants, I came to know the man in depth, taking the measure of a rare person: One with the wealth of experience and business acumen of a Midas-touch tycoon plus the depth of uncanny discernment of a sage — and yet always with the compassion of a truly great human being.

LET me cite instances. In those tumultuous days of rugged nation-building following Singapore's sudden independence, the Government faced nerve-wracking challenges. They had to make rough and tough decisions, not always the wisest or most balanced.

And the bank found one of its prime sites gazetted for an acquisition on distinctly unfair grounds. The bank's managers were incensed and consulted the best lawyers in the land. We were assured we had a cast-iron case. Even then we went further and sought learned opinion overseas. We retained a top-flight Queen's Counsel with impressive acquisition experience. He summed up his unhesitating advice in three words: "Go to court!"

But in the end, Mr Chin Tuan said nay.

He ruled against fighting the Government.

"I do not agree with all the Government is doing, but it has an unenviable time keeping the country going now. This is not the time to fight the Government… we have more to lose by winning," he said.

And then he added with a smile in consolation to his managers, "We will make back this loss in other ways…"

THOSE were also the torrid times of politically-motivated industrial unrest: Singapore's era of endless strikes and work disputes. The left-wing trade unionists let past no opening to vilify Mr Chin Tuan and his ilk. He was the top man in many established firms (OCBC, Raffles Hotel, Robinsons) and his political stance had always been right of centre. So his was the ready face of the ugly employer, the image of the oppressive capitalist. He had to endure acrimonious attacks. Yet, despite the venom spitted out at him in those encounters, at the end of the day after the dust had settled, historians would often uncover one sparkling little footnote — a gem to sign off those clashes of passion on a shining note of a great man's compassion.

To give one example: After the angry words and allegations, after all the agony of industrial action, in the course of which some 300 OCBC employees walked out during a 12-day strike, the parties finally arrived at an amicable settlement. During the work stoppage, those employees had suffered loss of pay. But when everything was over, they found help extended to them, ex-gratia. Quietly, a sizeable sum was passed on to their union to distribute as relief for workers who had lost earnings in the dispute. The money did not come from the bank. It was a personal donation made by Mr Chin Tuan.

And then there was that occasion when the vocal trade unionist, S Woodhull, publicly denounced Mr Chin Tuan and threatened to call a strike over the termination of two sales-girls although they had been dismissed for cause: Their employer, Robinsons, had caught them red-handed, stealing from the department store.

Even as Woodhull ranted on, Mr Chin Tuan stood his ground. He told the unionist that he would rather close down the store than back down from his stand. He made it clear that was no idle threat. He reasoned, "Reinstating these two girls would condone, if not encourage, theft. The store would be finished. So we might as well wind up."

In the end it was the unionist who backed down.

There is a sequel to this incident that took place some years later, recently dug up by researchers. Woodhull had been detained by the Government for his part in a communist plot. Upon his release he decided to go to London to study law. Quietly, Mr Chin Tuan provided him financial aid for his studies (and even bought him an overcoat!). He said of his erstwhile enemy, "He was fighting a cause. We had an honest disagreement. There was no animosity…"

SOON after the War, long before other companies followed in like manner, Mr Chin Tuan initiated enlightened staff welfare practices in OCBC. He launched a comprehensive staff welfare package that included holidays and a bonus scheme based on corporate results, as well as training schemes for self-upgrading, both locally and abroad, and scholarships for children of staff. And he initiated a company provident fund scheme which multiplied savings through the bank's expert husbanding of knowledgeable investments.

AT THE individual level, I recall occasions when he would veto his managers' recommendations to end an officer's services for inefficiency or incompetence. He would say, "In his younger days the man served the bank well. I'll talk to him. I'll make sure he knows why we're letting him go. But let him save face. We should let him retire early."

WORKING so closely with him, it was only natural that I came completely under his spell. I quickly learned his style, and when he put me in charge of overseeing the development of the bank's new 52-storey head office building, his past tutorship served me well while his ready hand continued to guide me through the awesome task. I went on to lead my team of great executives and consultants through that mission, putting into practice his words: "A good manager learns how to use people who are better than himself."

I MADE numerous decisions during my tutelage under Mr Chin Tuan. Many bore fruit in satisfying ways and won me plaudits and recognition.

There was, however, one decision I made in my mind that never bore fruit — for it was never tested.

In those days a few of us close to Mr Chin Tuan used to be invited to accompany him in his food forays into odd corners of the country. The man was an accomplished gourmet and he knew where to go for the best cuisine — including the most unlikely coffee shops tucked away in Chinatown and other crowded areas.

I recall worrying for his safety during some of these expeditions into "wild" country. He was a wealthy man, a potential candidate for kidnapping. He was also a man against whom some people might have felt grievances, real or imagined.

As I walked with him in some of those crowded streets, I began to develop a habit of looking searchingly to left and right, studying faces and clusters of people, more than once in my imagination even anticipating a gunman dashing out, revolver in hand, firing away at him.

What should I do in such a contingency?

I had a decision to make, something to firm up on beforehand in my mind. His was a life infinitely more precious than mine. So I decided and I was ready. There was no longer any doubt in my mind exactly what I had to do — I had to leap out there in front of him, block off that bullet aimed at him!

That great leap never happened. But it could have. In a way, a pity…

It would have been a fitting tribute to a great man — and sharpened the point in this story: My great leap forward (no way goofy)!

A Lonely Candle For Grandpa

WHY was everyone so quiet — and so long-faced? What was happening? The little boy only knew it had something to do with his Grandpa. Something really strange — and terrible!

He had so many questions to ask. Grandpa had never behaved so strangely. He loved Grandpa and Grandpa loved him. So why didn't Grandpa hug him when he came home that day? Why didn't he carry him up in his arms and kiss him as always? Why did he rush off to his room? Why didn't he come down to join the family for dinner — or for anything else? Why did he spend almost all the time alone in his room all through those long days he did not go to work? And why that weird mask on his face that made him suddenly like an alien from MARS!

He heard the adults talking anxiously about Grandpa, but he could not understand what they were saying… something about some horrible illness. They whispered the word: SARS!

Grandma tried to explain to him. "You know, your Grandpa is a doctor, right? He sees patients every day, and so sometimes he gets germs passed to him by them, right? Most times it's not bad, because there are medicines he can take that will make him okay again…

"But sometimes there comes something new and terrible like this sickness called SARS. Doctors don't have the cure for it yet. And it can kill people…" Grandma went on, her voice suddenly hoarse. "So anyone suspected of having the sickness has to be kept separated from other people. They have to be quarantined so that they don't spread the germs to others…"

"You mean Grandpa has got it? Grandpa has got SARS?" the little boy was wide-eyed with terror.

"No, no! It's just that he's not sure. The Health Ministry phoned him to tell him the chilling news: One of his patients had been diagnosed with SARS — and he had died! Grandpa discovered he had a fever, only very slight, but fever is an early sign. And he had been seeing a number of patients with fever. Without being ordered by the Ministry, he immediately decided on his own he had to do the responsible thing.

"He acted at once. He closed his clinic and self-quarantined himself at home. And once home he would not let any of his family come close to him…"

The little boy felt so afraid for Grandpa but he understood what Grandma said. When he next saw Grandpa looking at him from the inside of his room, he instinctively made to go to him, but he saw Grandpa firmly shaking his head. So they froze and stood apart…

And then the boy saw Grandpa's big eyes warming up to him, and beneath them Grandpa's familiar smile — though now hidden behind the white mask. And he smiled back at Grandpa.

THEN one day they held a party for Grandpa — a celebration the family would never forget.

There Grandpa stood, by himself in their garden, an isolated figure, very much alone. When he sat down, it was on a chair set apart. Grandma and the rest kept a distance away from him, watching him intently as he peered at them over that mask over his mouth and nose.

His colourful birthday cake looked wistful — but Grandpa even more so.

They lit the lone candle on the cake. They moved aside for Grandpa to blow off the flame.

Grandpa stood silent for a moment before his cake. Making his birthday wish? No need for any of them to guess — surely to be freed from SARS!

Would he now blow off the flame? No! Trust him to think better than to chance spreading germs on to the cake that the family would be sharing.

He took a serviette and fanned off the flame with it. The family clapped. And they sang *Happy Birthday* to Grandpa.

HAPPILY Grandpa's self-imposed 10 days of quarantine came to an end. His slight fever had come down. After the allowance of that safe period since contact with his infected patient, he was now sure he had not contracted SARS. He returned to work. The episode was history.

But the image of Grandpa and his lonely birthday celebration would always remain in the family's mind.

And one little boy would never forget the lesson of responsible behaviour his Grandpa taught him.

This story, though with some fictional details, is based on a true (and touching) family episode when MP Dr Tan Cheng Bock went into self-imposed quarantine during the SARS crisis in Singapore.

DISCOVERIES

ASK THAT WHY

MY FRIEND Hannah carefully cut off the ends of the chunk of ham before putting it into the oven to bake. It occurred to me she did that every time she baked ham. I don't.

"Why?" I asked her.

"I learnt cooking from Mother. She's a great cook, you know? She always cuts the ends off," she explained.

"Why?" I repeated.

"I've never asked her," Hannah confessed, adding although I did not say a word, "yes, you're absolutely right. I must ask her why…"

What was the reason for discarding the ends? The handed-down wisdom of generations of ham-bakers? They knew things we did not know? Cutting off the ends made for better cooking? The opening of ends allowed the ham's tasty juices to burst forth in all their glory? Or might there be sinister elements inimical to good health or exquisite taste that could be conjured up in the hell-heat of ham trapped between tied ends in an oven? Or perhaps it was only to enable more flavour-enhancing heat to get in when obstructing ends are removed?

Whatever the reason, we would surely learn something valuable from Hannah asking her mother why.

"WHY?" was an important question to me at a high point in my working life. Without much by way of relevant experience, I was put in charge of building a multi-million-dollar sky-scraper, the OCBC Centre. I was the man appointed to be CEO in charge of the project, head of a team of experts. Mr Tan Chin Tuan, my chairman, had that extraordinary faith in me. And he allayed my worries as to how to respond to the nitty-gritty details of the challenge. I was then a newcomer to the organisation, a non-professional among top building professionals. I was as lay as they came, in fact the layest of them all, an almost absolute know-nothing. More specifically I knew nothing of answers to the myriad of problems of skyscraper building.

But the old man put in my hand a magic wand. He gave me an invaluable bit of advice, how to do my job as a non-expert in command of a team of experts:

"You don't have to know how to find the answers — all you have to know is how to ask the questions."

Armed with that counsel, I sallied forth.

I never asked so many questions in my life.

And most of them began with: "Why?"

And at the end of the day, as my expert consultants told me, I made them think hard, down to the basics — and often review their initial recommendations too. I learnt — but they learnt too.

"WHY?"

Why do children naturally ask their so many "whys"?

Isn't that the key to learning — the opening of door to wisdom: Perpetual curiosity, the mother of discovery?

"Why can't we eat candy for dinner?"

"Why do we have to eat veggies?"

"Why does it get dark at night?"

"Why must we sleep?"

"Why do we have to go to school?"

"Why must Daddy go to work?"

AND sometimes one answer to why only begets another:

"Why do you have to stop playing with me to watch TV?"

"To know the latest news."

"Why?"

"So we can know what's going on."

"Why?"

"To know what to do."

"Why?"

"To do the right thing."

"Why?"

"To know when to stop you asking why. Just stop asking why!"

And sometimes even that still begets:

"Why?"

OFTEN we jump to the wrong conclusion, good or bad; often we miss something, that could be great or at least illuminating, all because we fail to probe, omit to ask why.

When a teenage niece of mine came to stay in our house for a few days, I heard her humming the tune of our national anthem, *Majulah Singapura*, every morning as she prepared her own breakfast, and the verse would often be repeated too.

"What a patriotic little lady! Such love for country!" My heart warmed up to our young Singaporeans. Yes, they could teach us older folk a thing or two — a moment of discovery, I thought.

I could have lived on with that grand illusion. But my wife was more curious — she asked her "Why?"

"Oh, just a habit I learned from very young…" she began.

"And a good one too," I wanted to comment, still brimming over with overflow of gush for the child's exemplary patriotism. But before I could do that, she went on:

"*Majulah* sung twice is just about right for doing a soft-boiled egg!"

A moment of discovery.

Majulah will henceforth secretly tickle me with a less grave note.

ON A more serious note, an elderly colleague who had just lost almost all his hearing for good, announced the sad news to me in these words:

"I've been struck with what they call profound loss of hearing."

I did not know how to respond. He went on, "Thank God for it!"

And with that he seemed ready to move on to talk about other things.

Was he being cynical? Sarcastic? Was it sardonic humour — that thanksgiving to God? Still, should I let it be? Leave him with the privacy of his caustic acidity?

AN EARNEST look on his face encouraged me, almost wanted me, to ask why. I asked why. I was glad I did — I learnt something.

"At first I grieved for my loss," he said. "Then I heard that one of my contemporaries, the envied genius of our class, had Alzheimer's. And I met another of my peers. He was a bad case of Parkinson's... By comparison, the small cross given to me to bear is something I should thank God for, right?"

My "Why?" taught me perspective and philosophy.

BACK to Hannah and the end of her ham story.

Did Hannah get around to clearing up that question about cutting off the ends before putting the ham into the oven?

She did.

The next time Mum came over she asked her, "Why?"

And Hannah thanked me for putting the question into her head. Yes, she had learned something. Not what she had expected after all those years of faithfully following Mum's practice: Chopping off the ends before putting the ham into her oven.

"Why? Why? And you've been following me all these years?" her mother went, "Hannah, you're a silly girl! You needn't have chopped off the ends."

"Why, Mum?"

"Just look at your oven — it's bigger than mine!"

THE JUNK

ANDRE was angry. He had trusted Somchat. And Somchat had let him down.

The man, a foreign worker he hired from Thailand, could not express himself as well as his Singaporean employees, but he was hard working and helpful. And Andre's many Thai tourist clients liked the ever-smiling man. So too Andre's Thai business contacts in his tour operation.

So when a recession took its toll on the travel trade and Andre had to down size his operations, he decided in his mind to retain Somchat although he had to let go about half his team of 10 staff.

Part of his cost-saving included a snap decision to move to a cheaper rental space suddenly vacant and up for grabs in a good location. On the eve of moving day, Andre came back to his closed office late at night more for sentimental reasons, though he told himself he should check if his staff had cleared out their desks and put their things into those big cardboard boxes provided by the moving contractor.

As he moved around the premises cluttered with boxes of office property as well as personal belongings marked with staff names, something shiny in one box caught his eye. The thing was all wrapped up but for a tell-tale corner exposed by a tear in the protective brown paper.

Andre recognised it even from just the tiny bit revealed. It was his missing antique Chinese sailing boat! He had looked out for it while he hurriedly packed his own office things but could not find it. There was not enough time to go over everything again, so he had just emptied the rest of his things, including things in packages and boxes, big and small, all into the movers' big boxes.

He tore off a corner of the torn brown paper. Yes, he was right: It was his precious junk!

The junk was a gift from a major tour operator from China,

called Chin Wu, whom Andre had looked after very well with Somchat providing his ever-ready help. Andre remembered Chin Wu's words as he handed over his junk, "This is a collectors' item — one of a kind, I assure you. This gift is to show how much I value your friendship…"

Andre checked the words on the box. It read: "Somchat — personal."

He could not understand it. How had his precious junk ended up all wrapped up in a box containing an employee's things?

And Somchat, of all people!

Somchat was someone he had grown to trust. Surely the man was no thief. There must be a mistake. Andre left the junk wrapped up in the box. He would ask Somchat about it the next morning.

"HOW come my Chinese boat got into your box — that special gift to me from Mr Chin Wu?" Andre asked Somchat casually, expecting an easy explanation that would clear the matter up.

Instead, Somchat looked startled and confused. His English worsened as it always did when he got agitated.

"I... Mr Chin… Sorry! That junk is mine. Not yours. You make mistake. Mr Chin gave me. That one not yours!" he went, and his face got redder and redder.

What Andre did not like at all was the way Somchat held on tight to his claim — and the junk, even hugging the thing to his body.

That made Andre really angry.

And Somchat began to tremble, becoming even more incoherent and finally completely tongue-tied as all his colleagues shook their heads and wagged their fingers at him and joined in to reprove him.

"How could you do such a thing, Somchat?"

"Steal from the hand that feeds you — that's really

bad!"

"Hasn't Mr Andre treated all of us like family?"

Suddenly Somchat burst into tears and stretched out both hands and pushed the junk into Andre's hands, saying, "Okay, it's yours! Take it…"

But Andre was already too far hurt. He had been betrayed by someone he had trusted.

And after that, how could he keep Somchat?

It was an unhappy goodbye.

Somchat, inarticulate even at that parting point, said, "I don't what to say, Mr Andre. How to explain… But someday, somehow, I will come back and explain…"

Andre shrugged that off. He trashed all memory of that dishonest man. There were a few letters from Somchat after that, but Andre did not bother to wade through the man's garbled writing. Why struggle through all that bad English? He wrote the fellow off.

Not long after, Andre's staff told their boss some news they had picked up: Somchat had started work with a tour agency in Jakarta. It was a move up for him, for the agency had its office in a prestigious building that housed a five-star hotel.

Then came the shocking news: The hotel had been bombed by terrorists! Many people died. Among them, Somchat.

ANDRE now felt sorry for the poor guy. Except for the dishonesty over the junk, Somchat had been a likeable fellow. There had been a bond forged between them through the years — before that miserable junk theft.

The man's farewell words came back to him: "Someday I will come back and explain. Somehow I will explain…"

Well, that was the end of Somchat — he would not be able to come back and explain.

Alone in his office after all his staff had left for home, Andre looked idly in the boxes in his room, some left untouched all those months. He easily found the junk that

Somchat had surrendered to him. He put it on his desk. He felt sorrow as it all came back to him — the way Somchat had struggled to explain himself.

Mechanically his hands began to rummage through the other boxes. It seemed as if some force were propelling him to dig into those untouched boxes. His eyes then caught a familiar glint of metal. His heart pounding, he yanked it out of the place in which it had lain buried.

It was a junk — identical in all respects to the one on his desk... two of the same, the junk claimed by that Chin Wu to be unique — "one of a kind!".

Perhaps even more than two... that was entirely possible: That Chin Wu had not been a truthful fellow. He had exaggerated the worth of his junk as a collectors' item. And yes, it was also likely that, undisclosed to Andre, Chin Wu had presented Somchat that other junk...

Andre had to sit down.

He felt shame and remorse. What a stupid fool he had been to let that worthless junk destroy the precious bond between Somchat and him after their years of working together!

He saw once more the tears in Somchat's eyes. His own eyes turned misty as he stared at the thing he had swiped from his former employee: That junk on his desk for which he had sacrificed something truly precious. And the last words of a friend now dead came back to him once more:

"Someday I will come back and explain. Somehow I will explain..."

SLEEPING WITH AN UNSAVOURY CHARACTER

ALEXANDER prided himself on being notches above ordinary mankind. He prided himself on knowing more than other guys. He prided himself on being able to carry his person impressively so as to look important, reliable, absolutely top class. In short, Alexander always prided himself.

He was proud too of his wide reading. In all topics including esoteric stuff such as psychology and behaviour patterns, and physiognomy — among countless other things. In particular he was proud of one talent: With one glance he could instantly assess people he came across. Few among mankind could pull wool over Alexander's eyes. Alexander was sure of that.

Alexander went for a pleasure cruise on one of those luxury boats that sailed nowhere while passengers ate, drank, danced, gambled and indulged themselves silly.

It was "full house" on the boat, and to his dismay, he found himself obliged to sleep in a two-bunker cabin, sharing the twin accommodation with a character he did not quite care for, a fellow with a one-sided smile and slinky slit eyes. Furthermore the fellow even revealed that his name was Kon. (Alexander later asked the purser for the spelling of the name, wondering if it could really be that appropriate, with a C.)

Alexander stared at the fellow, taking in all that telltale swarthiness of complexion, unkempt stubble on chin, twitch of cheek, general nervousness of demeanour — and the fact that Kon tried to return stare for stare but could not hold his end of it. He looked away, in fact turned his whole body away.

Alexander prided himself now that he had done it again: Summed up someone at first sight. This was a bum. Not to be trusted. Distinctly unsavoury.

Fortunately he and that fellow would only be together a couple of nights and most of that time they would be unconscious — in dreamland. He had only to make sure his valuables were safely locked away. Perhaps he should get the ship's staff to keep them in their safe each night.

The bum tried to make small talk. He smiled many weak

smiles. But soon he realised that he could not hope to chum up with his cabin mate. He too must have concluded they were of different worlds. He made no more attempts to fraternise.

THAT evening, after he had tried his luck at the poker tables (and actually lost money despite his priding himself on being able to read others' minds), he called at the purser's office to hand in his money and valuables for safe-keeping.

"I'd feel safer if you kept these for me. I'm sharing my cabin with a total stranger — and frankly I don't like the look of him. He doesn't seem the honest kind, the kind I could trust."

"Absolutely, sir. I understand, sir," the purser replied, like one seasoned to deal with such requests.

Alexander was given an envelope which he duly filled, signed, sealed and handed to the officer. And then he was handed a record book to sign as well.

His duty done, the purser became chatty.

"You know, you're not the only guest here tonight to feel that way. Just before you, only half an hour ago, another gentleman came in here with the very same request, saying quite similar words. He's sleeping in a room shared with an unsavoury-looking character. He too wanted us to keep his wallet in our safe."

"Really?"

Mildly curious, Alexander looked for the gentleman's name in the register — and found it:

"Kon."

QUEENIE'S INHERITANCE

"TEN thousand dollars! How come she gets so much? A mere maid, and Mum leaves so much to her? What was Queenie to

Mum? She must have been one very cunning cheat — a schemer who worked on the helpless old woman!" Sol, the son, waxed hot and furious.

It was irrelevant to him that he, as the only offspring of his widowed mother, was to get the lion's share of the estate's worth, some $10 million. Mum's bequest to him was her huge bungalow house and "all my bonds and equities". Out of her residual miscellaneous assets, she willed $10,000 to Queenie. And whatever remained available after all disbursements was to go to a charity she supported, the Pink Leopard.

"There are a few things to be settled," David, the young lawyer, had told him. "There's the floating cash from that large tranche of bonds and equities sold but not yet actually re-invested by her fund managers at the time of her demise — about a million dollars. Strictly speaking, that's not bonds and equities. But I don't think the charity would be so uncharitable (ha! ha!) as to contest that portion on what appears to be a technicality: Arguing that, being actually cash, not yet reinvested into bonds and equities, the sum should not be yours but theirs."

Sol was not worried about that. Paula, who headed the Pink Leopard, knew the family well and was a reasonable person. And reasonably friendly too, though, on his part, he had never shown much friendliness towards her — until now. Indeed he had often grumbled openly about Paula's successful appeals to his mother.

DAVID had called a meeting with Sol and Paula, and the maid Queenie too.

Sol and Paula came early, before the maid.

"I don't accept that my mother's maid should be getting such a bonanza. How come your firm, as her lawyers, allowed my mother to do a dumb thing like that? She couldn't have been in her right mind!" Sol ranted away, repeating his gripe.

"As I explained to you before, it's her money. She can will it any way she wants... and she was in her right mind at the time," David said softly but firmly.

"How can she be in her right mind, David, once it's been softened up? I'm sure that Queenie's no angel. She must have been scheming all along, working on the old lady, buttering her up with flattery, jumping to her every whim and fancy. And, no doubt melting her heart with sob-sob stories about her own poor family at home. Manipulating her where she was most vulnerable because of her need for family to be around..."

"Because you were not around for her?" Paula came in. She knew the old lady. And Queenie. And Sol, too.

"That's none of your business, Paula! But actually I was busy with my projects, bogged down with my overseas business deals. I just could not find the time to come home. And anyway, it's not as if she had no resources to use to take care of herself..."

"You never came home even when we phoned you to tell you she had a serious fall and suffered painful fractures. Not even when she herself asked you to come. You were just not there for her. Queenie was," Paula went on, relentless.

"That Queenie! No doubt she rubbed that in!"

"No, she did not. In fact, I heard your mother complaining a few times that you did not care for her anymore. I saw her tears. And Queenie would tell her each time not to judge you too harshly, that you must have been really tied up, otherwise you would have come... Queenie defended you!"

"Ha! You believed that? Come on, get real! That must have been for your benefit, while you were around. God knows what she could have told her when they were alone!"

"Believe what you want, Sol. The fact is Queenie did take wonderful care of your mother when there was no one else around for her, nobody to keep her company, to listen to her, pray with her, tend to her needs... she gave her the love she needed. Something beyond medical care and food and service. Queenie was closer to her than you were. She was like a daughter to her."

"A daughter? Good grief, you must be a bigger fool than I thought! That slimy woman was doing all that stuff to toady up to her, to get a big fat ang pow from her — most likely, she went all out to poison her against me, do me out of my inheritance... like a daughter, indeed? Hah!"

AT THAT moment, Queenie arrived. And the first words she said, breathless and shiny-eyed, were:

"May I say thank you, everyone? I'm so grateful to Mum for that big inheritance she gave me in her will!"

"Mum? Don't you call her Mum! Don't you dare call my mother your Mum!" Sol burst out like a madman, his arms actually going up, as though ready to strike the maid.

"Don't be silly, Sol!" David intervened quickly, "All maids call their employers Mum! It means nothing!"

"It means something in her case," Paula would not let it pass.

"What's wrong, sir? Did I say anything wrong? Did I do anything wrong?" Queenie's eyes were wide open with shock at Sol's hostility.

"Wrong? You bet, you scheming woman! I'm going to expose you. I'll take you to court. I'm willing to spend a fortune on it. I can afford it. I'm going to make sure that you don't get a penny. And I'm going to make sure you get punished for trying to swindle a defenceless old woman who was ill and dying. Just think of the logic of it: You're not family, you're just a maid, how the heck could you ever inherit such a big sum? You took advantage of a defenceless old woman! I promise you: You'll go to jail! Don't you know that you can be jailed for trying to cheat?"

"I don't know, sir. I never asked for the money. Please, sir, I won't take it if you don't think I should. I don't want to go to jail, sir. Please, sir, don't be angry. I swear I only did everything I could for Mum, for your mother, out of love — not for money!"

Queenie was now on her knees to Sol, in tears, frantic with fear.

David could not find his voice. He was shocked into silence at the sudden drama.

Paula was not.

"Look here, Sol, you're going too far. You're terrorising the poor woman. She's got a right to the money, you know?"

"She's got a right to repudiate her inheritance, Paula. And she's just done precisely that," Sol said in triumph, not about to let the moment go.

Turning to Queenie, he said, "Will you sign a paper right now? Say you will not take the money, that you do not make a claim for it? Write it out and sign it now, and I'll forgive you. I won't prosecute you!"

"Yes, sir. Anything you say, sir!"

That was too much for the others there.

David looked about to come to life and say his bit. But he had still to find the precise and legally correct words.

Paula beat him to it.

"Sol, let's make this crystal clear to you. Your mother has the right to leave whatever sum she wants to a maid who has been so faithful to her. And Queenie has the right to take it…"

"And Paula, I have the right to contest her inheritance. I'll sue, I promise you. And with a good lawyer, I'm sure I'll have a good chance of winning, too!"

"Yes, Sol," Paula admitted.

And then in a dead serious voice, she added quietly as though thinking aloud, "Just as the Pink Leopard has the right to contest your claim to that cash floating pending re-investment — that lot of bonds and equities after they cease to be such. And I'm sure we'll have a good chance of winning, too."

David found his voice at this point, "Paula does have a point."

And to help Sol to do the wise thing, he added in his best lawyer's voice, "And the Pink Leopard will have a chance of winning, too!"

"So back off, Sol!" Paula's voice growled low as a leopard ready to pounce.

QUEENIE got her inheritance.

TOLEDO'S PASSING

SUMIKO TAN, the seasoned *Straits Times* journalist now editor, once devoted an article to a simple domestic event: The passing of her dog. I found her words edifying. Especially as Pat and Karen, our son and daughter-in-law, had just had to go through the same grief.

And (to a lesser degree) me too.

Their golden retriever was sent to our home when they found it impossible to manage two babies and an ageing big dog, not to mention a home body cat that hardly went out, all crammed into an average apartment. Our bungalow house seemed a natural alternative for Toledo, having become a kind of old folks' home complete with large garden for roaming if not romping (and if and when it came to that, vegetating with the vegetables), not to mention fellow residents of corresponding vintage: My wife and myself.

I have to admit that I was not exactly sold on the idea at first. I had been chased and bitten by dogs three times in my life, so I was by no means your head-patting, lick-loving, rabid dog-lover. But *ole!* Toledo learned to live with me, and I with him. I got used to his natural super-friendliness towards all humankind. He got used to my psychopathic non-friendliness towards all canine-kind.

When he first came he was everywhere in the house. He loved the place. At first he roamed all over the premises — and I was no longer lord of my castle. But we soon fixed that. Not without loud barks of protest, I began to set the OB markers. With secured grille doors and gates, I defined the inside of the house proper as out of bounds to him, leaving the garden, covered terrace and garage as his domain, subject, of course, to my right of access any time (a right I was no longer eager to exercise in view of loss of exclusiveness).

At first he would determinedly picket our entrance way, vociferously declaiming his objections to the segregation, hoping perhaps that I might relent and recognise his right to mingle with other of God's creatures and allow him in.

But my response was masterly inactivity and he finally accepted the inevitable.

It took time but we arrived at a kind of *modus vivendi.*

And over time Toledo and I even bonded, though on a strictly-no-licking understanding. Dogs have a way of getting to you — God did not give them soulful eyes for nothing.

Then Toledo took to parking himself in our car-parking spaces, refusing to budge despite our loud honking. He had to be physically dragged away! Later he would even sprawl his massive body over our welcome mat, blocking ingress and egress, regardless of our vociferous urging to move aside.

We did not realise it then. The dog was trying to tell us something — but we were just too dense to understand.

Toledo was ill — very ill. And then he started to go down-hill fast. He was diagnosed with secondary cancer. Pat and Karen took Toledo back to their apartment, more a home of love to him than our house, congestion regardless. Soon they had to make that painful decision: To put their dog to sleep.

After Toledo's passing, I wrote out my condolences to them:

"We do not know if dogs have a soul (or equivalent thereof) but once I read in some religious writing that animals have something called an 'animus' — but that kind of 'dogma' could be just dodging that mother of all questions: The dog gone soul question.

"Whatever the answer, I have a feeling that when we ourselves are about to cross that border to Heaven we might just hear a familiar barking and sense a sudden rush of body of animated fur — and maybe even get anointed with yukky licking of feet… we thought we might let you know our thoughts (and prayers), whether or not this helps a bit or at all…"

In his passing Toledo did his last bit for us and kind of bonded our family closer together. And on the metaphysical plane he took us to a new openness of mind. You might even call it a higher threshold of spiritual insight…

Shakespeare put it well:

"There are more things in heaven and on earth than are dreamt of in your philosophy."

A Remembered Hallmark Of Friends

EVERY time I get one of those beautifully printed cards so inspiringly worded, I remember my old cronies in the Social Welfare Department where I spent some truly happy years. Not that those guys, a stingy bunch, had a habit of splurging on expensive cards. In fact there was only one card that I remember them for — it was *their* Hallmark. And even that one, they did not give actually to me.

I was then up for a promotion interview. For my great leap forward, from the time scale salary range of ordinary civil servants to the superscale grade — a take-off to the heaven of the stars of the service. I was naturally tense, and my colleagues sweated with me though they assured me it was in the bag.

"Who does not know the fantastic job you did in the relief operations for the 16,000 victims of the recent Bukit Ho Swee fire? How can they not recognise you for that?"

I was grateful for that encouragement. The standards for breakthrough into the super grade were rigid and I knew I had at most a 50-50 chance, there being so many other superb performers among my competitors.

As I left my Department to go the Public Service Commission for the interview, my three closest buddies told me they would wait for my return.

The Commissioners asked me tough and probing questions that showed their high expectations. But after an hour of grilling, I sensed that I was winning them over. They were now going into areas that showed they were evaluating how I could fit into higher duties.

At length the chairman conferred with his fellow committee members. They all nodded and kept smiling, which was a good sign. The chairman said I could go. I felt I had established enough rapport, and so I boldly asked whether I had got the upgrading.

The chairman looked at his colleagues who nodded like they were assenting to an unspoken question. So he said, "Young man, normally we don't say this to candidates. But if I were you, I'd go and celebrate."

I FLOATED out of the room, on cloud nine all the way back to my office where my buddies awaited my return.

The moment they saw me, they asked eagerly, "You got it?" They did not wait for my reply. It must have been written all over my face. Or perhaps it was true — they had all along been 100 per cent confident about my chances and did not need my answer.

That would seem the case for they straightaway handed me a beautiful Hallmark card with printed poetry plus their penned congratulations ("We knew you would make it to the Superman grade! Let's go celebrate!"). And they announced that they had already booked a table at a nearby posh place for dinner.

So we went to our celebration do, those friends of mine who proved they had greater faith in me than I had myself.

Thank God for buddies like these! I congratulated myself over and over again. We drank more than we should've done. We left the premises, singing steadily, walking unsteadily. We wisely decided to leave our cars behind and go home by taxi. My pals left first as I had to make a toilet call.

As I waited for a cab outside the door, I remembered something those guys had given me, that Hallmark card of theirs. I felt for it in my pockets to fish it out to read once more.

Just then the waiter at our table came rushing out to me. "Wait, sir! Here's an envelope one of your friends left on his seat. Must have dropped from his pocket or briefcase." He handed it to me. It was addressed to me. I opened it. I found a Hallmark card: A lovely card with lovely poetry, different from the card given to me earlier — with moving words of consolation.

And on it my friends had penned their own words:

"Never mind about not getting the promotion. Forget it. It's more important that you deserve it. And hey, you're sure to get it before long. So, let's go and get drunk and drown our sorrows!"

That was my remembered Hallmark of friends.

Hope *Wan Liao!*

"HOPE *wan liao*!" Elsie announced the crisis: It was all over for Hope!

"She just told me so herself. It's been coming for a while, but now Frank's gone and done the karate chop. He's told her he's divorcing her."

We sipped our cafeteria coffee in silent empathy with Hope, a dear friend for long years.

Then we talked about Hope and Frank, once actually voted in our church group as the model married pair. And we began to throw up other names — other friends, other marriages broken up through the years — good God, so many!

"What's the world coming to?" Denise, reasonably happily married, at least for now, voiced her unease. "What's happening to family values? What's the good of wedding vows? For better or for worse, in sickness and in health, till death do us part — huh?"

"God, why so many failures, so many broken families?" Helen asked God.

I wondered aloud if God was the party to question and threw in my two bits. "It's the things changing so fast around us — to hell with old-fashioned self-control, no inhibitions about anything at all, women now leaping in with men in unbridled pleasure sprees, the media and the Internet running wild and naked right into homes, old values becoming side lined as too fuddy-duddy for new situations, no new values replacing them…"

We were quickly into even deeper gloom and doom, extrapolating our gripes into neglect and dumping of children, feuds within families, social clashes, endless wars, corruption in high places, and soon on to terrorism and non-existent weapons of mass destruction, and beheadings and other current favourites — generally, the implosion of human relations…

"What hope does the world have?" Denise summed up for us.

Clouds had darkened the sky outside. We parted company in that dismal atmosphere, real and metaphorical, no solution found.

"Yes, it's a black world we live in. What hope is there, indeed?" I rumbled within as the oppressive skies above rumbled in like tune.

Then suddenly against the grey clouds a shadowy face appeared — someone who had taught me something when I pointed to the sky outside the window by his bed:

"You can't see it now, but it's there. Behind those clouds it's there still: The sun. It's there and, in fact, that's why you can see the clouds…"

And the man went on to talk about good things to be found even when things look bad…

I decided to go and see him.

BONG was a new friend, a retiree happily staying with his son's family till he became bedridden, and so he got further retired — into a retirement home. He had certainly good reason to be cheerless, yet he smiled most of the time and he was always reaching out to others around him who needed cheering up.

I recalled the afternoon we first met. I arrived at his home with a bus-load of church friends on a mission of goodwill and mercy: A Christmas carol-singing call. Our noisy group descended on the home's half-asleep old folks, like sudden angels from on high, high and mighty with self-crowned halos, sweetly (or at least so we thought) singing over the plains, loud and long in our disharmonious repetitions of *Gloria in Excelsis Deo!*

We had come to bring Bong and his fellow-residents good cheer — plus, of course, our goodies bought at cheap sales.

Some of the old folks reacted downright grumpily. A few

actually scolded us for interrupting their siesta. Bong came to our rescue. He cajoled his comrades and calmed them down, in the end actually getting everyone to switch to friendly mode, applauding our efforts and joining in the singing. His mediation saved our mission of goodwill.

I asked the nun in charge about him. "Bong's an incredibly joyful person... you know, he's practically dumped by his family? They visited him less and less often. And finally the lot of them just emigrated away."

I sought a chance to speak to Bong, one to one. It must be hurtful getting dumped. I wanted to ooze sympathy.

Bong smiled and deftly changed the subject.

Nearby I noticed a sad-faced resident looking in a daze at a family photo by his bed. Next to him someone was complaining softly to his visitor about neglecting him... so many long faces around!

Bong did not focus on them. Instead he pointed to a lady nearby who was gently pulling a blanket to cover an old man who was dozing off. "That's Ah Tuck and his daughter... isn't that a touching picture?" I hadn't noticed, but now I did.

And then graphically, with drama of facial expression and gesticulation, he told me about how another resident shared some finger-licking-good sour *kana* (preserved fruit), a present received that morning, with someone who had no visitors. "Now, doesn't that just make you feel great? There's such a lot of goodness around in the world, isn't there?"

A visitor's little child joined us, urged by his mother to share his box of Smarties with Bong. He offered Bong only the black and brown chocolates, carefully separating off the red and green and other bright-coloured ones for himself. Finally he had only two Smarties left, one red and one black. He offered Bong the black one.

With a twinkle in his eye, Bong asked, "Can I have the red one, please? It'll make me really happy if I can have at least one red one."

The boy hesitated. He looked at Bong, then at his mother. It was a tough call. He put the red one in his hand. He offered it to Bong.

"You see what I mean? There's a lot of goodness in the world," Bong said, as he laughed and took the black one instead, raising happy smiles all around.

SO, COMING out of that dark evening with my friends drenched in despair about Hope, I instinctively sought the company of my friend Bong.

No words were needed. His smiling eyes and the memory of his infectious joy at once dispensed me the consolation I needed.

Yes, hope is never, never, *wan liao!*

Goodness and joy are always there, behind whatever dark clouds, waiting to be uncovered…

FAMILY GEMS

FATHER'S PRESENT

IN MY seven-year-old heart, I felt let down.

I could not understand it. Father had promised me a very special present if I did well in my Primary One examinations in my new school. I did not know what it would be, but from the way Father mentioned it, the present had to be something really special. Not just another bar of chocolate or pencil box. Not anything ordinary.

Earlier that year (1935) somehow my family got me into SJI (St Joseph's Institution). My uncle worked that miracle: getting my elder brother and myself into that premier school. So we moved from a nothing school, the ramshackle old Royal English School (long since deservedly demised), to an everything school.

Despite my age, I was placed in the bottom rung with the six-year-olds. If I did well enough I would leap-frog past the next level to join the others in my own age group.

Father urged me to do my very best. "Do well and I'll give you a very special present," he distinctly said.

I did well. I was not first in my class, but still I was a credible eighth boy in a class of 40 — and that was well enough for the school to grant me my leap-frog wish.

I CAME home shining with the joyful news of my double promotion. Father said he was happy, but he looked preoccupied.

And that was it. He totally forgot something important — my very special present for doing well!

Indeed he was immersed in his frowning silence and gloom most of the time then. Seeing my disappointment, my uncle pulled me aside and told me why Father looked like that. He had just received another of those letters from China.

Letters from China were always from my grandfather, his father. And they always made Father depressed. They brought nothing but devastating news: Calamities like drought or flood, crop failure, famine, illness — and, of course, they asked for money to be remitted home *"joo kin joo ho"* (the faster the better)!

Father had a heavy burden to shoulder. As eldest son, he had to support not only his own family but also his father's, ever since Grandfather got himself deported back to China by the British. Father's pay as a bank clerk was not much. He had to support his family as well as his own father's family in Singapore, so it was a tough life for him. In addition, now and again, he was called upon to remit money to help support his father's second wife and the second family fathered by him since his return to the old country.

Being filial to his father's appeals naturally took precedence over spending on his own children.

Promise or no promise, Father was dead broke by then.

I felt utterly dejected. I did not say a word to anyone. I just buried my head in my books. I cried, but only in my heart.

He promised me! He has not kept his promise to give me a very special present for doing well…

Father at last noticed my long face. He took me aside. He bent his head down close to mine, forehead on forehead, took hold of my shoulders, and looked me in the eye. And he said softly, "I'm sorry, I even had to borrow tontine money to send home to my father in China. A son has always to say yes to his father, no matter what… so I don't have money left to buy you your present. But I want you to know this: By doing so well you have made me proud of you. That is something I can promise you every time you do well: My pride in you as my son!"

I could not help it. My eyes turned red. The first reaction in my heart was (and I might even have let it burst out): *Big deal!*

But Father's eyes continued to search mine. And I was suddenly drawn into the earnestness and love reflected in them. He was appealing for my understanding — something he desperately needed.

A son has a duty to his father. Fathers just have to put their own fathers before sons, before themselves! Right?

Out of the turmoil and confusion inside me, something stirred. Perhaps it was my Chinese genes, centuries old but still strong enough to assert themselves. They led me the way they had led Father.

Sons always put parents first… Chinese filial piety.

"Right! And that's our big deal," I spoke out of a heart maturing fast, "I do well, and you be proud of me every time I do that…"

Father was indeed proud of me.

He made that pride abundantly clear. He spoke about me to every single one of our relatives, and to all our neighbours, and his office colleagues and friends — and even to total strangers. If he had the money he would have put out advertisements in the papers.

I too kept my side of the deal.

After that eighth-boy placing in my first year in SJI, I went on to score my real successes — one each year for Father.

I achieved first-boy placing for every year-end examination from the following year right through to my last year in school.

Courtesy of a father's very special present: A nothing present that became an everything present.

Gone Home

LITTLE Steffi, that bright two-year-old, is picking up words at breakneck speed. Never mind meanings — those things can follow later.

She toddles into my lounge. Her eye catches something

familiar — the corner of a picture sticking out from beneath a pile of other framed pictures. She tugs at it till it is clear what it is: A picture by a Myanmar village artist created from coloured stones stuck on a board. It was a parting gift from Steffi's former nursemaid, who left the family months ago.

"Nice," Steffi says as she holds it in her hands. She adds in a softer voice, "Auntie!" She is telling me that is something from Auntie? It is something that touches her? Perhaps more — more than she knows how to put words to?

She misses her?

Does she know where Auntie has gone? I can find out:

"Steffi, where's Auntie?"

"Gone home," Steffi answers straight off. She must have asked that question too — and her Mummy had given her the answer.

Does she know what "gone home" means? I don't think so. The process of knowing what words mean comes in stages as she hears them over and over again in different contexts.

FOR example:

"Where's Baby Ryan?" That was a question I once asked Steffi when I came out of the toilet to find her playmate no longer with her.

"Gone home," Mummy replied for her.

"Gone home," Steffi repeated that reply on her own behalf. Baby Ryan had returned home to his house as he usually did around that time. Steffi had, and will continue to have, that kind of situation to be a context marker to colour in what "gone home" means.

"GONE," as a word on its own, Steffi is also learning to understand. She hears it often:

Daddy has "gone" to work.
Mummy has "gone" to the market.
Her dog has "gone" for his walk.

Auntie has "gone" to the shop downstairs to buy something.
The rain has "gone" away and little Steffi can go out to play.
Daddy has "gone" to England for a meeting.

"Home", as a word on its own, Steffi understands better if not completely. It comes up more often:
Come Steffi, get in the car, we're going "home".
Grandma and Grandpa are at "home".
We're off to fetch Daddy — Daddy's coming "home" from England.

"Home" is not one place. It is many places. It means a happy, comfortable, familiar place, a nice place people go back to.

Is it far off? Or near? Hours off, or days and weeks away?

Or even forever?

Auntie has "gone home". In time, little Steffi will learn there is a further off going away from her — to a further off home, a kind of Never-Neverland, a place in the world, but not her world.

Steffi's 12-year-old cousin, my other granddaughter, Colleen, is 10 years ahead into meanings of "gone home". Of course, much higher all round in the learning curve of meanings. But even for her there will still be depths of things to learn.

SOME time in time to come, both Colleen and Steffi will be told some old person (like Grandpa) has gone "home" to a new meaning of home. And, that will add that ultimate meaning to their embrace of "home" — beyond time, beyond world…

And then for them, hopefully, "gone home" will extrapolate into an infinity of meaning: An ending departure that is also an endless arrival. A going that is also a new kind of remaining. To a place that is not a place but a state of mind, or rather of soul. Amid whys and no's that will resolve into acceptance and peace. Visions of a future and forever togetherness.

"Gone home" will then unveil its last and lasting meaning.

Colleen and Steffi, just hold fast to your child-state openness to meanings. Do not follow those who grow out of openness to fall through the trap door into closed minds. Do not deny those coming vistas of meanings that will stretch all your way, on and on, from here to eternity:

To home in heaven.

NEW MAN KIND

My old man.

Mary calls Tom that. That's what her generation calls husbands. Old as a term of affection, not age or era.

But their old men do belong to one era of time — and the species has evolved. Quietly, almost imperceptibly, the men have become something else.

"What? Cook?" Mary would have raised her eyebrows in surprise if she had been asked that about her husband, Tom. And Tom would have probably dropped dead. No sirree, men do not cook for the family, no way! Men do not do kitchen stuff. Nor do they baby-sit, do laundry, or clean house. Mary's man would have felt a sissy to don an apron and do a housewife's chores. So would all his buddies. Macho, or at least macho-looking, never caught doing non-macho things — that's what men had to be.

For some men, even pushing a pram called for execution with consummate circumspection including due put-on of nonchalance, if not a deliberate display of embarrassment.

Coo-cooing to baby was, of course, absolutely taboo — at least in public.

And real men just do not change diapers.
Neither do they pee or poo a toddler. God forbid!

MARY and her old man invited us out to dinner at a beach restaurant with their son Pete and his family. The older men and women were there first. The young couple and their two-year-old infant arrived, blowing in like a gust of fresh wind in a flurry of fun and laughter.

Pete carried little Susie, kissing and baby-talking the giggling child all the while. Kate followed behind carrying the baby's things. Macho or not, father had a relationship going on with baby, mother conceding and coming along one step behind.

As we sat at the table, Pete joined in feeding the baby, even going "ummm!" with each spoon making its way into the little mouth. All that with aplomb and natural ease.

And Pete turned his head and smiled at us, the old men and the old women — and we suddenly felt absorbed and accepted into the warm wholeness of that family togetherness. Family togetherness that drew no boundaries to define male and female roles.

Apparently reading our minds, Kate confirmed, "Yes, Pete bathes the baby too. And puts her to sleep…"

And no doubt do those pee and poo things for baby too. You bet!

Yes, Pete is man unshackled. New man kind. Freed to be father and mother. To be all things that are family. He and his generation have re-defined man in family, man's role in household.

No longer like our generation, shackled in single dimension, man and woman defined by a gender, man and woman each with a one-face family agenda.

No longer *old man*. Pete is *new man*, he as parent as she: New man kind.

THE BROKEN WEDDING SET

IT WAS a free and easy family-and-friends buffet — Singapore *chin-chye chap-chye style* (no-fuss hodgepodge grub), home-cooked stuff plus hawker fare laid out at side-counters, random seats at our dining table with additional chairs at other smaller tables plus our staircase steps.

Someone, one of those merciless and loud-mouthed auntie types, remarked candidly on our old dining plates, still good except that the green bamboo motif on them was now hardly visible: "*Aiyoh!* So faded! And you still use them?"

"A wedding gift — an original C K Tang full dining crockery set," Sylvia explained.

"What? A wedding present? So they must be 50 years old, right? And you still have the set complete?"

"All except one dinner plate," I came in with an embarrassed smile, ready to make my full and frank confession with that relentless auntie in charge of cross-examination.

"How awful — one piece breaking a perfect set! And by now, surely a collector's item too…"

"Tubby broke it," Sylvia laughed as she looked at me.

"Good grief! How could you?" the cross-examination went on.

"Easy!" Sylvia continued laughing, "He threw it out the window!"

"What? You actually threw it out?"

"And on the night before our wedding too!" Sylvia put on her best look of martyrdom.

"Let me explain," I said, now the centre of rapt attention whether I liked it or not:

"THAT night something led me to take another look at that magnificent set, just delivered to my house a week or so earlier. We had left the costly crockery mostly still unwrapped in the huge cardboard box it came in. I opened the box and removed more of the brown paper that cushioned and covered each piece. To my horror I discovered white ants crawling all over the top pieces! Frantically, I unwrapped them and took them all out, leaving only paper and those unwelcome insects behind in the box — or so I thought. It was only after I threw the box with its contents, paper and termites and all, out from a rear window into my backyard space that I thought of checking whether all the pieces in the set had been safely retrieved. They were — all except one, one miserable dining plate.

"I rushed downstairs to my backyard. I rummaged through the paper in the discarded box. I found the missing piece, all right. It even looked all right. But when my hands picked it up it crumbled — a thing of beauty shattered beyond salvation! I felt utterly woeful.

"The next day we got married in our church. It was a perfect wedding. Everything went off smoothly. Then I told my wife about our broken wedding set — the one iota of imperfection to a perfect day!"

"*Aiyoh!* What a terrible thing to happen — such a bad omen for your wedding!" Our auntie came out pat with her ready prognosis of evil, no doubt out of force of habit.

"Bad omen for our wedding?" Sylvia and I both went. We looked at each other. We smiled. We did not need to rebut with words.

AND yet things did happen to us — things that broke us, perhaps like the breaking of that plate…

Like when we quarrelled, both standing firm on our own ground. But then we were two individuals with our own strong personalities and views. And we always made up.

Like when our second child David died, unexpectedly stillborn. That was a terrible blow. But we moved on and within a year God sent us a replacement second child, John… And David was to come back to us in later years — unexpectedly, in a different way, and yet still David. (But that is another story…)

Like when my widowed mother, with her own lifelong set ways, her inarticulate grief in heart, came to live with us. And Sylvia, for all her sympathy, began to suffer that loss of soul tranquillity when there is no longer one sole woman beneath one roof — well symbolised in our Chinese hieroglyphic character (*an*) for peace. I suffered the torment of being torn apart into two. And worst of all, each of us unable to share without hurting the other, staying mute, yet feeling the mutual silence.

Like so many other broken things, perhaps forewarned to us in the breaking of our wedding set with the shattering of that one piece…

AND yet, a perfect set, surviving intact through all those years of our life, would have had no meaning — beyond our fading away with the fading of design.

One piece broken right at the start prepared us to accept other things in our life yet to break — without fatal crack to the almost-perfect set we still have and cherish.

No, one broken piece does not a wedding set break. Indeed, that one broken piece prepared us for imperfection.

It made our wedding set.

THE EYES OF MY FATHER

IDENTIFICATION of people in the archive spaces of the mind often distil down to one thumbnail image: Some clothing or the way clothing is worn, some act or attitude, a speech habit or a favourite phrase, a peculiar gait, a touch, a heady scent or a nauseating body odour. Or one unforgettable feature of body or expression of face.

My summary image of Father, now dead four decades, is

his eyes — the goodness in the eyes of a man who lived his life doing good for others.

They told me how, as eldest son, he looked after his siblings; how from his teenage years he pitched in to help his mother and the family left behind in Singapore by his banished father. He went to work early for his (and their) keep. When he landed a prize white-collar job with a British bank, he was able to marry and raise his own family as well. And, Grandfather in China, hearing the great news that Father was now a regular wage-earner, promptly wrote and asked for his cut. Father responded with filial piety remitting what sum he could spare to help support his father — and the old man's new wife and children in China.

Fortunately the cost of living was incredibly low in his time. The lowest denomination of currency was a quarter-cent coin and you could buy a decent meal with that. So his sumptuous salary of $18 as a bank clerk in the prestigious Hong Kong and Shanghai Bank went a powerful long way.

Outside his family circle he helped people he knew, and others he hardly knew. And as one of the few English-educated youth in Chinatown where he lived, he was often asked to read and write letters for others.

He joined a mutual aid society — a welfare group that helped its members (and others) in emergency need, especially when bereaved. He ended up the society's treasurer — a life sentence.

His services were also eagerly sought to tutor neighbours' children weak in studies. Sometimes he was paid, sometimes not.

When one of his office colleagues needed to borrow money from the bank for a big bang for his only son's wedding, Father was the only one to gamely stand as debt guarantor despite the real risk of repayment default.

He was the one his colleagues turned to for help when, in danger of punishment for some mistake, they needed an advocate to plead with their boss. Often he had to undertake to supervise them personally to ensure no repetition of fault.

And when his Chinese supervisor needed leave beyond his exhausted entitlement to recuperate from ill health, he undertook to cover the man's duties in addition to his own. He had to work late into the night — and that, and many other chores and stresses for others, in due course of time took their toll on his health.

He was everybody's friend in need.

And so, in the end, his eyes told of he kind of man he was to all — they spoke compassion.

I NO longer remember the details of those last weeks of his terminal illness. There was a time when every iota of those days of agony were memory treasure and I could recount them, blow by pain-filled blow, to anyone.

Now all that is eroded away.

Except that one treasure: His eyes.

Right to the end, his concern had been for us — even when he no longer had reason to worry about us. Because of his sacrifices, all of us were doing well. Care and love shone out of his eyes right to the end. Pain sneaked out too but that was quickly suppressed.

When he died and those eyes closed for good, I grieved for him with a grave sense of loss, the loss of those eyes to the grave: *Never again would I see those eyes!*

MY BROTHER Charlie gave the best years of his life to serve as a Brother of the Gabrielite order in Boys' Town helping lost young people find their way to get back on track. After that he gave another chunk of his life working for the blind. But my eyes were blind to the shine in Charlie's eyes. Until someone remarked to me how much he looked like our father.

I studied him up close.

I saw Father's eyes.

AND I began to see those eyes in other people too.

I saw Father's eyes in Catherine's — my sister who spent a lifetime caring for her family, then went on to help care for others through her voluntary church work.

Beyond Charlie and Catherine, those compassionate eyes are everywhere.

The world is full of good people — care and compassion shine out of so many. Only we often do not look to see that light in others. For when we focus on people in our unlit mode, they too turn lightless eyes on us…

My working life, a good part sweated out in a materialistic world, raising solid buildings and making solid money for the banks I worked in, toughened me, made my eyes as hard as hard-hat or gold-bar.

Attitudes, like concrete, harden over the years and stay hard…

But natural elements take their toll on them, so concrete can crumble, and they can be hacked down. So my soul drew hope from the good example of others — and grew with compassion.

For compassion is contagious — from eye contact on to soul contact, and we succumb to compassion.

So I learn to respond to others…

I AM in touch with a remote family member, not often met before, someone who has recently given birth — sadly, to a girl with Down's Syndrome. Mother has come to accept and cherish the baby. And father too. They are celebrating the baby's baptism. They are having a meal at their home, to present her to relatives and friends — such as will come their way…

I am on my way.

I wondered what to say to them, how to shine on the baby. I look in the mirror. I saw the look that was all I needed to bring them:

The eyes of my Father.

WEDDING PARTY FOR A COOLIE'S SON

"DAD, Sylvia and I have decided. There's no need to spend on a wedding dinner for us," I said.

Dad looked doubtful. My elder brother had gone off and entered a Catholic religious order, so marriage was out for him. I was Dad's first son to get married.

I could read his mind. He was thinking of his co-workers in the Hong Kong and Shanghai Bank where he had been a clerk ever since he was 18. And surely I had my office friends to consider. And Sylvia, my wife-to-be, a doctor, had her hospital colleagues too.

The whole big gang would have to be invited to celebrate with us.

"A wedding dinner will have to be a big affair, and in a posh place too. It will cost a bomb," I said.

"I can borrow from the bank," Dad offered immediately.

"No, Dad! We can have a tea instead. And we can pay for that ourselves."

And Sylvia nodded her firm support.

Dad still looked unsure. I quickly added, "We can have it at the Adelphi Hotel. That's a top class venue. Tea there will cost a bit more but it won't cost us a bomb like a Chinese dinner."

Mother chipped in to say she would cook us a big meal at the family house as well to do the right thing by close relatives.

Dad did not exactly say those words made famous by a classic Singapore TV serial, "This reminds me of a story…" but it obviously did, for he went on to tell his story.

IN HIS bank he had under him a *coolie* (as Chinese labourers were called in his time) and a *peon* (as Malay office boys were called then). Ah Seng and Hassan were much older than him, and they had served the bank for longer too.

When Ah Seng's son got married, the *coolie* spent a fortune on the celebrations. The highlight was a lavish 12-course Chinese dinner at the Wing Choon Yuen in Great World Park, then the Number One favourite restaurant of rich Chinese towkays. The *coolie's* meagre savings were not enough to meet the expenses, so he obtained a loan of $1,000 for the feast, a prodigious sum in those days. The bank lent him the money at a special interest rate, normally only granted to favoured big clients.

"Hong is my only son. I have to celebrate this important event in a big way. It's the grandest moment of his life, and mine too!" Ah Seng told his office colleagues, refusing to listen to their advice not to splurge so much on one night of feasting and drinking. The show was for family and friends, and Hong was all he had to show for. Ah Seng's mind was set. There had to be an extravaganza, no matter what the cost.

However, Ah Seng privately confided to Dad, "Hong has promised me he will help me repay the loan once he finds work and has money coming in."

So Ah Seng had his grandest moment.

And after that moment he spent the rest of his working days, a sentence of nearly 20 years of hard labour, slaving away to repay that loan. Without fail, the efficient bank he worked for faithfully deducted the instalments of principal and interest from his monthly wage.

Hong did find work and did have money coming in. But he did not help his father repay the loan. By the time Ah Seng stopped work, a spent and sickly man, he had only a paltry sum left to see him through his sunset years.

"You mean Ah Seng's son didn't help his father with any repayment at all — after the old man incurred that heavy debt for his sake?" I asked.

Dad did not answer directly. "Hong's marriage did not

work out. He had a roving eye, and a roving itch. Before long he went abroad for good, deserting his wife and leaving his father with that extra mouth to feed! After that Ah Seng heard nothing from Hong for years. Then, after Ah Seng retired, out of the blue a letter arrived. Hong revealed he was now in Macao. He had been there for some years, working in a casino. And apparently he was doing okay…"

"So, he sent his father some money?" I asked.

"No. On the contrary, he wanted Ah Seng to remit him money — and a big sum too. *From his retirement savings if he had the money? If not, could he borrow from the bank again?* He said he was on to something absolutely fantastic, the biggest chance of his life to hit the jackpot, a sure fire get-rich-quick thing.

"He asked his father to believe him: Yes, together they were going to make pots of money. *I swear to you, that is the truth*, he declared to his father…

"Ah Seng knew his son. Yes, when Hong talked like that, it was most likely the truth. Pots of money could be theirs!

"*Truth and pots of money at last from Hong?* As if that matters now? Ah Seng tore up his son's letter."

AND then Dad went on to tell us, by way of contrast, the story of Hassan the *peon*, who also had an only son. He celebrated his son's wedding quietly, quite within his modest means. No need for a loan from anywhere.

Over the years he saved enough to invest in sundry goods stall when he retired. And that modest business prospered.

Hassan was now the owner of a shop, doing well enough to ensure a comfortable living for his son, and the generation after him.

THERE was no need for Dad to ask us, "And the moral of the story is…?"

Also no need for him to confirm whether he endorsed our wedding tea decision.

TOUCHED BY A TAN TOCK SENG ANGEL

IF HAVING no pulse means a person is dead (or nearly there), then I was dead (or nearly there). I was three then, too young to remember the details, and anyway my mind was dead to the world. Mummy filled me in on the full story of my childhood crisis.

It was the second day of the Chinese New Year. We were getting ready to go to Grandma's house for her usual family dinner with lots of relatives. As we were about to leave, I started to poo. In those days, I pooed whenever I could. Then I started to puke as well. After Mummy changed my clothes (and her own), I promptly started all over again, and I continued pooing and puking myself to pieces in Daddy's car.

(Later the doctors said I was suffering from septicemia. Somehow the bacteria had got into my bloodstream and mounted a massive attack on me.)

By the time we reached Grandma's house, I was a horrible mess. I was already limp and faint. Daddy carried me in. The guests there were shocked.

Grandpa told me that I kept on saying, "I want to see a doctor…" He said, "You forgot Grandma is a doctor." My Uncle Pat, also a doctor, was there too. Both examined me and agreed, "Better take her to hospital!" Grandma grabbed a tablecloth, wrapped me in it, and the whole family rushed me off to Tan Tock Seng Hospital.

At the hospital they must have been surprised to see us, a solid mass of people crowding into their Emergency Unit. They must have been relieved to discover there was only one patient — little me.

Grandma told the nurses I was in crisis. So I got into the emergency room at once. My parents and the rest were left outside waiting and praying. After what seemed like eternity to them, a worried nurse came out and told them they could not get any pulse from me! That must have been a terrible moment for Mummy and Daddy and all my family there.

They rushed me to the ICU (Intensive Care Unit).

It was now touch and go. One after another, four doctors there tried to get my pulse going again but to no avail. Then, by a miracle, Dr June Lou, the very experienced head of the Paediatric Ward, suddenly turned up at the hospital. According to the nurses, she would normally not be there that early in the evening, especially as it was a holiday too.

She knew exactly what to do. She succeeded in getting my heart pumping again! So I lived.

Mummy said I was touched by an angel:

Yes, Dr June Lou!

I think of Mummy, Daddy, Grandma, Grandpa, Uncle Pat, Dr June Lou, the other doctors, the nurses, our maid Jovie — all who were there for me that night.

And I know I was touched by more than one angel!

(This true story was written by Colleen Goh Li En, then aged 11 — with a tiny bit of help from Grandpa: Me!)

IN LIGHT VEIN

A Super Performer

ONCE upon a time Supramaniam was a top name in the esoteric circle of Singapore's saxophone players. That was when he and his idol, the world-famous "Satchmo", were both young and strong in lung. ("Satchmo" was of course that lovable Louis Armstrong of sainted memory — who could ever forget his classic rendering of that piece, *Oh, when the saints go marching in…?*")

Now in his 70s, Supramaniam, known among old-time friends as "Supermaniam" or more candidly as "Superman", could still flaunt a mean sax and hold hip youngsters goggle-eyed with his magic instrument — though for health reasons he had now to keep himself under rein, which was not easy for a man born with swing in his soul.

So when he gave in to persuasion and went to that get-together of former cronies and other jazz-lovers, those spiritual denizens of old Dixieland just would not let him go home. He and his old girlfriend Bonnie (both now spouseless through bereavement) had to go up on stage again and again to help all present that night relive the good old times — he blowing his sax and she singing her blues…

And a good time was had by all.

Not without its price to pay.

After the wee hours of that lively night, Supramaniam, who lived alone, had to admit himself into hospital, more as a precaution than out of immediate need. A friend sent him there straight after the party.

He could not afford a private room. So he checked into a C class dormitory sharing space with other men, a few middle-aged but mostly elderly.

He slept through the noisy hospital morning with its frequent interruptions by nurses and others. In the late morning he woke up feeling more himself.

He found two visitors seated beside his bed. Two cute and

curvaceous young things. They had been waiting patiently for him to wake up. They had only adoring eyes for him — to the envy of some not-that-sick male patients in nearby beds.

The girls looked familiar to Supramaniam.

Yes, they were there last night at the musicians' reunion — among his swooning admirers!

He said hello to them. They cooed and twitted like happy birds — and the hearts of the erstwhile Romeos nearby ached to witness such adoration even as they puzzled over the weirdness of it all. *What was all that about? What did that old bag of bones have to deserve such adulation?*

A delivery man came in with a bouquet of red roses for Supramaniam. There was a note with it.

"It's from your old girlfriend, Bonnie!" the girl who opened the note screamed out in delight.

"Ooh my goodness! Ooh wow!" the other girl gushed and almost swooned. "Shall we read it to you, Superman?"

Superman? The girl actually called the old fellow Superman? The other patients were intrigued, and they craned their necks forward so as not to miss the message.

"You'll love this!" the girls said in unison when they silently read the contents together. Then one of them read the message out aloud:

"Superman, what a wild time we had last night. We did our thing on stage — and we wowed them, didn't we? I'm still dizzy over your fantastic performance! With ecstasies of love, from Bonnie."

Fantastic performance? Ecstasies of love? Those other patients around the old man could not believe it.

And the girls squealed and clapped their hands. "Wow! Wow!" they went.

Yes, those girls certainly knew what that Bonnie girl meant.

And so "Wow!" went the other men too, a look of respect now shining out from their eyes. They did not know exactly what performance that Bonnie was talking about. But that did not stop them guessing — and their imagination naturally ran wild.

After a while the young things sighed and said they wished they could stay but they needed to run. The men around sighed too — they too wished the girls could stay and need not run.

And all those pairs of ogling eyes followed the swaying hips as they wiggled their way to the exit of the ward.

At the door, the girls turned around and their dove-like eyes and luscious lips smiled one last time for their Superman.

And then, they said their farewell in words of unequivocal love that could not but set the eavesdroppers' hearts racing away. Dangerously and uncontrollably, even if not really comprehending:

"See you again, Superman."

"You really and truly sent us last night!"

"Yes, all the way to heaven!"

And then the eavesdroppers almost dropped dead (some had to press the emergency button soon after!) as the girls blew kisses and pouted and winked. And said loud and clear and unabashedly candid to the old man:

"Thanks for your glorious sax!"

Sweet Nothings In High Decibel

YEARS after graduation Jean remained her same old self — incorrigibly the mischievous girl of the class.

So, Ruth should have known better than to take Jean's words at face value. But that was Ruth for you, naive as a baby, easy to lead along, ever the diffident young thing (though no longer that young).

She and her classmates were now of that age-band that people looked at with the question mark in their minds: Married?

Some were, some just cohabiting, some divorced or separated, some still single.

In that last category many were genuinely happy to remain unattached, and many reasonably happy, even if not so all the time (depending on moods and definitions of happiness). And many were still in the running but now less unrealistic in expectations and more open to matchmaking overtures, SDU (Social Development Unit) aid, the lot…

Ruth belonged to this last category. She had one problem. She held herself back too much. She had gone out on introduced dates, SDU outings, auntie introductions, everything. But when her date showed signs of interest in her and she liked him and mentally checked him off as a definite possible, she would suddenly become coy. And a wall of doubts would come up.

She would wonder how he really and truly felt about her. Whether she should wait some more before responding, before speaking her own mind? *What's in his mind? What does he really think of me? Is it too soon to let him know what I think?*

Ruth could not forget the tears shed by her cousins: June, who in her early Twiggy 20s, was "led up the garden path" by a Don Juan with no sincere intentions. And at the other end of the scale, Fatima in her fat 40s, who was wont to spill out her own love fast — only to find men shying off just as fast.

And so at an early milestone on the road to romance, Ruth would suddenly switch off her engine to become dumb and unresponsive. And men would give up on her as cold fish. Her most promising dates would end with many words from the man — and suddenly few or no words from her (though she would come off with lots unspoken in her heart).

All because of that phobia of articulating her reactions.

If only there was some way she could hear what they were really saying in their hearts as they sat chatting with her, turning on all their charm, spewing out their sweet nothings… and if only she could know if and when to say what she felt!

"DEVAN'S a good man. He's not only good-looking and a giant of a guy, he's such a caring soul too. You know, he's in that church group that visits dying people in hospices. And he's from a landed property family. So you ask: How come he's still unhooked? I'll be honest with you. He's got one problem. He's very hard of hearing. If you say anything soft he won't hear you. So you've got to talk loud with him. I've given him a great report about you through a friend. He's interested. So we've arranged a date for you at Joe's Coffee House this Saturday night. Okay?"

Jean's eyes looked earnestly at her. Ruth had to say okay. Ruth would have anyway.

JEAN'S precise specifications made Devan unmistakable. He rose up at once to greet her with a smile and a fleeting touch of hand, no real physical contact. Just the right thing: Step one on a first blind date.

He spoke loudly. Jean was right. He must be quite deaf. Only deaf people talked that loud at close range. Fortunately it was a Saturday night at that popular eating place — so it was noisy and loud-talking was none too conspicuous.

He was indeed a good man. Goodness oozed out of every pore of him. He was earnestly dedicated to his social work, what he called "being there for the very ill on their last journey". He told moving anecdotes about the old and the not-at-all-old among the dying. He held Ruth spellbound. And other diners near their table too. They could not help overhearing his words — they came out booming to all. And Ruth felt she had to respond in louder-than-her-usual speech volume too.

He started talking about himself. And soon it was clear he

was himself really interested in her. All that also loud enough to be heard by all their interested neighbours at the nearby tables.

At first Ruth was more than a bit embarrassed, but soon she felt *"What the heck!"* She had to go along for the poor man's sake — let him express himself, and respond loud enough to him.

Even when the conversation became more intimate, it came out in high decibel. By then Ruth began to feel, for the first time in her life, release from repression: *Why worry?* Her heart was stirring with a strange exhilaration. And then, uninhibited thanks to more wine, he came out, this time less loudly, perhaps more for himself, but audible enough to her, with his candid confession:

"I find you most charming. I certainly hope this will blossom into a beautiful relationship!"

Ruth found it hard to respond to that remark. *Was a lady expected to respond to that kind of declaration?* Anyway, she was not supposed to hear that aside.

Ruth had begun to realise one fact: Yes, there was chemistry between them.

So as she looked down at her own large glass of lovely *Beaujolais*, she daringly spoke her response. To herself, in a soft heart whisper. *Soft enough so no one at the nearby tables could hear her — and naturally not Devan with his hearing handicap.*

"In my heart, I am also beginning to feel you are Mr Right, come to me at last. Thank God, I can say this out because I know you can't hear me… Yes, I like you too. Yes, this looks like love at first sight for me too. Yes, I too hope this is the beginning of a beautiful relationship… I feel good being able to speak my mind out like this."

All that in what she thought was a safe, inaudible whisper. Words she would never have uttered aloud to any man — were he not so deaf.

Then to her surprise, she heard Devan replying to her,

speaking words of love in an equally soft voice, "Yes, yes, yes! I knew it from the moment I saw you come in. We are meant for each other…"

And soon, they were both laughing — embarrassed yet exhilarated. They realised what had happened. That irrepressible Jean had tricked them. She had told each the other was very hard of hearing.

Such a silly prank!

But thank God for it!

Both had been fooled into candidly expressing their feelings, starting in high decibel innocently with nothing much, soon transforming into sweet nothings — that became sweet something. Something expressed clearly enough to each other:

Love. (Now exchanged in normal low decibel.)

TALKING WITH A MACHINE

TALKING with a machine is not everybody's cup of tea.

Yet it's something we've got to learn to do and live with these days. Dial any major organisation and you will have to work your way through the routine stages of quizzes, Stage One usually beginning with language choice, "For English, press 1, for Chinese, press 2… and so forth." That's only for starters.

After that you get hit by endless menus of numbers to press. Listen carefully because the machine speaks with its own accent and speed, it says things only once, and it does not explain what it's talking about. By the time you've run that gauntlet of numbers, you feel like you've had a number done on you — and, for elderly callers like me, you've probably forgotten whatever made you decide to sweat through that maze of numbers in the first place. That is, if you haven't (by grace of a merciful God) fallen asleep or dropped dead from stress.

You may try cutting in with a plaintive plea, "Can I speak with a human being, please?" Some of my friends have tried this but the machine at the other end only barks out orders, it does not entertain backchat. It blithely ignores you.

Sometimes a seeming flash of hope is provided. The machine actually says, "If you wish to speak to our customer service officer, press 13." So eagerly your fingers reach out and press that salvation figure, hoping luck will be with you.

For a moment the machine is shocked into silence. Nothing can be heard, not even new numbers. Then music comes on — and goes on and on. Then at last a tired voice comes on line saying, "Sorry…" You jump in and say, "That's okay" and start saying your bit. But the voice just goes on as though you never spoke, "…our lines are all busy. Please wait. We will attend to you shortly."

You say "Thank you" — and then you feel foolish because that voice sounds familiar. Yes, you're talking to that same machine!

If you are lucky you manage to establish contact with the human world out there. Then you will probably be given a party to contact — and you are asked to go back to square one, dialling again from scratch, and listening very carefully to press the right number at the right time.

Finally you do reach the line of the party you wish to contact. But either someone, presumably human, tells you she is out to lunch or a machine comes on again saying, "The party you have just called is not available. Please leave your message after the beep…"

You do — and hope to get a return call.

Which, of course, seldom ever comes. (Though, to be fair, that is not always the case. Occasionally you're truly blessed by heaven, and someone does call you back.)

Often the machine does its job and you get to where you

want — and it gives you the information you seek. It might even speedily do the transaction you want done, like paying a bill or transferring your money to some account or even buying something or other.

Indeed, once one gets used to it, it's convenient and saves time, dealing with a machine that doesn't require one to talk, only to press numbers, especially for things done frequently.

I do not exaggerate when I say one can actually begin to enjoy it. No need to wish anyone "good morning" or say "thank you". No hassle at all. And accessible whatever time of day or night.

Yes, one can get really hooked on it.

So much so, one can become truly stunned when unexpectedly confronted with a human voice answering instead of the expected machine voice giving the expected cues.

That actually happened to me.

One day I rang my bank to do a transaction that their machine at the other end and I have done hundreds of times till we had become true buddies, completely in sync.

To my surprise, a human voice came on. I thought at once that I had dialled the wrong number. But the voice said the name of the bank and added, "How can I help you?"

As I stayed dumb, the voice asked, "Who do you wish to speak with, please?"

I thought only for a second. I knew the answer to that one:

"Can I speak with your computer please?"

THE CHICKEN, THE EGG
AND THE PUPPY

DURING the Japanese Occupation, a new family of people-plus-chickens moved into the old bungalow house next door to the Gohs'. The Tays were not friendly. They did not invite the Gohs over, nor did they respond to the Gohs' invitation to come over for tea.

Their chickens were equally aloof except for one. The long-legged *kampong ayam* (village chicken) kept coming over, though never invited, in fact quite unwelcome. She was the kind of bird, all legs and liveliness, and a busy beak that would dig about everywhere for worms, leaving holes galore behind her. That was all right so long as she kept within her legitimate boundary and at least confined herself to hole-digging when she came over. But she did not. Instead of just hunting for worms, she helped herself heartily to the *kangkong* and other vegetables desperately trying to grow in the Gohs' garden.

Mr Goh complained about the foul play to the Tays, but it turned out they were passionate champions of fowl liberty. "God meant all his creatures to enjoy freedom from control," Mr Tay piously proclaimed. Freedom was a dangerous thought during the Japanese regime, but that was okay, the Tays were only talking fowl freedom. Besides, it was common knowledge Mr Tay had *guanxi* (connections), friends among the *Kempeitai*, the feared Japanese military police — a link ordinary folks like Mr Goh lacked.

So the Tays continued to let their hyperactive bird scratch gaping holes under the boundary fence and trespass over to the Gohs' land, and help herself to free salad.

POOR Mr Goh was at his wits' end. *How to stop that blessed bird from coming over?* He could only shoo the chicken off, which wasn't much of a deterrent. She would just return later. But anything more violent than shooing would certainly bring on the wrath of Mr Tay. The voracious bird was eating up his crops — and he could only look on hungrily, fantasising about eating her up in return. But that was a definite no, for Mr Tay's powerful Japanese friends might then come and eat him up!

IN THE midst of the frustration over such fowl occupation, Goh's son came with his irritating request, "Can I keep a puppy as a pet, Daddy?"

"What?"

"My friend has given birth to three puppies, and he says I can have one..." Donald explained.

"That's wrong. You mean your friend's dog has given birth to three puppies," Daddy corrected him.

"His dog is my friend too," Donald clarified. And he flashed as cute a smile as he could muster — something that most times worked on Daddy.

"Then, in that case, I suppose your grammar is correct," Daddy conceded, sweetened by the smile.

"What's Grandma got to do with it?" Donald wondered, but he zeroed in on the more important point first. "Is that a yes, Daddy?"

"No, no way! A dog will gobble up our food. And God knows we don't have enough as it is," Daddy sounded unshakeable.

"But, Daddy, people don't have to feed dogs these days. They know how to find more food themselves. They'll eat anything they find from drains or anywhere. And there's that Japanese restaurant down the road with all its garbage bins..." (Yes, dogs during the Occupation were effluent dogs, unlike today's affluent dogs.)

"No!" Daddy was firm. "That chicken from next door is already eating up too much of our food."

"But she also lays eggs on our side of the fence..." Donald argued.

"Shh, not so loud! She did that only once — one miserable egg," Daddy quashed the argument. "And Mr Tay doesn't know that. Otherwise he's sure to do something — at least, make a song and dance about it!" he added.

Donald had a sudden brain wave.

"If I can get the chicken to stop coming over, can I have

the puppy, Daddy?"

"Okay," Daddy answered. That okay seemed safe enough with that rider. Not a chance Donald could make that miracle happen!

THE next morning, Donald went out into the garden when he spied Mr Tay on the other side of the fence.

"Mummy, I hope I'll find another egg in our garden like we did before," he called out aloud as though talking to Mummy inside the house, loud enough to be heard across the fence.

There was a rustle audible from behind the thick creepers at the fence.

"Mummy, I've found something!" Donald suddenly sang out, dancing about excitedly with something in his hand and rushing back into the house.

It was not an egg, only a mushroom (and not an edible one, at that) — but how was Mr Tay to know?

The next day, Donald told the Tays' son, "I hope you'll let your chicken come over to our place more often."

"You're sure? I'll tell my Daddy," the Tays' son said — and did.

The next thing the Gohs knew, Mr Tay had filled those chicken holes under the fence line and reinforced their common border with boulders to prevent any more tunnelling for illegal social visits abroad.

All it took was one song and dance about a virtual egg laid on the wrong side of the fence.

And Donald got his puppy.

THE CRAZY JAPANESE RACE

TAKAYA and Takano were two Japanese soldiers who came to Singapore with the second wave of the Occupation forces. These were not at all wild men like those savages of the first wave. The two did throw their weight around a bit (surely only to be expected of any Occupation forces), but they were not heartless and cruel like those bloodthirsty warriors who swept down the Malay Peninsula with General Yamashita (later to be duly executed as war criminal) or the Gestapo-like *Kempeitai* (Japanese Military Police), who stayed on and detained anyone and grabbed anything as they wished.

T1 and T2 also grabbed some things they fancied but at least they always tried to pay for them, even if not quite the true value. And if they did any arm-twisting, it was purely of the metaphorical kind. Theirs was a kind of more benign thievery.

And the two Ts were fun-loving folks. They laughed a lot and their chubby faces and rotund bodies won them friends. These included Singapore people, even though theoretically enemies, among whom they came to be known as Tweedle-dee and Tweedle-dum.

But at times they too did some bad things. Like when they saw two local youths having fun racing each other on their bicycles and they wanted in on the fun act.

They asked to try out the bikes. They liked them and they wanted them. They offered to buy them but the boys did not wish to sell their bikes for their inflated Japanese money. So they compromised. They bought the bikes with something a little better than money: Cigarettes and MB 693, that VD control drug, which the Japanese soldiers could get from the army stores — stuff worth quite a bit on the black market. Even then the sum total of what they offered was just barely attractive, but the bike-owners felt it politic to accept whatever they could get, knowing that other Japanese soldiers might get in on the act and offer even less. And some might even use meaner means to get what they desired.

So the two Ts got their bikes. They practised a lot and became great riders. Soon they were showing off to their comrades the speed they could get up to and the fantastic climbing and other tricks they could do with those super bikes.

The word got around the camp: The two Ts had got themselves two amazing racing bikes. Their commandant, Major Mikimoto heard about the wonder bikes. And naturally wanted one of the bikes for himself — the better one of the two, of course.

He sent for the two Ts. He asked them which of the two bikes was superior. Takaya said "Takano's" and Takano said "Takaya's".

Who was right? How to tell?

The Major decided on a race to settle the question. He told the two Ts to report to him the next morning at Woodlands Point in the north of the island for a bike race all the way down to Newton to the south. They should ride as fast as they could. He would drive down ahead of them and wait for them at the finishing line in Newton. The race would prove which bike was the better one. The Major would commandeer the bike that crossed the finish line first.

"Sleep early tonight. Have a good rest. It's going to be a long and tough fight for you two tomorrow morning," the Major told them.

The two Ts kept a straight face, but after they left the Major, both burst out laughing.

"What a crazy race — sure to be a fiasco! No wonder they say our Japanese Army officers are dumb!" T1 said.

"Yes, it's sure to be the slowest race ever run," T2 nodded. "Who wants to win — and lose out?"

"Maybe by the time we arrive at our snail's pace at the finish line, the Major is going to get tired of waiting and go off, thinking our bikes are so slow both are not worth having at all!" T1 said hopefully.

"Still, we shouldn't dilly-dally too much. He's sure to have men watching along the way to make sure we're really doing our best — riding hard enough," said T2.

"Anyway, our Major Mikimoto is no pearl of wisdom, right?"

THE Major was not that stupid. He knew the two rascals would try to go slow on their bikes. But he had his way to get them to go all out — do their darnedest to win.

And T1 and T2 did pedal for all they were worth — sweating and panting all the way from Woodlands down to Newton.

The race was in fact a thriller. Certainly not crazy, and no fiasco. T1 was in the lead at the start, but T2 put in extra effort and passed him. Then T1 gave the race everything he got and surged ahead. But not for long. T2 called up every last ounce of his remaining energy and passed T1 just before the finish line.

Takano had won the race.

But he did not lose his bike.

Takaya lost his.

How come?

At the Woodlands starting point, Major Mikimoto, a pearl of wisdom after all, ordered a switch before the two Ts rode off.

He made Takaya and Takano swap their bikes.

A Lesson Well-Learnt

KON flashed his beautiful (though false) teeth in a pure white smile that, as he always prided himself, worked like a charm on prospects — at least quite a few, if not all. This prospect was listening and Kon, the property agent, felt he was getting somewhere with his pitch to sell an apartment to Shane.

Shane still looked like he needed a bit more working on. So Kon restated his sales blab in different words — and flashed that magic smile again and again.

"There are many professionals who live in the block," Kon repeated with measured emphasis in tone. He omitted to mention that some had also been moving out.

"Being on the top floor your apartment will give your tenant a great view," he said glibly. Actually the low-rise block was surrounded by other newer and taller blocks, though from the front window of that fourth floor apartment one could still catch a glimpse of part of a distant tree beneath a slice of sky between two overbearing high-rises.

"And being on the top floor means greater privacy, a treasure these days." (That also meant climbing more stairs and possible leaks from the flat top roof constructed years ago before waterproofing know-how advances arrived — but a first-time flat buyer like Shane probably did not think about such things.)

"I'm buying to rent out — you know, as an investment. Will it be easy to rent out?" Shane asked. Kon had anticipated that question. "Tenants always prefer the top floor," he told Shane, twisting the facts a little.

"In fact there have been quite a few leases signed up for the top floor units," Kon added. No need to say how long ago, or how many, he excused himself. *A good salesman should always present the best selling points, right?*

And, of course, no need to mention that other top-floor unit that had stayed vacant over most of the previous years though there were very short leases now and then.

"To tell you the truth, Mr Kon, I'm not knowledgeable about property investments at all. My dad helped me to locate and buy the house I now live in. I've never bought any property myself. And I've just come into some money and so I thought I might invest in a property…"

Kon beamed. He liked this young fellow. *So open — and so innocent! A dream client after his heart.*

"Tell you what — you're such a nice young man, I've decided: I'm going to help you. I'll arm-twist the owner and get him to reduce the price further by another five per cent. How's that for a bargain?"

Kon flashed his killer of a toothy smile again. That smile must be taking effect — he caught Shane staring at it with a reflective glaze in his eyes. *Hypnotised by the smile?*

So he impulsively reached out with a fatherly hand to give the young man a pat on his shoulder. To which the latter surprised him by abruptly pulling away from him.

What's wrong? Was the young man taken aback by surprise by his physical gesture of friendship?

Kon said nothing, but his eyes betrayed that he was baffled.

SHANE explained:

"Listen. I should tell you something about myself. Most of my life I've been unthinking and impulsive in making decisions. I was easy-going and, I must admit, not sharp enough. As a child I got conned all the time. Schoolmates would smile and hard-sell me their old and, often spoilt, toys — at their original prices. And anyone had only to tell me a sob-sob story, no matter how outlandish, and I would part with my piggy bank savings to help him. Neighbours would turn on their charm, and I would succumb to their sweet-talk and be persuaded to do their chores for them while they went off to enjoy themselves — and I might even hear later what they told others: What a sucker I was!

"My dad, an ever-smiling man, was normally a tolerant father, but he would still reprimand me, even if gently. Don't always trust charming smiles, especially when people are trying to hard-sell you something, he would say. Learn to make prudent decisions, don't just act on impulse! Each time, while he scolded me, he would still smile.

"I suppose over time I did learn to be less impulsive, though I did still go on making big bloopers…"

"So, that's how your dad gradually taught you that lesson: To make good decisions by yourself?" Kon interrupted, a little impatiently, anxious to get Shane back on track to making the crucial decision on buying the flat. Still he was able to keep smiling that irresistible smile of his.

"Yes, Mr Kon, my dad had to teach me over and over again. But the most lasting lesson was actually the last one he taught me — just a week before he died in an emergency surgical operation. I shall never forget that last, most important, lesson he taught me…

"As usual, I had committed an awful blunder in making a decision. I had agreed to stand guarantor for a bank loan by an acquaintance — someone I barely knew. He had a nice, smiling face and he showed me a list of other people, some of them known to me, who were allegedly helping him in his commercial project. Then the bank called me to say he had defaulted and skipped the country and they wanted me to pay up the rest of what he owed…

"My dad, already not well then, looked at me and shook his head. He called me to his bedside. *Shane, Shane! When are you ever going to learn to make prudent decisions? It seems scolding you is just not enough!*"

But he still managed to smile, his last big though weak smile for me…

"And with those words, with the toothy smile still on his face, he suddenly slapped my cheek with his hand! The blow was not hard at all, barely more than a touch, but it was totally unexpected, and so I felt the full sting of it — that first, and last, time my dad ever hit me…"

"That, Mr Kon, taught me a lesson I'll never forget."

"SO, SHANE, at long last, that taught you the lesson — that last time your dad impressed on you the hard way: That you have to make good and wise decisions, right?" Kon concluded, still smiling his toothy smile. He was ready to now steer the young man back to the psychological moment when Shane would make the positive decision to buy his flat.

"Yes and no, Mr Kon," Shane enlightened the property agent, for he had made his decision:

"That taught me not to trust a smile..."

INSPIRATIONS

A Caring Mother Comes to Toa Payoh

RICHIE could not understand it.

That dumpy old Maria Teo had only come to Toa Payoh barely a year ago. What was so great about her? How come she always got loudly hailed by the inmates of the Home as soon as she walked, or rather waddled, her ungainly way past their beds. All of them, unless dead asleep (*or just plain dead, ha! ha!*) managed a smile for her even if they might go on at once to grouching on their favourite topic: Their boring aches and pains — but even then, for her they grumbled in the good-humoured kind of way they never did for others, like him for example.

Why, the woman must be as old as, if not even older than, those inmates themselves!

And how much did MT really do for them? Aside from listening to their long-winded tales of woe? And holding their (yuk!) so clammy and scrawny hands? Or laughing loud asinine hee-haws with them as she pulled their legs with her none-too-witty jokes?

Yes, what did the woman bring for them in down-to-earth terms — money or food or medicine? In fact, her old clothes and her dowdy appearance betrayed what she was: A woman barely able to fend for herself.

And in contrast, here he was, a highly-respected professional from a top firm. One whose service to clients was measured in minute time-slots for relentless billing at no mean rate — a VIP to whom minutes meant money, and yet here he was, unselfishly sacrificing his precious time for the home, helping with administration and accounts, mounting productive appeals, organising countless committee meetings. And making handsome donations by GIRO out of his own bank account! Yes, even if he said so himself, he was one truly dedicated do-gooder who went all out to help those aged folks. In a really concrete way — unlike that MT woman!

How often had he not demeaned himself to become a cap-in-hand mendicant for the home's sake? Opened his mouth to brazenly beg his well-heeled friends for a dole for these poor people — pleading nobly for the cause of the hungry and homeless, the neglected old folks in our midst?

"How can we just carry on with our lives while we know there are people who will have nothing to eat unless we feed them, no place to shelter in unless we support the Homes set up for them…?"

Why, without him this home would surely collapse in next to no time!

And yet, which of those old people were ever grateful to him — except when obviously coached by the staff? Who ever genuinely smiled at him, warmed up to him, joked with him — in that stupid way they did with that nothing MT woman?

The Chinese inmates even called the woman "Ah Boo", the Hokkien word for "Mother". (The Indians called her Mother Teo; it was the Eurasians who called her by her initials, MT — and that to Richie was rich, for the woman had actually come empty, hadn't she?)

What did they call him? Nothing! Why, they hardly ever addressed him. When he looked at them, he would see mostly expressionless faces — that same mask of anonymity the very old always put on for the world, outside of the few specially admitted into their circle. Like MT.

Doubts began to nag Richie's mind. Feeding the hungry, housing the homeless — for what? Why waste time on them? Those people did not even appreciate him, no matter how much he did for them.

Was he doing anything wrong?

Impossible! Everyone in his own social milieu praised him. They all appreciated him for his noble work for the old folks

— everyone, that is, except the old folks themselves!

Richie teetered on the edge of giving up. Should he step down, ask them to find someone else? Let others take on the burden to feed the hungry, shelter the homeless in that charity home…?

THEN a social worker colleague to whom he had confided his despair, persuaded him to go with her to listen to a nun, a worker for the aged, who had just come to Singapore.

"She does glorious work. Such an inspiring person. Bound to be canonised a saint some day… just come along and listen to her. She may help you rediscover motivation, recharge your battery for what you do. Find out how she herself finds fulfilment in helping others…" she urged.

So Richie found himself in that crowd of 10,000 in Toa Payoh Sports Stadium that wet and cold Saturday evening, January 10, 1987.

Luckily he and his friend arrived early and secured themselves seats on the covered terraced seats, for the heavens opened up and those in the open field were drenched. Yet, amazingly, people stayed on, and despite the steady drizzle after the brief storm, people kept on coming through the afternoon.

The main attraction must be good, Richie thought, impressed by such fervour from spectators.

Fortunately, the heavens cleared up before the speaker arrived. She was a tiny person, an old lady in her mid-70s, dressed simply in a nun's habit that resembled a white sari with blue line trimmings.

Hardly impressive! She looked Indian, shuffled meekly like a humble Indian social worker, even spoke English with an Indian accent — though, as Richie had been told, she was European, not Indian. Her accent had developed while she spent the best years of her life in India.

The moment she started speaking, the entire stadium fell

silent, listening with rapt attention. Despite age and insignificant build, her voice was rich with power and impact, her presence quickly becoming even more so.

What she said held Richie rigid.

He felt as though she was addressing him personally — him alone, never mind the thousands around him.

"People — children or adults — are meant for great things," the nun told him, slow and deliberate.

"People are meant to love — and to be loved…"

There was a miraculous quality of divine proclamation in those words. Richie was transported despite himself.

God enunciating his commandments to Moses on Sinai, Jesus proclaiming the beatitudes on the mountain… Not just the words, but the way they came out — with God's love and tender appeal.

Simple words which yet were strangely intense with meaning and drama. Words that slew and swept aside his old mindset: Smug prejudices, selfish preoccupations, demand for gratitude and recognition… words with the mind-boggling power of bombs exploding and bullets ricocheting back and forth in his mind, illuminating his innermost self with dazzling understanding, transforming him…

Yes, that was it! He was meant to love — and so to be loved.

His old folks at the Home were meant to be loved — and so to love…

Absorbed in reflection, he missed the speaker's next few words.

Then once again her voice came through — and again she was talking directly to him. She was explaining love. Her words came out loud and clear, emancipating yet enthralling, as Richie felt rather than saw her eyes flashing out at him where he stood not far, yet too far, from her.

She was emphasising "the terrible, terrible hunger of loneliness and rejection".

The words echoed over and over in his head, and involuntarily he answered her aloud, "Yes, Mother!"

That was it! That was why the old folks kept their masks on to the world, never opened up to him — that was the something they needed to hide behind their facade of expressionless faces!

And that was what was wrong with him! He had not understood their greater need. Not for money, nor for food, nor shelter. Their need was for the listening ear, the kindly mouth speaking personal words, the touch that did not shrink back from ageing flesh…

And the nun's next words endorsed the enlightenment Richie had found:

"Hunger is not for a piece of bread. Hunger is for love…"

Richie suddenly found his eyes filming over, unexpectedly and uncontrollably overwhelmed.

Yes, this Mother in Toa Payoh was teaching him what he had failed to learn from that other mother of Toa Payoh — Mother Teo.

It was not too late.

Richie knew what he had to do — from now on he must first address that greater need, that need to feel wanted and loved, the respect of identity he owed those old residents of the Home. To him they were no longer inmates — but residents, fellow-inhabitants of a shared place in God's world.

And now the nun was speaking her final words — to him. Words that described him, yet showed him a new path, bestowed understanding, inspired resolve — consoling words of special meaning to the ecstatic heart of the man once ready to let go and run away from his home, one who had felt unwanted, unloved, homeless. The nun said loud and clear:

"Homelessness is not being homeless, it is the feeling of being unwanted, unloved…"

FROM that event came Richie's epiphany of soul — that coming of Mother Teresa of Calcutta to Toa Payoh.

A Dropout Drops In

THE media praised him. They held him up as a model eminently worthy of emulation by his fellow-countrymen: "Most Singaporeans tend to be *kiasu* (scared to lose). So they go for the sure money of the established professions or employment for regular wages. Few will take on the greater risks of entrepreneurship even with its prospects of greater rewards."

They went on to lionise Boey Buck Chang, their paradigm of enterprise. As a young man he had courageously "gone West" — invaded the US with his yummy mass-produced Chinese rice dumplings. And, as one of his journalist admirers summed it up, "the rest is history".

Of course he had now business problems galore to stress him out. So probably life might be easier for him with less business. But so what? The man was deliciously rich. The reporters hazarded some numbers, no doubt duly exaggerated, but who would gainsay them? Singaporeans who often went goggle-eyed with big numbers flashed before them lapped it all up.

He had a big heart and gave generously to charity, so somehow people still managed to like him despite being envious. Also he would champion underdog charities, less glamorous and more in dire need.

He was often wooed as a VIP guest to functions. People knew his admirers in the media would come too, so there was a chance their function might get coverage. He was even invited to address schools despite the fact that he was only a Singlish-spieling dropout, not having succeeded in completing secondary school.

One day he was delighted to receive an invitation from the old boys of a particular school. It was the graduate association of his old school, which unfortunately he had not been able to join as he had failed to graduate. Among the members were his former schoolmates, those brighter boys whom he had envied for having studied hard enough to move up till they got their "O" level pass, that passport to study opportunities in tertiary institutions and the working world's openings for jobs. He was truly happy that at last he was recognised by that august group of his old school's successful students — a drop-out at last invited to drop in!

The highlight of the evening came. After the crowd had eaten (and drunk) well, the president of the association stood up to welcome "old BBC" to their company. "Not to be confused with the British Broadcasting Corporation, though that should be apparent from the different English they speak, ha! ha! ha!"

That clever joke, even if at BBC's expense, went down extremely well, evoking hilarious guffaws.

He revealed that previous attempts to admit those who failed to graduate had not been successful as most members felt it of paramount importance that the eminent image of the graduates should be jealously safeguarded. However, in old BBC's case, he and his committee had, after careful deliberation and in due recognition of his generous donations to the alma mater, decided to create an honorary membership and confer it on him. He then read the citation and presented BBC the certificate of honorary membership.

Most of the audience condescended to respond with polite applause.

BBC was invited to address the gathering.

"Kindly make it brief," the president whispered, "members don't appreciate long speeches from outsiders."

BBC read from a prepared text, enunciating his words with respectful care. He thanked the graduates. He confessed frankly that he had tried to gain admission in the past but had not been successful. He urged the graduates to understand and sympathise with the attachment that old boys tend to have for an institution in which they had grown up in along-side friends and received their education, regardless of whether they had made the grade or not, examination-wise.

The graduates listened to him, some nodding (possibly because sleepy), many still shaking their heads. But as BBC went on in the same vein, some openly showed boredom and began to chatter among themselves.

"Do such loyal colleagues not deserve consideration? I strongly recommend that we open the door wider. I recommend that we create a new category: Associate membership for alumni who did not finish school with a pass."

BBC looked around the hall. He could see his carefully prepared words were falling on barren soil. In fact, one or two tables pointedly started on their "yamseng!" drink-toasting, according him scant attention.

BBC decided to depart from his speech, which had been corrected by and rehearsed with a friend. That text was getting him nowhere. He now spoke from his heart, appealing in a manner he felt more forceful, more frank, more himself.

"Let's be big-hearted, yah? Come on man, what you say? Can or not?"

With that departure he lost them.

BBC's eyes looked around. Was there not a single sympathetic face? He found one. The smiling man was seated at a nearby table. Good old Henry was the long-serving loyal school clerk.

And Henry reminded him of something — a painful something, though it happened long ago.

After his final year in school, BBC had sanguinely applied for the post that Henry now filled, as school clerk. He would have, like Henry, given his whole soul and life to the job. But he had been rejected as he had not passed his "O" level examinations. That was how Henry, "O" level qualified although from another school, got the job. And Henry had done well. He had received every annual increment going and was now, after nearly two decades of dedicated service, right at the very top of his time scale salary structure.

The president of the association, discerning the declining interest in BBC's speech, decided to interrupt the speaker to ask if there was anyone who had a question for good old BBC (hoping there would be no takers) "before we allow him to sit down and enjoy his meal with us?"

But one graduate rose, glass tilted and shaky in his hand, asking in a slurred but loud voice, "I'm sure we're all glad that old BBC has managed to succeed in life, despite not having graduated. Incredibly, he seems to have done well. But may I ask our dropout friend one question. Would he not have done even better if he had been able to succeed in school, pass his exams and become a graduate like us?"

A silence fell over the hall — from those not drunk. The drunks cheered.

The questioner lapped up the spirited support. He went further, "Tell us, BBC, what if you had made the grade? Obtained your "O" level? You would have done even better, right? What more fantastic successes might you have achieved? Where do you think you would be today?"

BBC met that challenge calmly — in fact he gave the question serious thought. Before he could speak, his eyes fell once more on Henry. The school clerk had his head down, hanging in shame at the behaviour of the questioner and his supporters.

BBC now knew exactly what answer to give. The multi-millionaire replied with a frank smile, "I would have been, from the time I left school right up to now — your school clerk…"

With that he bowed and stepped off the stage. And as he passed Henry's table, the school clerk, tears in his eyes, stood up, shook his head, and hugged BBC.

BBC looked at Henry in the eye. And in a soft voice he said what he had left unsaid on stage, something only to be shared with the faithful clerk who would also understand:

"And I'd be a happier, even if poorer, man, right?"

A STORY WITHOUT WORDS

FROM my chair in the waiting room I could see them. The couple in the adjacent meeting room had their backs to the large glass panel of the door separating us. They were seated at a round table facing their counsellor, my friend whom I was waiting to see. Nellie waved to me as she caught sight of me, and I signalled her: *Carry on, I have plenty of time, I can wait.*

I could not hear what the two were saying. My ears were severely deaf, even with my powerful hearing aids on. But their body language told me enough. They were your typical adversaries in marriage combat, quiescent for the moment but clearly still truculent and ready to shoot.

But they were in good hands. Nellie was a wonder-worker, seasoned in family repair.

The two in their set negative mode were saying their set negative things. I did not need hearing to hear them. Nellie knew precisely how much to let them let out, when to step in to stem the vitriol from getting out of hand.

She now gained control. In my mind I could hear the soothing tones, the soft voice of reason. The combatants were now more passive, if not wholly submissive.

I saw Nellie taking out paper, giving a sheet to each, earnestly urging both to do something. I could not make out everything she said but I could lip-read and guess snatches here and there:

"Write only positive things. Good things you remember about your partner — the things that once meant a lot to you…"

The two looked dubiously at Nellie, then at the blank sheet before each, then back to Nellie. Not once at each other.

I "heard" Nellie encouraging them, "Go on, give it a try! You can do it…"

I became fascinated, shamelessly "eavesdropping" on the session.

For a long while neither did a thing. Just staring at the

bleak emptiness of white before them. Nellie never gave up. She continued on with her gentle pushing.

Then the woman responded. She began to write, slowly and hesitatingly at first, more steadily as she got into stride.

The man saw her. He too grabbed his pen, but he seemed at a loss on what to write. Then I saw the woman's shoulders quiver almost imperceptibly as she wrote. The man looked at her, saw her face that was hidden from me. He looked away, but now he began to write, faster and more furiously...

Nellie looked on, eyes half-closed, edge of lips minutely curled up, silent and Buddha-like in supportive serenity.

After a while the two stopped. They looked at each other. Their faces were not visible to me but I could sense it — it was that palpable, that easing of hostilities.

They handed their sheets, now filled with writing, back to Nellie. She shook her head and said something as she motioned to them to pass their sheets to each other.

Both took them readily, read them avidly.

They now turned to face each other. The woman was in tears, the man was not crying but clearly moved too. They were not looking at Nellie now, they had eyes only for each other. They were saying something, both talking at the same time, the woman sniffing behind her tissue.

What were they saying? I could not lip-read talk muffled behind tissue and blurred by emotion. It was the crucial point and I could not eavesdrop — not a single word.

But what need was there for words?

Action spoke. They now touched, held hands, and soon they were in one each other's arms. My friend Nellie sat smiling in the background, happy to fade out of their lives, hopefully for good — or at least, until the next crisis...

(This story is humbly dedicated to the beautiful people who inspired it: Lim Seow Beng and his caring helpers at the HELP Family Service Centre in Ang Moh Kio.)

DEFINITIONS OF POWER

"POWER!"

The kindergarten teacher enunciated the word with explosive power, grabbing the attention of the toddlers in her class. "Does anyone know what that word means?"

Eager little hands went up. "I know!" "I know!"

"It's a man who makes *pow*," one plump girl said. As in *char siu pow* and other *pow* dumplings. Yummy, that power!

Another girl stood up and delivered an elaborate exposition:

"My Grandpa says there are some people who won't let other people do anything. They always want to do everything. Grandpa calls those people: *Pow kah liow!* Pow, pow, pow all the time. Power is that kind of people, right?"

"No, it's someone with lots of strength like Superman," a boy burst in with his definition. "He fights bad people and he hits them very hard — *POW!*"

And to illustrate, he transformed himself into such a power, complete with flailing arms and kung fu kicks, powing away verbally too.

"HOW would you define power?" the lecturer asked his trainee managers.

"Power is the force you need to have to get things done," said one young man. "As Mao Zedong put it so well: *Power comes out from the barrel of a gun.* That sums it all up. You must hold the gun — whether that's a physical weapon or a psychological means of coercion to make people obey you."

The lecturer shook his head and offered his less pugnacious, more standard, textbook management theory:

"Actually, Power is only one of three elements needed to manage. Power provides the fire power, the weaponry a manager has to be armed with to get things done, such as the power to hire and fire. Then there is Authority needed to mandate him to use the fire-power in specific situations. But Influence makes up the third ingredient, the most important one — his personal charisma that gets things done without having to flex his muscles of Authority or open fire with his Power…"

THE preacher talked about power. About Jesus on the eve of his crucifixion, announcing he was soon to be handed over to the power of men. The preacher set us thinking. Yes, man, made by God in his image and likeness, has been handed awesome power: For good or evil, to achieve great things, or nothing — or great evil. We try to play God with that power. Yes, we even kill God with that God-given power. All religions teach the awesome power of good — that man sometimes turns into awesome power of evil.

I RECALLED a man once suddenly empowered.

Buck See-toh had received one-third share of his late father's estate, the other two-thirds going to a half-brother and a half-sister, children of his father from other unions. Buck had never been close to them, and he promptly went back to no contact with them once the reading of the will was done with.

He heard that his half-brother, Zed, did nothing with his inheritance, merely letting it sleep on in fixed deposit until his own demise, when the money slept on in his widow's name.

His half-sister, Henrietta, had already joined some convent or temple before their father passed on. What she did with her legacy, Buck did not know. *Probably just handed over the money to her order — such a stupid waste! Money is power, and to waste it like that is surely a sin…*

Yes, to Buck, money was power.

"Power has defined me," he declared to his business associates upon getting his share, and he set out to enhance his self-delineation by making even more money. He was utterly non-discriminatory about ways and means. He focused solely on getting richer quick. He had no time for those who needed his help. They were of no use to him, so why waste time and money on them? He made few friends — but many ene-mies.

At first he did well. Then he took more risks, even going into shady businesses that promised high returns — or heavy losses.

In time all his money went. And his power, too.

He had never bothered to keep in touch with family, so he did not think they would help him now, even if he knew how to contact them. And he had no friends, so he had no one to help him.

All power gone, he ended up in a welfare home.

ONE day some voluntary workers came to visit the home. Buck, by then a changed man, was impressed by their genuine concern for needy people. He asked them about their mis-sion.

"Our founder was the late Sister Clare, an unknown per-son, just an ordinary nun in a convent. She came into some money and she donated it to start our society, providing the needed funds for facilities and staff. They say she inherited the money and she used that power handed by God to her to do good for others. And others followed her example with donations to support our work…"

Buck listened in wonder. The nun's name was not familiar at all — but it led him to think of his half-sister. They were, of course, not talking about her, but that could very well have been her.

How beautiful if it had been her…

He said to those good people, "Yes, power is not defined by what we possess. No, not even by our material achieve-ments. I realise this now: Power is defined by what we do for others with the power given to us. And in a way, all of us are given power. Some do good, some do bad, some do nothing. It is what we do with it that gives definition to power — meaningful definition."

Just as he was about to leave, the leader of the group turned back and said to Buck, "You know, it must be a coincidence, but our founder had the same surname as you. Sister Clare, before they gave her that ordination name, was also a See-toh: Henrietta See-toh."

Buck felt suddenly rewarded — reunited with family!

He was on the point of claiming relationship, but he stopped himself, rejoicing instead only within himself:

Share only in your heart that glory of your sister who richly defined power handed her!

ROSE FOR DAD

DEAREST Mother,

You must have seen me from heaven. You must have pitied me in my despair. I prayed to God for help and you must have put in a word for me.

Thank you! God knows what I might have done…

You know how well Dad cared for me all these years. Although motherless from my early childhood, in the past I never once had reason to feel forsaken by him. He was a good Dad, always there for me.

"You're so lucky! You have a saint for a father," my jealous classmates, many from broken homes, would say to me.

A saint!

I remember the day we came home from the crematorium. He sat with me in your large bedroom, too big for one person. We cried and cried.

He told me then, "Mum and I were a truly loving couple.

We hardly ever quarrelled. And when we did, I had only to come to her, sincerely sad with a rose in my hand for her, and all would be well. She loved flowers but, as you know, rose was her favourite. And, that's why, rose has become my favourite too!"

And mine of course — only to be expected.

He made a solemn promise, both to himself and to me, "There'll never be another woman for me after your mum!"

Never?

Hah!

WHEN I came home to Singapore on vacation from my Government-financed university studies after years away in UK, Uncle Joe and Auntie Amy met me at the airport — instead of Dad!

"Where's Dad? Why's he not here?" I wanted to know. "Something bad has happened to him?"

I was gripped by sudden fear.

They had to tell me the truth: Yes, something bad had happened to him.

He was now in hospital — that hospital where they treated people with AIDS!

Dad had AIDS?

How was that possible?

"Did he? Did he get it from..?" I asked Uncle Joe and Auntie Amy. They knew what I was thinking. They nodded sadly, and they told me more.

"Don't think too harshly of him," Auntie Amy said gently. "He was very lonely, especially after you left for your studies. That woman seduced him — and he fell..."

"It was his bad luck that woman had the disease. I don't think she knew it herself then," Uncle Joe added.

"But he swore me a promise when Mum passed away! He said there'd never be another woman..." That was the first thing I could think of to whimper out in my shock.

And then I let loose my feelings, screaming out my anger.

We talked a long while.

And Uncle and Auntie actually pitied him! And they asked me to go and see him!

"Your dad's quite ill. He's overcome with shame. And he misses you so much It will be good for him to have you come to him," Auntie said, placing her hand gently on mine.

"What? You're asking me to see him? Never!" I shook off Auntie's hand.

ALL next day, they did not give up trying to persuade me to go to him. He had done something bad, but he had been good to me, they kept on nagging me.

I could not stand it. I had to get away. I walked out of their house. I walked about aimlessly. So I ended up in church — which was not far from their house. It was empty then.

I went in to ask God:

Why? How could You let this thing happen?

God did not answer me. But I did calm down a bit. Perhaps that was how He answered me…

I remembered how I had loved Dad. And how he had loved me…

But still what he did was unforgivable! He deserved what he got! For being unfaithful to Mum, right?

And then I felt the opposite way: No, in the past, he had always been there for me. A small voice in me told me I should be there for him now.

Then again, I swung the other way, tears flowing down my cheeks in bitterness on Mum's behalf. And on my own behalf — in confusion and self-pity.

Back and forth, back and forth, like that.

"Dear God, tell me what to do? Give me a sign. Tell me clearly. Should I go to him or not?" I prayed in church. And then I walked out of the church.

I felt exhausted and depressed. For a long while I sat there, alone, on the steps of the church facing the empty spaces of the car park.

Nobody was around but I must have looked a sight, hair awry, eyes teary and dazed, quite lost in my own world of betrayal.

Then from the corner of my eye I saw a small car drive up and stop in the car park. I saw a man and a little toddler get out. I could feel them looking at me. The man opened his car door again and took out a bouquet of flowers. He pulled out one stalk. He passed it to the child. He pointed to me.

She stood there unsure. She started squeezing and plucking at the flower, pulling out petals, until it looked a bit wounded. Egged on by her father, she walked a few steps timidly towards me, and then stopped.

Tired of waiting for him and feeling indifferent, I closed my eyes.

Then one word, spoken in a tiny voice, called me back to the world:

"Rose."

I opened my eyes. The little girl was in front of me. She was holding out her rose to me, a sad-looking rose. Only that one word. She was obviously just learning to speak.

Her tiny finger now pointed to her father standing next to his car. And she said her second word:

"Dad."

And with that, the two disappeared into the church, unaware of the impact those two words had made on me.

God had answered my prayer. He had told me what to do — in those two words, passed through a child's lips.

I knew then I had to go visit him. Regardless of what he had done, I must go to him, a child's flower in hand — a sad rose, but a rose for Dad!

I went back into the church to thank God — your church, dearest Mother, your Novena Church.

Now, home from my visit to Dad, I write you this letter — my witnessing to your love and your intercession to God for me, dearest Mother of Perpetual Help!

Your loving daughter,

Rose

THE SINGER AND THE SONG

THE speaker at the mike meandered on.

The man was veritably venerable, well-respected and loved, but sad to say, deadly soporific. The hard walls magnified the torment to his listeners, rendering his words "full of sound and fury, signifying nothing".

I could make out phrases here and there, but not how they hung together. I heard of war and terror, earthquakes, plagues, famines and fearful sights, but I could not be sure. My befuddled mind made out only one phrase with certainty, and that was because he repeated it slowly and deliberately:

Great signs from heaven…

Despite those earthshaking things thrown at us, he could not shake up his listeners from stupor — indeed the words made things worse, for while the individual snatches did demand attention, as a package it did not deliver, failed to jell. Given idiom gap between him and us, and unsoundness of so-called sound system, the stress was monumental for those honestly trying hard to understand him.

And there were others before him whose words we had to suffer through.

The first man who spoke with a sing-song lilt, distracting and needing special de-tuning to follow. The lady who read so slowly that I felt like getting up to tell her to get a move on. However, as with my fellow-sufferers there, I respected the circumstances and held my peace.

I looked around. Yes, I was not alone. We were all in the same boat: Expressionless and controlled, saintly in our stony silence of profound suffering.

All except one person. At first I felt sympathy for the poor fellow, obviously unused to the kind of penitential patience we regulars could muster. He was finding the torment more than he could sit still for. He tapped his feet on the floor. He shifted his legs about. He shifted his eyes around. He let out deep sighs.

And then he did the utterly unforgivable thing: He voiced aloud his grievance to all around him, irrespective of the respected speaker still orating at the mike.

"Can't understand him at all, can't hear him!"

He had broken the code of silence. All our sympathy for him evaporated. I kept my peace. The others ignored him too. No one followed his protest lead. No one nodded. No one made eye contact with him. We just continued on in our frozen appearance of listening, glaze-eyed in our impassive passivity.

He gave up. He realised he was alone, unsupported in his uprising. He stopped his squirming. He even seemed to shrink a bit into his own frame.

I felt sorry for him.

I prayed for help from on high: What to say to the poor guy. I found the words.

After the speaker had (at long last!) finished, I caught the man just as he was making a hurried exit. I spoke divinely inspired words to him.

"My friend, the sound system was bad, and the speaker was not that great either. But the secret we need to learn is: Stop hearing what can't be heard. Stop trying to piece things together. Hear only the words here and there that you can hear. Accept them as what you are supposed to hear — and meditate on them. In other words, let them make up their song for you personally. Never mind what you can't hear.

Listen to the song, not the singer…"

I do not know whether those words of wisdom registered with the man at all.

They registered with me, myself. Suddenly.

I thought of those words here and there, the few words I had heard clearly enough — the speaker's disjointed mention of all those catastrophes followed by his dramatic pronouncement:

Great signs from heaven…

Yes, even if I could not hear the singer, I should hear the song, get that essence of message meant for me. Those terrible things connecting up into: *Great signs from heaven!*

It was time for me (and the many others like me) to be shaken up from our past complacency, from taking things for granted: We're okay, the world's okay, everything remains unchanged — all things staying as we were.

The WTC bombing in New York, the Iraq war, the ongoing acts and threats of terrorism and counter-terrorism, the not-quite-over disease potential for catastrophic human extermination — do not these *great signs* compel us to re-look the world we have taken for granted? And each one, at ourselves too…

Those words of wisdom I spoke were not for the stranger — they were for myself: The song I should have heard, never mind the singer.

The context was a church, but it could have been a mosque or temple, or any secular place, words we might hear anywhere. Words to act on.

Yes, listen to the song, not the singer…

THE END OF DAYS

HECTOR and Yogaratnam live in the same high-rise block, Hector on the highest floor with that great sky view, Yoga on the lowest with only that not-so-great traffic view, one floor above the void deck.

They're home from their work, the end of their days.

HECTOR drives himself hard, earns top money, comes home as always still tightly wound up. He has had a hectic day. Demanding bosses, colleagues whose reliability (and unreliability) he has to gauge with circumspection, customers and suppliers loyal only as long as its to their advantage. Deadlines, and more deadlines. Phone call after phone call. Stacks of mail, electronic and snail. Irritating home calls from wife with family problems. Even at lunch, his handphone gives him no break, snarling his guts up with problems hotter than the spicy mix in his *rojak*.

He has brought his briefcase of urgent papers home in that usual sanguine hope he can tackle the lot of them. But his wife talks endlessly — for she too has homework for him that can't wait. And his children bring him their problems.

At home as at office, the pressure continues: Decisions, decisions, decisions!

And his handphone does not let him off, buzzing intermittently for attention.

Hoping for a break he turns on the TV.

Ah! Breaking news!

Surely the world's offering of disasters, wars and calamities, must, in comparative juxtaposition, provide him relief?

No, instead they launch him on orbit into tangents of anxieties.

The news suggests implications on business.

He hurriedly jots down notes on his "to-do" list.

Now at last in bed, his wife snoring away, Hector tosses

about. With his last drop of wakefulness he tries to work out solutions to problems that will come tomorrow.

His last thought, a fleeting moment of wisdom, as he surrenders to sleep is:

Is this the way to end days? Is this the way to spend days?

Is this the end, the purpose, of days?

But Hector has no time for philosophical cogitation. His body demands rest. He sleeps. Fitfully. And so he slips into that uneasy oblivion from which he will emerge into the mad rush of yet another day.

There is no end to his days…

IN HIS bedroom way below, Yoga reads from a good book — a treasure he has found, something in harmony with his reflective mood.

He too has had a full day at the office. But he has switched off, mind-wise, phone-wise — all wise.

He has laughed and talked with family. He has done his exercises — physical and spiritual.

He switches off his bedside light.

He intones his constant mantra: *Be still, and know I am God…*

Be still… His mind stops wandering. Becomes still.

And know… His mind touches that awareness, infinitum of understanding, that leap into embrace of universal being.

I am… He is conscious of the Being, the Entity there, reaching out to him: Love ever there, Love into which he begins to merge:

God.

The purpose, the destination:

The end of days…

To Pat With Love

THERE is one simple act that is the greatest gift passed on to us by our Creator. It blesses both him who gives and him who receives.

It is to reach out with hand, and heart, and touch another living thing with compassion.

I dedicate this story to all God's creatures gifted to do that — to pat with love.

The evening we came home from a short holiday away, we were told that one of our neighbours' mongrel dogs was no longer around. The two mutts looked much alike — ancient, scanty of hair, lethargic, though one was a little more lacklustre than the other. They were probably siblings of same vintage.

The tyke more far gone was gone. We did not miss the scraggy thing one bit. But our neighbours' normally quiet house seemed even quieter.

The next evening as I watched from the upstairs window next to where I took my coffee breaks from my work on the computer, I saw the bereaved one amble around the sad, empty field, stopping by some miserable clumps of plants and sorry-looking broken pots, sniffing around morosely, like he could be re-living happier sniffing times with the dear departed, peeing dejectedly here and there wherever that act of canine blessing seemed called for, in evoked response to lingering fragrances of one no longer around to share moments with…

Then, as though fatigued by the unaccustomed workout, the sad animal flopped down on the front porch, on an old rug now too big for one dog alone. Still he lay on one side only, leaving ample room where an absent loved one used to sprawl alongside him.

After a while I saw the animal stretch out a scrawny paw over that empty space. Was it my imagination or did he actually pat his brother no longer there?

THE door of the house opened. The pale-looking daughter of the family came out into the porch, a small girl barely of school-going age. She was obviously out to do that thing children do after school: Study from a homework book while pacing about — in between distractions. She too began to meander around the field, uncannily observing those same stop-stations, those almost-ritual stops, a kind of "Way of the Cross", that her dog had meditated his way through earlier. (The girl naturally did no peeing.)

But she repeated those rounds several times. Then her pilgrimage over, she went to sit on a chair next to where her remaining dog lay spread out on the rug. She carried on with her reading and study. And as she did her homework, her hand reached down to the dog and patted him.

At first the dog did not react. Then suddenly he let out a howl of uncontainable grief. Whereupon the girl yelped out too in softer human idiom and let her book fall, as she knelt down from her chair and leaned her face over the body of the forlorn one.

From inside the house a face looked out. It was the girl's mother. She watched. She did not come out. Clearly she was that kind of wise mother who knew better than to interrupt a lesson of love being learnt…

From the secret peeping point of my coffee corner hidden among coconut fronds, I took all that in. And my hand spilt coffee in compassion for dog and child and mother…

After a while the girl went back to her homework, leaving the animal asleep on the rug…

Out came the girl's mother. She too began to do a pilgrimage around those clumps of plants and broken pots, studiously poking about here and there things which did not seem to me to need poking.

At length she came to where her daughter sat, her chin on

her hand, her eyes on a page that I had not seen her turn for a good while.

It was now Mother's turn. No words were needed. She reached out with heart and hand to the girl's head.

To pat with love.

And so I could not help but do it too. Though only in my writer's way: Tell the story.

With heart, and hand, on keyboard — to pat with love...

MEMORIES

Bruce Lee At
Costa Del Sol

THERE are times when bravado can save your skin — aided and abetted by the right attendant gestures.

That happened to me once when I was checking out Costa del Sol, that beautiful Mediterranean coast of Spain. I was with a Singaporean friend. We were young and curious about the insides of bars in different countries and after sundown we felt compelled to pursue our diligent research in that direction on that Coast of the Sun.

We were attracted by one particularly boisterous bar and went in, presuming that a crowd meant endorsement by those in the know. We found ourselves the only Orientals in the room steaming with hot-blooded Spaniards, some already quite liberated by liquor.

We ordered the local beer, Matador, which naturally the bartender understood. The local folks there sensed the sudden presence of aliens. A hush fell on the room, eerie because everyone there had been simultaneously voluble.

"O-oh!" I exclaimed, looking at the tough-looking men around us, probably fishermen from the coastal vessels who had come in for a bit of rowdy fun after a hard day's work trawling in the boring sea.

My friend read my mind: *Maybe we shouldn't have come in here.*

"These tough characters could be the local mafia — letting off steam after their weekly meeting…" my friend whispered his fear, worse than mine.

One burly man, swarthy and tattooed all over his arms, swaggered up to me, backed by a few other equally villainous-looking toughies. He looked me up and down. Sizing me up? He needn't have bothered. I was obviously several sizes down from him.

God help me! Give me inspiration for what to say — and how to say it! I prayed in my heart as I waited for the worst.

Suddenly Senor Goliath asked, "Cheena?"

Not wanting to say nay to the fellow, I just nodded.

Up went his beefy hands in a strange and alarming stance. I automatically fell back a few paces.

"Kung fu?" he clarified what his two upheld hands were all about.

"Yah! Kung fu!" I said, holding my hands up too, like those Hong Kong stars, all fists and legs — plus appropriate weird yelps.

And I was inspired. "Bruce Lee!" I uttered.

That seemed to make him happy. He nodded vigorously.

Then I did my bravado thing. I yelled out my version of several long-drawn-out screeches, as unearthly as I could pitch them — the kind Bruce Lee routinely yowls out as he chops and kicks everything real or imaginary within sight with his fists of fury and limbs of death.

Those yelps saved our skin.

That, or maybe the final yelp my friend was very quick to holler out — to the bartender with a signal clear to every bartender in the world, a sweep of upheld glass embracing the entire bar:

"Drinks for everyone!"

WHEN A FIRE BURNS

THE hotel manager asked to see me personally.

I was then the Deputy Secretary, very busy general facto-tum to the Permanent Secretary, in the Ministry. His hotel was a top hotel in the country. I was curious. I made time for him.

"I'm not sure how to put it..." the elegantly-dressed man

began apologetically. "You recall that recent fire in Singapore that made nearly a hundred attap house dwellers homeless? That was in your Minister's constituency. He came out with a public appeal for donations for the victims and our hotel promptly responded. We announced we would organise a grand charity dinner in our ballroom which happened to be available…"

"It was low season then for the hotel industry, right?" I interjected.

"Er… yes. We pledged to donate the proceeds to the cause."

I nodded. "Yes, I remember. That gesture got you wide media publicity. And, I read that you had a full house. So you must have raised a tidy sum for the fire victims?"

The manager turned red.

Then he said, "Unfortunately, no! You see, this was the first time we did this sort of charity thing. I must admit we miscalculated — we got burnt. We made lavish arrangements as befitting our prestigious hotel: The food was top of the menu. We even put on a top-class floor show. We did not specify any minimum donation — we thought we could count on the generosity of our diners. We thought our regular clientele would be the ones to respond.

"What we never envisaged was that so many other people, especially those from the community centres, the not-so-affluent neighbours of the fire victims, would take advantage of the donation function. For them it was a chance to savour the luxury of a top-class hotel. They secured invitation cards — and they gave only paltry sums for what to them was surely the experience of a lifetime. We were dismayed when the accounts came in after the function. There was so little left after deducting our costs, which you will appreciate must be high as we are a five-star establishment…"

"Just how much did you collect for the fire victims?" I asked a little impatiently.

"$9,000," his face went red as he mentioned the four-figure takings — as though he had just said a four-letter word.

"What?" I was surprised and did not bother to disguise it. Indeed I decided to step it up to explosion decibel: "Only $9,000? After you got all that hullabaloo from the media, after the hurrahs from everyone? All that hype for your hotel — for a miserable $9,000 for the charity?"

"We are embarrassed," he replied defensively but kept his eyes down, duly crestfallen.

I let the embarrassing silence sink in for a minute or two.

"Could you inform the Minister for us?" he asked in a soft voice.

I thought of saying "Let me think about it."

Instead I went on a different tack, "Do you really want me to do that? Tell that to the Minister? I think he will take it very badly — and I won't blame him one bit! Don't you want to think about it — discuss with your directors whether there's more you could do?"

And on his way out, I added pointedly, "And how do you think the media will react when this gets out — even if we assume the Minister says nothing? Especially after they've been lionising your hotel no end. Can you imagine the righteous indignation — articulately expressed and widely disseminated?"

A FEW days later the manager came to see me again. He informed me:

"Our directors have discussed what you said. They asked me to thank you for your wise advice. We have come to the conclusion we should top up the figure, adding a donation of our own for a very good cause…"

And he handed me a cheque for $30,000 to pass to the Minister.

Poisoning Staff

TO OUR horror, we discovered we had been poisoning staff.

With our mass poisoning stuff — polluted water!

Staff in our head office building, with absolute faith that our tap water was potable stuff, had been serenely consuming our supply piped down from our roof-top tank. And that tank had also been surreptitiously, and most foully, moonlighting as graveyard to a variety of insects — and even one tiny rat!

Mea culpa!

As Facilities Manager, I was then in charge of the building's facilities, including the water supply.

I immediately declared an emergency, turned off the supply, and got in the technicians to work round the clock to clean up the tank and the pipelines. I also fired the cleaning contractor who had been lax. And I hired in a new gang more on the ball.

The incident understandably led to a heightened hygiene concern among our staff.

First, our staff canteen and its kitchen came in for meticulous scrutiny and endless complaints. And then the old air-conditioning ducting system and its potential for circulation of germs and dust worried many sick. We brought in expert consultants who did loads of actual rectifying — plus reassuring semblances of such with detergents and deodorisers.

But awareness had been stimulated and questions continued to crop up. Which was not bad — except for the excess of anxieties from the few who would never trust our environment (or poor us in Facilities) again.

The main focus stayed on our water supply.

"Just imagine that. Packs of huge rats floating around belly up in our water tank — and we drinking water from that source! Ugh!" I never heard the end of that squawk, no matter how frequently we were now checking the water. And somehow the little rat had also grown in size and multiplied into a tribe!

I knew we had to do more than the routine. The situation demanded a Rolls Royce job on our water.

I called in a chemist friend who had become an authority on water purification. He advised me to implement a costly but thorough cleaning (and maintenance) process which included adding a certain chemical into the tank water.

"Has it been used elsewhere?" I asked.

He said yes, in Manila.

And he told me about the Manila experience, which had also taught a good lesson to all in the business.

It was announced to the people in Manila that the process was to be launched on a certain date. The day arrived. And right from that D-day, the authorities received endless complaints from the public and the media about the condition of the water.

It's worse than before. It tastes awful. Not fit to drink! That summed up the widespread complaints.

"What the public did not know then was that a mishap had in fact delayed the project in Manila and the new process had not yet been implemented. You can imagine the red faces among those loud and public with those complaints when that fact became known!" said my friend.

"And after the process was implemented?" I asked.

"No more complaints!"

We checked with the health authorities. My expert friend's recommendation (plus its successful use in Manila) was good enough for them — and for me. We mapped out the schedule for our implementation — and then we launched our programme as we had planned.

We revealed the details and announced when we would be adding the chemical.

D-day came, and with it came also immediate complaints about the quality of the new water.

Some zeroed in on the colour:

"So cloudy! Puts me off drinking it."

"Sickly-looking! That's what comes from adding chemicals to clean water from our reservoir…"

Some phoned in about the odour:

"If you smell hard, you'll find it stinks like hell!"

"Smells worse than medicine."

A few complained about the taste:

"Never tasted anything so horrible."

"Worse than before processing!"

"Even the rat water tasted better!"

We gave our consumers a few days. Then we announced that, for an important internal reason, we had decided to defer the new processing, so in fact the water complained about was no different from before. It was the old water.

We did not announce that important internal reason — what the Manila experience had taught us.

And there were no complaints when we implemented the process.

"Dad, Run For Your Life!"

DEAR Son,

You said something to me three decades ago, that has not only stayed with me all these years, but has exalted meaning in my life.

I was then in charge of putting up a 52-storey skyscraper and feeling oppressed by the onerous weight of that task. I was overworked, unfit and often unwell. I was in that blur when, out of the blue, you came at me with your scary words as if some immediate danger were about to befall me:

"Dad, run for your life!"

"What?" I came out of a blur, breathless in sudden panic.

You calmed me down and explained.

My lifestyle is all wrong. I work late every day. I carry home files. I never relax. I don't eat right. I do no exercise nor take time off for other leisure. I suffer bad moods — and I have recurring stomach ulcers.

In fact my doctor had already advised me along those very lines. Eat regularly and properly. And learn to de-stress. I promised him I would. I wasn't sure how but said I would try. Apart from advice, he prescribed medication.

"Your pills will cure me?" I asked.

"They'll help," he said, adding with a sigh, "but you'll be back again before long. You executives are all alike. Too achievement-orientated. Work too hard. You don't eat, or you eat rubbish. And you won't relax… so, you'll be back — with your ulcers."

I left, knowing that I would try to live by his prescribed advice for a while — then, I would slip back. There was something missing in that lifestyle prescription he gave me. It lacked specifics.

True enough, before long work pressure zapped my resolve — and my ulcers gave notice of a comeback.

"You need to exercise, Dad," you zeroed in on what was missing — what needed focus.

I laughed. What exercise? All my life I had never exercised. I was never one for games. Who had the time anyway? Once the day started, it was work, work, work all the way till darkness covered the surface of the earth.

You said, "Exercise is the key. It will keep you fit. And give you appetite for food. And it will relax you — de-stress you."

I laughed again. Me exercise? That's a laugh! I didn't golf. (Too time-consuming!) I didn't do tennis, nor badminton, not even ping pong. I certainly did no soccer. I could not swim (not even float to save my life!)

"So what do you suggest I do?"

"Run," you said.

"You mean, as in walk fast?"

"No, as in jog, Dad."

And then you passed me a book. You said it was a runaway best seller then — *Aerobics* by Dr Kenneth Cooper.

I promised to read it as soon as I could find the time.

Of course I could not find the time. Soon I could not even find the book.

Then, arm-twisted by family to take a break and go on holiday, I agreed to go to the Cameron Highlands. It was not far from Singapore (and so, not far from my building job).

I found the book among the many items put away for reading when I could find the leisure (ha, ha!) and I packed it in my travel bag. You were then away and could not come with us, so bringing your book along was, in a way, taking you with us — to talk with me (even if you'll be talking about running).

And I read it on the way up to the hill, and in the holiday lodge.

I found the book hard to put down. It was more than about running — it was about the miracles that running could work. Authoritative as a medical doctor's counsel — convincing and encouraging as from one who had been through the mill himself.

A spellbinding guru was urging me on.

I toyed with the idea of jogging.

Back home I would have been too embarrassed to even think about going jogging. At 40-plus, getting somewhat pot-bellied, I would have died rather than have our neighbours see me galloping about in running shorts! No, I'd never have pounded that first step.

But there, in the wilderness of the relatively uninhabited hills, invigorated and intoxicated by the mountain air, no neighbours' eyes to pry me shy, no mocking tongue to wag and say me nay, I could start to run.

So I did.

First of all, at a slow crawl around the fringes of the golf course. Then on the second day I picked up steam and did more — faster and longer. From the third day on I was hooked.

I ran and I ran.

I have not stopped running since.

I found my health improving. My appetite was now great. My heavy-headedness was gone. So too my pot belly.

And soon I found my stress going too. Exercise gave me meditation time. I could think about things undisturbed while jogging. And I could also ponder over things other than my old perennial concerns of work and deadlines. I could enjoy greenery and birds and breeze and clouds and God's sunshine — and God.

Since that first run at the Cameron Highlands I have kept up my daily running.

For 30 years now.

I built my skyscraper (and went on to other high-rises), enjoying my tasks now — no sweat! My gastric problems are history. My diet has become easy to observe, easy-going and enjoyable eating, no way spartan at all. My meditations during my long jogs have sublimated into silent praying — peace-bestowing encounters of the spiritual kind…

Yes, running has given me better life.

Someone asked me recently, "At 76, do you still jog to stay fit?"

"No, as a matter of fact, I don't any more," I replied honestly. "I jog to stay alive."

Yes, I still do my daily jogs, though at a much slower pace. Jogging has kept me physically fit, mentally alert and spiritually bonded with *Life*. I believe that without my daily dose of revving up my system, I would have long lost my quality of life — perhaps life itself, to say nothing of quality.

More than that, daily jogging has now blessed me with

both struggle and surrender. Fighting the good fight to keep meaningfully alive. At the same time accepting the finish line to come when I have run my course. And most important, being able to say at the end of it all: I have kept the faith. With life — and *Life!*

So, thank you, son, for what you said to me that time when I was 40-plus and not in the fittest of shape of body and soul — those momentous words of yours of more vital import than you knew:

"Dad, run for your *Life!*"

LIKE me then, you are 40-plus now — and not in the fittest shape. I pass back to you that message:

"Son, run for your Life!"
Dad

THE HIDDEN THINGS OF DARKNESS

BRIGHTNESS is an assuring thing. What is dark makes us anxious about hidden things, so we tend to dread and pre-judge the dark: Evil things must be lurking in there!

But there are times they can surprise us — the hidden things of darkness.

MANY in Singapore know my brother Charlie. To them he is brightness: A shining beacon. A man of goodwill and affirm-ative action, he has dedicated all his life to doing good things for others. He makes good things happen, standing up for what is right, regardless of consequences to himself. And even when only a child, there were occasions he had to suffer consequences: Punishment for standing up for his siblings and others.

In my mind he is always my protective elder brother. I watched him grow to manhood with a tough independence and strength of spirit — the kind born of upright mind and compassion.

I remember my two other brothers, Robert and Hock, in another way. By contrast, they were passive — and sad beings. Things happened to them all the time. They were the suffering ones in our family.

Both were unwanted from birth. They were farmed out to be nursed by strangers poorer than our poor selves. (We then depended on Father's meagre salary as an office hack, but at least our family had that precious blessing: Regular income.)

Yes, my younger brothers started life without that natural nourishment others take for granted: Mother love.

War came and Father lost his job. We faced poverty. Father defaulted on only one payment for their services, and those foster-mothers promptly dumped Robert and Hock back on us.

Mother was already stressed out by what fate had thrust on her: That brood of her four remaining little ones at home. And that was not all. Custom had condemned her to that Chinese young woman's fate worse than death, a calamity not uncommon then: Daughter-in-law slavery in a large family that lived by that time-honoured old-fashioned code of daughter-in-law servitude. She had to spend her waking hours in domestic drudgery, serving an autocratic mother-in-law and ordered around by her many unsympathetic siblings-in-law with no other menial help.

The sudden return of those two cast-off brats caused something in her to snap. They came home to a brooding mother, one hair trigger removed from berserk animosity.

Hock, the weaker of the two, did not survive his hapless homecoming. He died and was disposed of. With despatch. One day he was around, the next bundled off to God knows where.

Yet he was the more fortunate one…

I recall Hock as weepy, grimy, under-nourished, with stick-like legs wobbly with rickets.

Today, much too late, I feel infinite sadness. But at the time of his demise, devoid of feeling, I forgot my dead brother promptly, scrubbing my mind aseptically clean of that filthy little alien who had invaded our world.

Yes, coldness of heart — that is something children pick up from their elders. And grow up with. Unless, along the way, somehow they find salvation…

My other younger brother Robert was different from Hock. He was one hard-boiled kid. He survived Mother. He took in his stride the raw deal life handed him. He suffered derision in front of siblings, scoldings and beatings, deprivation of food, red-hot chillies rubbed onto his lips, endless abuse as an outcast.

But like Charlie he too grew to manhood with a tough independence and strength of spirit — his own brand, the sullen kind born of anger.

His habitual darkness of mood at times made me uneasy. I remember looking at the blackness that was his constant countenance as he sat by himself brooding in his private world. And I remember wondering about his menacing darkness: What hidden things, what hate, what evil lurked in there? I must have verbalised those thoughts to my other siblings. And surely Robert must have heard them.

Yes, brothers sometimes hate with fearsome hatred. But Robert's was actually a protective hardening of skin. He needed that to survive assault and indignity and unlove — and then to allow later, surely by the grace of God, that germination of empathy for others, in time unexpectedly born out of his darkness…

I was the brother in between Charlie and Robert — the one with no great hate, but no great love either. Somehow, I had become Mother's favoured son. Good things just happened to me, and I accepted them. Bad things, I simply ignored. I took Charlie's precious brotherly ways for granted. I paid precious little heed to Robert's woes. Sure, I was now and then uncomfortable about Robert but I always played it safe, tacitly siding with Mother in her frequent onslaught against our despised one.

Love for others, like Charlie's all through his life, is beautiful. Hate against others, like Robert's in his childhood years, is ugly...

But how does one describe a torpor of mind, like mine, towards a brother's torment?

THANK God, I learned humanity as I grew up. From Charlie as an unassuming but persistent mentor, from the Christian brothers in my school who imparted me compassion, from realities of hard life under the Japanese during the Occupation, from taciturn Father especially from posthumous memories of him and his papers inherited by me.

And yes, from Mother too, during (and after) those years of her long-drawn-out suffering in body and spirit, as she lay helpless and wretched, stricken with diabetes and heart disease, eyes seeming to plead for mercy and relief, mouth mute in her agony of atonement, in the purgatory of her dying years...

But even then it took me more years before I appreciated my brother Robert for what he had to go through, for the man that he was quietly becoming — his blossoming into a thing of beauty...

SO, AT first I did not understand the significance of it when, on my birthday in 1984, out of the blue Robert sent me a bouquet of flowers. It was the first (and only) time I had received flowers from a man. That surprise gesture took place after Mother had passed on at age 78. With the flowers came a strange note in which Robert begged my forgiveness.

What on earth for, I wondered?

And he asked me to read something in The Bible: St Paul's first letter to the Corinthians, Chapter 4.

What was that all about?

Mystified, I looked it up. Two points stood out in St Paul's words — about not judging others, and about God bringing to light "the hidden things of darkness".

I could not follow.

I gave up.

In those days I was a busy executive, general manager of a leading corporation, and up to my neck with work. I was fully focused on corporate objectives, I was what management gurus called "achievement-oriented". I had no time for any other concerns, certainly none to spare for unproductive pondering on the likes of my brother Robert, whatever he was trying to say through abstruse scripture...

Later on, however, I did remember something relevant to Robert's message through flowers and scripture. Two or three years back he had sent Charlie a letter, very emotional and unclear — a violent outburst against his treatment by Mother in childhood. And he had also bitter things to say about his siblings.

Charlie, saintly as ever, was unruffled — his sole concern was for Robert: How to help him come to terms with what he had gone through. He sent me a copy of the letter asking me to understand and pray for our brother. He advised me to take it as Robert letting out steam — giving vent to years of unfair treatment and hurt. The anger in Robert's words did upset me then — but only for a brief spell. I shrugged off my feelings as unproductive and filed off Robert's letter into dusty oblivion. I returned to my equanimity of no-feeling.

FIFTEEN years on and Charlie has journeyed on with his sharing of compassion. Robert has also moved ahead in his maturing of soul that had begun with Mother's death. (I believe that she was doing her unfinished business, her mother's thing on him, resolving his anger, guiding him towards forgiveness, lifting him up into sympathy for others, especially those with breaking or broken family problems like his own childhood experience.)

Robert went beyond forgiving Mother — and others that needed forgiving. He began to speak of her, and us, with genuine love. And to help others with his church work in family counselling.

And on All Souls' Day he is the one who, every year without fail, goes dutifully to pay a son's respects to his mother's remains in her columbarium niche — now the most loving son among his brothers.

RECENTLY I came by chance upon Robert's old letter to Charlie among my old papers. I could not believe that I had really read that letter before, but I must have done so, though what Robert was trying to tell us I did not get — then.

In his letter he told us about canings and humiliations. How he had to eat leftovers after the rest of the family had finished eating. How, like a dog, he was given the bones to lick after I had eaten off all the meat. How a pencil, a treasured belonging, was snatched from him and given to his younger sister. And I read with horror how on two occasions he was nearly strangled to death by an almost deranged mother, saved only by loud cries of fear from his older sister Catherine that brought Mother back to her senses…

And I also read with shame how I had rejected him time and again when he turned to me for monetary help that he needed then as a young man starting out in life.

Yes, I had read that letter before. And yet I had never done that: Read that letter. At the time I had read only anger. His anger in writing it. And mine in reading it. And I did the kindest thing I was capable of then. I put it aside. I clicked on to my no-feelings mode. And I erased from memory that offensive missive.

And my brother with it.

NOW, really reading that cry from nearly two decades back, I finally understood my brother Robert. And I marvelled at the transformation I had not really noticed till recently. Yes, he had become a greater man than I could ever be — perhaps, even greater than my brother Charlie, the one who had always been somehow, almost effortlessly, good.

Only a good mother working from heaven above, could have made someone with Robert's wretched beginnings, shine out with such saintly forgiveness and compassion.

And St Paul's words, quoted to me long ago by Robert, no longer mystified me. What was within that blackness of my abused brother's countenance was not evil, nothing to be prejudged and feared — it was goodness, and indeed brightness, waiting to shine out as, in St Paul's words:

"The hidden things of darkness…"

THE PRECIOUS HEART

I REMEMBER her as a caring woman from my childhood days. She was family — and yet she was not.

She cared for us. Cooked our meals, cleaned for us, watched over us as babies and toddlers and school children. She loved us.

Father paid her two dollars a month (the going wage in those pre-war days) plus food and lodging. Her food was leftovers and her bed was a straw mat on the wooden corridor floor outside the children's room.

When the war came and our family could no longer afford to pay her wages, she asked to continue to work for us for just food and lodging. There was no other option for her as she had nowhere else to go. After the war she stayed on, only getting paid wages again after Father found work. By then she would have stayed on regardless, having become part of us.

I suppose you could call her our foreign maid except that she was not much more foreign than ourselves. (We had come to Singapore one generation earlier.) We never felt different from her, no less Chinese, certainly no more Singaporean — the word "Singaporean" not having even been thought of then.

She spoke Chinese as we did, although her Hokkien Chinese dialect came out more sing-song than ours. What she spoke was actually the Chawan dialect, close enough to our Hokkien tongue to make her less alien to us than say, the Cantonese or Hainanese Chinese. She wore the same samfoo clothes as the rest of the women in our family did except that hers was consistently an insipid plain top and black trousers.

What her real name was I never knew.

Everyone just called her Ngeow Boh (Hokkien for Mother Cat, the Mother part being an honorific). Neither in appearance nor disposition was she feline. If anything she was more bovine being big-boned and substantial, indeed to us children she was large enough to be elephantine.

Ngeow Boh was well-loved, not only by us, but by our neighbours too. She got on especially well with our next-door neighbour, Auntie Ah Geck and her little daughter, a sweet child called Ah Poh ("Precious"). Auntie Ah Geck would give Ngeow Boh old clothes and odds and ends. And whenever she returned from a shopping trip to Chinatown and came over with delicacies for us, she would always have a separate servant's share for Ngeow Boh.

Once she even gave her some costly herbs to relieve her asthma. In gratitude, Ngeow Boh sewed little Ah Poh a patchwork blanket just like one she had made for me. Ah Poh told me she felt really nice in its multi-coloured warmth on rainy nights. I said, "I know."

AS NGEOW BOH grew older, she talked about returning to China, and we sensed our parting with her would come soon. She had saved a little money — not much but enough to get her back home to live frugally with her own children's families without being destitute and a burden.

She started to make plans. She would go down to Chinatown to discuss with her "sisters" in their "coolie house" or common workers' address — a kind of home-from-home place to go to when off from their employment accommodation.

One day she came home to our house, flushed and breathless with excitement.

"Luck has befallen me," she announced with a broad smile. And she shared with us what that wonderful piece of luck was. While in Chinatown, she went to a remittance shop that she used to send money home to China. Just outside the shop she met ("by happy chance" she said) a poor, sad-looking man who showed her a beautiful jade pendant in the shape of a heart. The man told her he was in urgent need of money to remit home.

"He was looking for a buyer for that prized possession. He had to remit money to his very sick mother. So he was selling his precious jade heart at a loss, a fraction of its worth. Another woman was there before me and she was pleading with him for time to raise the purchase price. But he told her, sorry, he could not wait for her as his need was immediate. He said all he needed was $88. I had just over that amount ready — the sum I was about to remit home…"

So Ngeow Boh bought herself the pendant for $88, a princely sum in those days — and a big chunk out of her life savings.

Father examined the pendant. His face fell.

He looked sadly at Ngeow Boh. He did not speak.

But there was no other way to tell her but straight. "You've been cheated," Father said. "This is not jade. There are many stones that look like jade, but are worth less. This one is worth much less. In fact, I think it has little market value…"

Ngeow Boh turned pale. She did not say a word. She did not cry. She just stared at what she had bought for a long while. Then without a word she took the thing with her to the only private place she had in the house: The bathroom behind the kitchen.

And for a long time she did not come out. Mother had to call her out for dinner. She did not eat. She went to bed. I don't think she slept at all that night.

The next day Auntie Ah Geck came over, her Ah Poh in tow. She had heard how Ngeow Boh had been cheated. She asked to look at the thing.

At first Ngeow Boh would not show it to her.

"Aiyah! What for you want to see it? Yes, yes, I'm been a stupid old woman. I've gone and let myself get cheated of my savings, that's all!"

But Auntie Ah Geck insisted.

"Ngeow Boh," she said, "I know something about stones, precious or semi-precious — just let me see it."

So Ngeow Boh brought out the pendant. Auntie Ah Geck looked over the stone carefully. "Yes, Ngeow Boh, you've been swindled. This is not real jade. But still it's got some value of its own even as a kind of coloured stone."

Then to everyone's surprise, Auntie Ah Geck made an offer for the fake jade. "Look, I've been thinking of buying something like that for my little Ah Poh. Will you sell it to me for $60?"

Everyone was surprised. Even little Ah Poh.

Ngeow Boh did not know what to say. Mother looked at Auntie Ah Geck. Their eyes seemed to say things only the two of them understood then — warm and friendly things.

"Take the money, Ngeow Boh," Mother advised. "Not

many people will want to buy that kind of stone. This is your chance to reduce your loss — and you can help Ah Poh get a nice present too. Everybody ends up happy, right?"

Ngeow Boh, who had been uptight and depressed, relaxed and allowed herself to be persuaded.

And little Ah Poh got her unexpected present…

YEARS later, I came across Ah Poh, now a college under-graduate, a sophisticated young lady, and understandably no longer answering to the name "Ah Poh".

I met her at a meeting of volunteers for a project that not many do-gooders sign up for — visiting HIV patients at a home. Genevieve looked the image of her mother, with the same warmth and friendliness. And goodness of heart.

She was wearing a familiar pendant — a gift from her dear mother who had passed on.

"You're still wearing that thing? Ngeow Boh's so-called jade heart?" I asked. Momentarily we shared an unspoken memory.

"You know that thing's got no value at all, of course? Your mother was really good, helping Ngeow Boh when she did, but what she passed on to you was not a precious jade heart…"

Ah Poh smiled. "No, Mother did not pass me a precious jade."

And then she added:

"But heart, yes. She passed me a precious heart!"

A Contract On His
Cha Boh Lang

AN OLD civil service colleague told me this story. I cannot vouch for its truth but it seems credible: I have lived the old

Singapore setting to it.

In the days before law and order became better established with independence, there was a Singapore businessman who had his finger in many pies. Kong made money fast partly because he was unhampered by scruples, though he took care never to stain his own fingers. As a property developer, he had to overcome stubborn obstacles to his projects, including pig-headed landowners and squatters who would not come to terms with him. To get his way he often used unconventional means — covertly, of course. Dirty work should be discreetly done. Better still it should be contracted out.

Kong knew one Tua Bak who was in his way a kind of businessman. He operated an unusual business, available only for a reasonable price to a very select group: People who needed stubborn opposition softened up, no questions asked. In a nutshell, Tua Bak's people did those many things that businessmen could not safely do for themselves without risk of staining their good reputations or even running foul of the law.

Tua Bak's people were efficient and absolutely discreet. And they accepted all consequences of mishaps. Their operatives would stoically suffer jail terms, even death sentences, if and as necessary — no one else implicated, no extra charge. They had helped Kong in tight spots in his business. Such as "negotiating" with squatters to accept settlement, prevailing on contractors to accept Kong's offers for disputed extra work, persuading debtors to pay up, softening up overzealous inspectors (whether by bribing and/or bashing), vandalising properties of people who needed to be instilled with an attitude of cooperation — generally providing him with effective facilitating service on those frustrating occasions when normal measures failed to produce results.

Over time Tua Bak had become more than a business associate — he was now a trusted friend. Kong jocularly referred to him as his secret weapon, his DDT against pests in business — Director of Dirty Tactics.

NOW he needed DDT to resolve a personal problem: Do a needed extermination.

"It's my *cha boh lang*, Amy," he opened the subject with Tua Bak, using the Hokkien common word for "woman" by which Chinese folks refer to their wives or mistresses. Amy was one of the latter. "She's being unfaithful to me — and after only one year with me. Even with that bad heart condition of hers, she carries on with others behind my back! I suspected something, so I got an agency to trail her — that's how I found out, though she doesn't know that I know… that woman really has a bad heart!"

Tua Bak shook his grey old head and sighed. "So disgusting, isn't it? Women nowadays are so shameless — no morals at all! They act like they're same as we men! Especially those English-educated women like her, all the same, *buay kian siow* (shameless). *Aiyah!* What's our world coming to?"

Kong appreciated his friend's sympathy. He confided, "I really regret leaving my Mei Lan for this cheap whore. You know Mei never fooled around — not before, not even now, after I've left her. And she's as pretty as Amy, prettier in fact…"

"Mr Kong, why don't you talk with Mei. Tell her you want to dump Amy. Say you'll let her come back to you. Admit to her you were wrong, tell her you know now that Amy's the wrong *cha boh lang* for you!"

"In fact I did that, Tua Bak. And you know what she said? She can never forgive Amy. She hates her. She can never trust that hussy so long as she is alive. She still bumps into her now and then — at the heart-check clinic they both go to. When I pressed her to come back, she said, *No, not as long as that hussy lives!*" Kong paused to let those last words sink in.

Tua Bak pondered on what Kong said — or rather, left unsaid.

Then he started thinking aloud for Kong's benefit: Pushing people around was one thing, exterminating them was another — careful planning was necessary. He could think of no one in Singapore he could trust to do a job of that order and stay undetected. He would have to go out of the country to recruit foreign talent.

"I'll have to put out a contract on her, get a specialist from outside — like Thailand. Someone who's really an expert, Mr Kong — someone who'll do the job neatly, and go back home at once without being detected. It will be costly."

Kong nodded. He could afford the cost. "Yes, get someone from outside. But make sure it's someone who's been here and knows his way around," he stipulated. The local police net could tighten very quickly, once they latched on to any crime.

"Of course! No problem. Trust me, brother…"

After a moment's thought Tua Bak spoke up again. "I have it — the man for the job. He's a lab assistant who's worked here for a short while, a year or so ago, before he returned to Bangkok. He knows you. I think you may even know him. Remember when you were hospitalised for your heart…"

Kong interrupted him, "Please, I don't want to know any details. I don't want to know the man. The less I know the better. I leave you to handle the job. I'll be going overseas with some business group soon. Do it then. Better for me to be out of the country when the thing, whatever it is, happens to Amy, right?"

"Okay, boss. You just leave everything to me. The more I think about it, the more I think my Bangkok friend is the man for the job. As a lab technician, he knows a lot about drugs, and Amy has heart problems… we can make it look like heart failure or something…"

Kong liked the idea, but he put his finger to his lips to silence his enthusiastic business associate. The less details he knew the better.

TUA BAK'S assassin from Bangkok flew in a few days after Kong flew out as a respected member of a Singapore trade delegation on a lengthy visit to Japan and South Korea.

The hired contractor was glad for the chance to return to Singapore. He liked the stylish girls available along Orchard Road; he had happy memories of pretty and easy pickings.

The assignment was dead easy and the pay-off handsome as hell. And he knew the Kongs. He had got to know Mr Kong when the latter was warded in hospital, and he had also met his *cha boh lang* then. He remembered too her disclosure that she had to watch her heart too. It was a pity he had to do a job on her — such a charming lady! But a job was a job. A man had to do what a man had to do.

He found out that the lady was due to visit her heart clinic soon. Arranging to bump into her by accident was easy. So was getting her to have a cup of coffee with him at the clinic canteen. Likewise, slipping a fast-dissolving tablet into her cup was a cinch…

He made sure the lady finished her drink. The pill was a sure-fire thing, a timed-release drug. It would look like a sudden heart attack — while she slept that night, that sleep from which she would never wake up. He would be out of the country by then, happily on his way home, enjoying a delicious meal served by those delicious air hostesses on Thai Airways…

On arrival home, he phoned his cryptic report to Tua Bak. "Job done as planned. Party will depart tonight. Send balance of payment."

Kong, impatient for results, phoned Tua Bak from overseas soon after.

He spoke only one word. "Done?"

"Yah!" Tua Bak confirmed. "Expiry deadline tonight — maybe already."

Kong breathed a sigh of relief.

Amy was history, thank God!

The next day his plane landed in Singapore. He was ushered with the rest of the delegation to the lounge reserved for VIP passengers. There, family members could also gain admission to meet them.

Would Mei be there, he wondered? The news of Amy's demise should be out by now — so Mei might just be there to welcome him back into her loving arms. He suddenly yearned for those arms with a longing of a love-sick young man. His heart began to beat faster in anticipation of the beautiful white flesh and curvaceous body of his Mei.

His *cha boh lang* was there all right.

But it was not Mei.

Amy!

Why? What went wrong? Tua Bak never ever failed before!

Then the truth struck him: That stupid foreign assassin must have made a blunder… God! The fellow had exterminated the wrong *cha boh lang!*

It was more than Kong's bad heart could take. His head went spinning. And to aggravate his feelings of disaster, Amy rushed towards him, jumped at him, and hugged him, and kissed him with those most loathesome hussy lips of hers.

And in his frantic struggle to free himself, Kong tripped and collapsed on top of her, squashing her flat with his dying mountain of dead weight flesh, giving her such shock, such sudden stress that the woman's weak heart went fatally wonky, too…

OUT OF
THIS WORLD

His Three Mothers

IT HAD happened so many times you could call it the story of his life:

"You don't understand me, Mother! I wish I knew how to say it. How I feel. I do care for you; I do love you… but I don't know how to tell you. I just can't!" he screamed at his mother. A silent scream in his heart. Outwardly, he was poker-faced as always. And he moved away — as always.

From childhood Kevin had that phobia for talking and sharing feelings face-to-face with anyone — especially people he cared for. Most especially, Mother.

Perhaps it was because as a child he loved his wonderful Dad so much.

And then missed him so much.

Mother suddenly hated Dad! Kevin could not understand why. Everything had been okay. And then Mother threw Dad out!

Mother had discovered that mysterious, unforgivable thing: "Your wonderful Dad was cheating on me!"

Little Kevin could not understand. *How had Dad been cheating? Had he been finding answers to problems dishonestly, peeping where he should not, or secretly doing something bad with someone — like boys who cheated during school exams?* Mother never explained it to him.

Kevin asked too many questions for her liking, and he whined too much about missing Dad. Mother just blew up every time Kevin mentioned his father.

One day he bawled his heart out — *how he missed Dad!* And Mother screamed at him, "Shut up! You'll never see your bloody Dad again!"

Bloody Dad? How did Dad get bloody?

"Is Dad dead?" little Kevin asked.

"He's as good as dead! You're never going to see him again!"

That was when he threw a tantrum and hit Mother with his little fists — and Mother, angry with him as never before (or after), slapped him on the face, and sent him spinning down to the floor.

As he grew older he understood…

God, how poor Mother must have suffered!

He thought about speaking with Mother about it. He tried. He put it off. He could not.

He grew up that way — silent like stone. He could never speak his heart to Mother — or any other person. Not even Aunt Agnes, Mother's sister who looked so much like her. She never married, had no family of her own, came over often, and was like a second mother to him.

HELP came to Kevin.

A friend took him to those Novena prayer sessions where the compassionate Fathers encouraged people to pour their hearts out in petitions to Mary, the Mother of Jesus — the Mother of Perpetual Help. And people actually wrote letters to her, beginning with, "Dearest Mother…"

Yes, he could do what those thousands of others were doing. He could write, if not speak. That way he could express what he felt! And he need not be embarrassed for he would be addressing someone not of this world?

He heard the moving things other people wrote in their letters (all anonymous). These were read out each week by the Fathers — letters that asked her for help, and letters that thanked her for help received.

I am not alone. So many others need, ask, and get, that help.

He found he too could write letters like those. To that Mother, to whom he could openly, and yet secretly, let out those feelings cold-stored for years in his heart.

That was the way he found to speak without having to speak — to talk to a "dearest Mother" invisible yet present and listening.

He became quite good at those letters. He wrote again and again, bringing his letters every week to slot into collection boxes in the church.

And one day he was anonymously held up as paradigm, as the Father read out one of his simple but moving letters to the packed church:

"Dearest Mother, I was dumb when I came to you. I could not speak out my thoughts and feelings. You have given me this wonderful gift. You touched me. And showed me how to find speech. I listened to the letters others wrote to you. I prayed for your help. And I found I too could do that — write what I feel. You have given speech to a dumb man. Thank you! Your loving son."

After that public bouquet, letters to "Dearest Mother" became a habit with Kevin. That was the miracle that gave release to his pent-up feelings. He was no longer a suppressed Zombie.

BUT still he could not speak, nor write, to his own mother.

The blow on the head he received from Mother was long forgotten by his conscious mind — but perhaps not by his subconscious mind. He remained as always, polite with Mother, but he could never pour his heart out to her — as he could with his other Mother, that "Dearest Mother" at the Novena.

Mundane communication was no problem, so long as they were about passing matters that did not matter.

The time came when he was faced with a passing matter that did matter.

The doctors discovered that Mother had advanced cancer. She was dying, soon to pass away. Time was running out. Suddenly so many unsaid things needed to be said. Especially love. Childhood anger no longer existing needed to be revealed as healed. Yes, understanding, forgiveness — and love…

But Kevin, even at Mother's death door, still could not

speak to her. Nor even write to her — as he could (and did) to his "dearest Mother".

He sat down and wrote his longest letter to "Dearest Mother" and in it he poured out all those thoughts and feelings of a lifetime of unspoken love for Mother.

He went to the church with that letter to pray for that help: To be able to reach out and touch Mother. But he knew in his heart, he would never be able to break through that wall that blocked out speech — the long dumb years had set up a solid stone barrier.

He prayed till he broke down and cried.

In his grief and confusion he forgot to put his letter in the box, leaving it in his trouser pocket where he also kept his handkerchief.

He left to go to Mother who had been moved back to her ward from the intensive care unit. Mother was still conscious but deathly pale. Aunt Agnes was with her. Nobody else, for Mother had few relatives.

Seeing Aunt Agnes with Mother made it worse for him.

There was Mother dying, and next to her, "Mother" alive!

And all his life he could speak out his heart to neither.

He broke down. In agony he cried. In agony he tried and tried. To say the things in his heart. This last chance he had…

He could not.

The words just would not come out.

"Why, God? How, God?" In grief and in frustration, he cried out in such an overwhelming flow that he had to pull out his handkerchief to wipe away his tears.

Aunt Agnes put her arm around him, and took him out of the room, and told him, "Go home and rest. This may be a long watch into many nights. Come back later after you have rested. We'll take turns to be with her…" She had been a nurse and was in better emotional control.

WHEN Kevin returned, he found that Mother had gone.

"Why, why?" he sobbed out his grief, "Why couldn't I do it? Why couldn't you wait for me — to hear the things in my heart, the love I could never say to you?"

"But you did say them! And she did hear them. We heard them together," Aunt Agnes said.

Kevin did not understand.

"The letter you left for her on her bed when you left?"

"What letter?"

"The one you wrote beginning with *Dearest Mother?*"

Oh God! Oh, my good God! That letter? I must have forgotten to leave it in the church, and it must have dropped from my pocket here!

"A beautiful letter," Aunt Agnes hugged him and said in a voice hoarse with emotion, "I'm proud of you, proud to be your mother from now on — as I promised your mother…"

And she went on to recount Mother's last moments.

"She was so moved by your letter as I read to her. The way you spoke about all the things you could not say to her before. You should have seen it! How her eyes shone. How she cried and smiled at the same time, as I choked through your touching words. How she took in every word — down to your goodbye signature, 'Your loving son'.

"Your words were the very last words she heard… and as she went, she answered you. She said, 'Yes, my loving son… I love you too.'

"She smiled as she went. You can see it — she kept her smile on her lips for you."

Kevin, though in turmoil of grief, was transported to ecstasy, lifted to high heaven…

Here was Mother sitting by him, Mother alive and talking to him. There also was Mother dead — but still smiling. Yes, with her last breath, she too had found the words of love she could not find to give him in life…

And Kevin found his own physical voice:

"Thank you, dearest Mother!"
This time to all his three Mothers.

LIFE IN A MONSTER WORLD

ONE moment Chua, an athletic and handsome young male, was making his way confidently about in the dark — the next, those frighteningly bright lights were turned on, full blaze, exposing him to certain attack in that cavernous place: The kitchen of the monster men.

Chua, his reflexes sensitive to the minutest of air movements, fled even before he looked up and saw the thing he had to fear most — one of those gigantic beings who lived in that palatial house, its hideous eyes fixed balefully on him!

Chua's legs ran helter-skelter in search of sanctuary, zig-zagging this way and that to evade attack.

The monster roared and gave chase, pushing aside towering chairs, clumsily trying to pulverise Chua with his massive feet and lunging at him with a huge pole.

Chua headed for his favourite hiding place near the wall, a dark alley nearby. He scampered frantically into it — that passage behind the monster's skyscraper of a kitchen cabinet. Here he might be safe, at least for a while. The place had provided him refuge before. After a few tries, poking at him with his pole, the giant would give up and go.

Not this time! This time the monster was ready with new technology, a biological weapon.

Chua heard the "sssh" hiss, felt the sting of poison drops and knew that the giant had resorted to that gruesome ultimate weapon! Chua's comrades in the secret underground hideout they shared had whispered about it — that deadly release of lethal chemical spray from which none ever returned whole, if at all! Chua knew his life was on the line. He had to throw caution to the wind, get away instantly.

Fortunately he knew the lay of the land. He squirmed out of the cul-de-sac through a slit at the back of the cabinet, through the inside of it, then out again through a gap under the door — out into the naked glare of the kitchen lights. He did not, could not, care any more whether he would be seen. He sped towards the door that led to the terrace hoping to reach the jungle of overgrown vegetation outside. The massive door was closed but that was no problem for someone as small as he was. The gap between the door and the floor was all the space he needed.

Thank God, the monster was still peering behind the cabinet and did not notice his escape. Chua breathed a sigh of relief. He had escaped extermination for another day — or so he thought.

Outside in the semi-dark, half-lit by the crescent moon, he stood momentarily still as he took in his surroundings. And then he froze, for now he had walked right into a new danger: The Monsters' gargantuan pet, the sadistic creature they called their "cat" was there in front of him, on the terrace floor, its body heaving gently in sleep.

Chua knew he had to be dead quiet, move slowly with care. The slightest noise would arouse that monster. He crawled a good distance. Then he almost died from sheer fright as one big feline eye suddenly opened — green and mean. At once the beast sprang to its feet, wide-awake, both petrifying eyes focused malignantly on him.

Chua did not wait. He dived into the dense foliage. The unknown was to be preferred, whatever its perils, better than the slow torture and certain death this sadistic animal could mete out to living things smaller than itself!

The cat jumped in after him. But Chua was already hidden by foliage, a safe distance ahead of it. And he kept on running as fast as his legs could carry him, for long as he could hear the fearsome creature trampling the tall grass behind him.

After a while the noise grew faint and Chua knew that once more he had cheated death.

Or had he?

Now he picked up a tell-tale movement and a sound, a hiss — and he knew a new danger had arrived. He stood completely still, aware that snakes sensed movement rather than saw their prey.

A massive solid torrent of slimy skin slid past Chua. The smell of the giant reptile was so strong it was almost overbearing. It seemed like ages, but at last the hellish train of monstrous flesh passed and disappeared — another danger survived!

Chua waited till the kitchen lights went off, signalling it was safe. Chua's mind focused on one thought: How was he to get back home — back inside the house of the monsters, in the comfortable darkness of the enormous kitchen, the world in which he and his comrades eked out their perilous lives, concealed in secret crannies out of sight of the family of giants during the day, emerging at night to scavenge for food in the relative safety of the dark. That was their life — the hard world that was their lot to live in.

Chua, on his way home, kept a lookout for the monsters and their cat — and others intent on exterminating his kind…

Chua did not complain — in fact he somewhat relished the thrill of adventure in ever-present danger. But he had heard a few older (and less agile) ones moan: *Could there be more abominable conditions than these under which they lived?*

Those older ones hated living out their existence side by side with those loathsome creatures — giants a thousand times their body size, in features resembling the repulsive monkey species, alien beings hostile to the point of insanity. What else would account for those monsters' compulsive violence against them, ever ready to smite them dead the instant they caught sight of their kind?

Yet these same Monsters glorified themselves with the pompous name of "Sapient Man", as opposed to lesser species of earlier Man; and they called Chua and his ilk by a name which sounded like a bluster of bigotry: "Blatta Orientalis"! Worse, they accused their tiny fellow-creatures of God, even without any evidence whatsoever, of being carriers of germs (as though they were not) and spreaders of disease — justifying their compulsion to exterminate Chua's entire species!

But despite the atrocious environment, by the grace of God the small creatures, especially young ones like Chua, felt life was not too bad — that is, while they survived the genocidal war waged by the monsters. Naturally resilient and optimistic, apart from the above-mentioned grouches, they simply carried on living each day as it came, taking whatever came their way. Living dangerously, enjoying the exciting life, feasting away on the monsters' leftovers as though that was abundance, though ever ready to scurry for cover at the first sign of their enemies — they accepted their lot in life.

And Chua's grown-up comrades even fell in love, did that mysterious thing called copulation, gave birth to babies, lots of them. So they enjoyed what little daily life the good Lord granted them in those dark and dank holes they called home. And that existence of theirs had gone on like that for countless centuries in that relentless world dominated by the monsters.

Yes, only love-making really made life worth living…

But love also led them into fearsome perils.

As it was to be for Chua.

Now on his way home, he had made good progress, as he dashed from shadow to shadow, crawling his way back towards those safe crannies in the monsters' kitchen. He was at the terrace, just outside the kitchen door, on his last lap to sanctuary, when it happened! A head-swirling scent hit him and paralysed him to a standstill.

He saw her: Cha Boh, a female he had heard the guys talk

volumes about, although he himself had yet to enjoy linkage with her — or any other female for that matter. For Chua was very young, in fact still a virgin. And that voluptuous lady was overpowering, steamy with that come-hither perfume that she knew would reduce males to putty.

Yes, that was the scent of love that the guys had told him about! Until this magic moment, Chua had never been exposed to it, that seduction fragrance irresistible:

Pheromone.

The vision of the lady alone, inviting and waiting on the moonlit terrace, sent Chua's heart into a mad gallop as that indescribable first sex-thrill raced through his whole being. He forgot everything else, forgot the need to stay alert to the menaces that beset the open terrace. He emerged boldly, brazenly, from the shadows, exposed himself completely in the light, ran around the female excitedly, naked in his frenzy of arousal, not a care in the world except to mate with this luscious creature!

Cha Boh, too, seemed to like Chua. With a flirtatious wiggle she ran off, but not so fast that Chua would not be able to catch up with her. The two began to dance about, dodging here and there among the shadows, in a kind of foreplay. Then they came together in the shade of a giant potted plant. And there they threw all caution to the winds — and passion consumed them.

It was as the guys had told him: Pyrotechnics with stars scintillating and bells ringing… so elevating, so heady, a thousand things happening at once, everything so real and yet so unreal.

And then the next thing Chua knew was: Cha Boh had abruptly disengaged herself and disappeared!

In that same moment Chua saw the mammoth furry paw swishing down from high heaven, smashing at him, into him! And he felt the awesome agony and exquisite ecstasy of his guts spilling out over the floor even as he saw yet more fireworks and stars and heard even louder bells!

But his last thoughts, his last feelings, remained with the numbing hangover of that climactic moment of his life, his first and last moment with Cha Boh. That made life worthwhile, worth thanking his maker for, even though life for him had not been long, would be no more now…

The monsters' cat had got him!

But (what the heck!) even if he was in the throes of dying, even if he was nothing but a lowly insect to the world, he was still God's happiest creature:

Kah Chua — cockroach.

MAX THE MIND-READER

THAT Tokyo assignment looked a prize posting and career-wise an upward-propeller. Max thought his colleague Tahir wanted it. When the boss mentioned to the two of them that Tahir might be the man for the job, Tahir turned red (with excitement?) though with the man's usual modesty he began to wax unworthy. So Max jumped in and backed the choice of his friend. That clinched it. The boss decided: Tahir got the posting.

Max only knew that Tahir truly did not want the Tokyo posting when, as they came out of the boss's office, Tahir let out a snarl, "Fine friend you turned out to be! Now I'll have to uproot myself for a year or so…"

Max wished he could read people's minds correctly. *All of us make wrong moves when we make wrong assumptions, especially about what goes on in others' minds, apparently myself more than the rest of mankind!* Max felt awful.

So, the next time in church to do his weekly praying thing, Max petitioned for help from above.

And suddenly, out of the blue, divine help was bestowed:

The gift came to him!

There he was, meditating assiduously at that evening service, when the guy next to him began to distract him, shuffling those big feet of his about. And then Max heard the clear whisper.

"This blooming service goes on and on. And it's crowded and hot like hell. Good Lord! What could have possessed me to come here? Should have gone straight to the bar to wait for my friends instead…"

The guy was actually spouting those not-quite-holy words to him, a total stranger, there in the middle of a solemn service!

Max glared at him. The guy did not look back. In fact his eyes were serenely closed, therefore impervious to any glare. His lips were piously still. And yet there he was, with his face devout and more grumbles in the same vein audibly rumbling out of him. *The fellow could speak like a ventriloquist without moving his lips?*

Max looked around him. Surely others around heard his words too? No, they were unperturbed. Max was the only one who could hear him. And the guy was not even addressing him.

It's my imagination, Max thought. But that wasn't it. The guy went on and on, mouthing mutinous mutter. All the while eyes shut, mouth motionless, face inscrutable — and blissfully unaware that scandalous thoughts were leaking out of him!

"You shouldn't be thinking thoughts like that here!" Max reprimanded him in a whisper. The man started, turned red, and said (or rather, thought), "How did you know?"

"I can hear your thoughts," Max explained — for his own benefit as well.

The guy's thinking went haywire after that, and as soon as the service was over, he slunk away.

AFTER Max left the church he got into a crowd. Then he saw

her: The comely young lady who stared at him, then averted her eyes.

And once more it happened: The whisper came to him — from her direction, her mouth not moving, her eyes not even looking at him:

"Wow! What a hunk, that handsome guy. He looks familiar. I think he could be the stranger I met (and kissed) last New Year's Eve. At that crowded free-for-all bash at Orchard Road. I'm not sure. It was chaotic then. The place was jam-packed. And I was half-drunk… I wonder if he remembers?"

"Yes, I remember," Max replied to her. She was startled. She stared at him, the question flashing in her mind, "Can the guy read my thoughts?"

"Yes, the guy can," Max responded, helpful and frank — perhaps too frank.

"He's kidding! But how? How does he do it?" she went on in her mind.

"Well, this is how: I was praying that I be able to read minds — and suddenly the gift came to me!"

Her eyes opened wider. "He may be cute — but he's so creepy…" She did not have to say it.

"No I'm not creepy at all!"

Her eyes spoke uncertainty, now mixed with a little fear. She went on to recall how, when the countdown went to zero, they kissed — and did not let go all through the singing of *Auld Lang Syne* — it was that long! And yes, she liked that! And then suddenly they were swept away, carried off, separated by endless waves of cheering men and women.

Hey! Got to be careful! He hears every word in my head…

She blushed at her thoughts and pulled the reins on them. She decided she should not stay. She slipped off — once more out of Max's life. It was too unnerving for a girl to be with a guy who could read her every single thought, unexpurgated!

Max's eyes searched for her in the mass of people around

him. He focused on each face. And the faces responded with their thoughts. He received them all at one go: A cacophony of confusing thought-chatter deafening to his newly-gifted thought receptors. He switched off the roar and hurried away, heading for his MRT station, careful not to switch on again to the madding crowd.

MAX boarded the crowded train with a small group that included a tired-looking woman heavy with child.

"Hope some kind soul will offer me his seat. I only need it for the next two stops," her thoughts came out to Max loud and clear.

There was a young man seated near the entrance with his eyes serenely closed. "Better not open my eyes, otherwise I may have to offer my seat to someone or other," his thinking told Max.

Another man, a bit less self-centred, was vacillating in his mind, "Should I offer my seat to this pregnant lady? But I have many stops to go… wonder how long she'll keep my seat before I can have it back again?"

"Yes, you should offer her your seat. And don't worry, she'll only need it for the next two stops," Max assured the man. He got up at once and gave the woman his seat. Then both looked at him with the same thought. *Could he really read my mind?*

Max answered them, "Yes, I can."

"He's kidding," the man told himself.

"I'm not," Max corrected him.

AMONG the passengers Max now spotted a nervous-looking guy. He kept stealing looks at an elderly woman with a thick gold chain around her neck.

Max read his intent. The scoundrel was thinking about his modus operandi: Follow her to her housing estate, try to snatch that necklace when they are alone, perhaps as she enters the lift.

"Don't!" Max warned him quietly. "Don't do it. Or I'll report you to the police!"

He said, "I don't know what you're talking about! You're *siow* (crazy) or what?"

But he thought, "Could he be a detective? Could this fellow be trailing me?"

"Yes," Max answered him, "This fellow could be!"

"How does he know what I'm thinking?" he asked himself.

"By reading your mind," Max answered.

He got off at the next stop.

MAX reached home to his sister's apartment where he was putting up.

Thank God for a sweet sister like Candy — and an understanding brother-in-law like Butch! Without them, I would not have a place I could relax in, a place I could call home — unlike Dad's house where I had to live with incessant questions and criticisms. Those thoughts he did not need to read — they were his own.

Candy and Butch were in the living room watching TV. *Yes, those two folks were angels to him, letting him have their guest room all these months, not one word of complaint about anything, not one demand, always giving way to him…*

Max felt so blessed to have them as family — especially since his tiffs with Dad, never really serious but still off putting. Those irritations were why he had sought shelter with Candy.

"Hi Max, have you eaten? We kept some dinner for you," Candy went, solicitous just like every time he came home late.

But this time before Max could respond, Candy went on. Or rather, her unspoken thoughts went on: "Why doesn't he ring to tell us whether he'll be coming home? He thinks this is a hotel or what? So annoying!"

Max stopped in his tracks. That was news. There was more news to come.

"When will he realise he's taking things too much for granted? He should make up with Dad and go back home where he belongs," Candy, her sweet smile betraying nothing, thought on.

Then Butch came in with his thoughts, his eyes still glued to the TV. "No privacy at all for us since he came and parked himself here. He's a real sponger. And such a thoughtless young man! And just because he's family, we can't complain! Wish he'd wake up to things and go back home…"

Max could not speak. He did not know what words to speak.

"How can we say anything? We don't want to hurt him. But surely he should be able to figure it out for himself!" Candy's thoughts now beamed over to him.

Max went to his room.

So, that was the truth! This was not home to him — not any more.

Time to go back home — to his Dad's home, at least until he could use his CPF savings to get his own pad.

Max decided to go home the very next day.

And Max was learning. There was more beyond smiling or expressionless faces. After a while he found he did not really need to read thoughts behind faces. He learnt perception, how to hear more than just words openly said. He could read thoughts — the natural way other people do their mind-reading. Yes, he was learning.

He decided he did not want that gift of mind-reading any more.

He knelt down and prayed that what had happened, all that mind-reading stuff, all would be just a dream — from which he would wake up in the morning.

YES, it was all just a dream — from which he woke up in

the morning.

He was still living in Candy's apartment.

But not after that day.

No Bodies

THE Professor seemed to float about in front of us, smiling strangely as he airily posed us that spooky question of his. At first we took it as a didactic kind of joke. Then we realised he was dead serious. The question became gripping. More eerie by the minute till it verged on the alarming — and entered the world of the terrifying:

"What if nobodies are really that — no bodies?" He let that sink in — let the few giggles in reaction die a natural death. The darkening sky outside lent creepy ambiance.

"What if nobodies are beings, whether of our world or not," he continued in his softest Boris Karloff voice, "who do not possess bodies that we truly see — only bodies that we may fleetingly see, and then lose all recall of them?"

He left us suspended on that question mark for a spell before he went on, "Think back to those moments when we walked in crowds. People are all around us — yet we recognise few, if any. We assume they are real. Real people, like us. Are they? Can we be sure?

"What if they are not? Can they not be from another world? Another planet? Or a spirit world? Or only figments of our imagination? What if their bodies are not real bodies — only virtual images around us?

"Do you not sense a natural restraint about reaching out to them, knowing better than to do that, instinctively respecting their other-worldly existence and committing no trespass into their private domain? And if you talk to some of them, do you not only sometimes get a true human response? More often, only a blank stare or a cold shoulder as the other party ignores you, moving on as though never addressed? Like a being not of our world? Perhaps one who has borrowed a body or assumed the appearance of one while with us?

"And surely there must have been times when you have felt this: You stand in a crowded street or a packed train, and suddenly you experience that isolation that tells you that you are utterly alone, notwithstanding the bodies around you? Your sixth sense tells you the bodies about you are no bodies!

"What if we live amid a mass of nobodies?"

HE LEFT off, letting silence stay suspended in the air. Then one student bravely put to him, "Professor, is it not possible that what you sense then is the illusion of aloneness — not the reality?"

"How do you know what is the illusion, what the reality?" the Professor questioned the question. "I only postulate a possibility. I ask for an openness of mind, a readiness to question apparent reality."

Then he came to the climax of his challenging questioning. "Look around you now. Look at your classmates. Suspend disbelief and let me put to you a thing apparently wild. Keep a complete openness of mind, and ask yourself: The people around me now — are they, everyone of them, real bodies? What if some, or all, are not? Stare hard, be utterly cynical about what your eyes and ears tell you. Are they real? Close your eyes, and then open them again. What do you see? Do you not see some of them fading away, or getting fuzzy around the edges?

"Yes, yes! Let me unshroud the truth! Look and look again, really hard. Are not some of them looking away in embarrassment?

"…and now some even actually fading away?"

I looked around in amazement. It was true!

That dark Indian boy Ramoo was turning pale, and even as I stared at him, he rose and left the room. So too did other young people, some even could be sobbing as they went.

No bodies? Beings all this while posing as live people of our world — now scurrying off because exposed for what they were — no bodies?

I looked at our old Professor, my eyes now wide with admiration. I realised I had never really known him.

Here was someone of solid stuff! Or was he?

Even as I stared at him, he seemed to change. He became transparent, more and more crystal-like. I could now see right through him.

And then he too was gone! He also was one of them — a no body!

During those few seconds concentrating on the Professor, I had not paid attention to the rest around me. Now as I looked around myself, I was stunned. I was alone, absolutely no body within sight at all!

Where was everybody? Where had they disappeared to, suddenly and utterly? Who were they? Why was it they could be here with me, people I have known for some time, and then abruptly all gone?

Were they ghosts? Souls of people dead and gone, allowed to come back to be with me for a while?

They could well be! That could be it — all of them, including the good old Professor, were dead people, now spirits and body-less.

Yes! For now my memory stirred and I recalled that sudden terrorist attack on our institution — one fell swoop with explosives that took away all my friends and blasted their bodies into the nothingness of no bodies!

Could that be it? I escaped? I alone was survivor?

My memory came back with more. It called up more images. Myself in an ICU unit. Indeed just a moment ago, all manner of drips attached to me. Doctors and nurses rushing around trying to zap my body up…

Then everything starts to dim away. And all is quiet.

I must have made it. That's why I am still somebody, still have my body.

Automatically I looked down on my body to confirm that as fact. The growing darkness about me and a strange sensation of smoke and mist made it hard for me to see.

I had to see myself — in the flesh.

I noticed the reflective ceiling glass over the hospital table on which I lay. It was like a mirror. That should do it: Reflect me, at least some part of me. That should affirm I had body, was some body.

I stared at it, twisted my head about to search for reflections.

What I feared most was there — or rather, not there.

No body.

WITH no body to hold me down, I could now stand up. And walk about and look around.

And then, one by one, they came to me. I could see them all — Professor and my friends just gone from me. And family and others long gone from me. All no bodies like me.

But now no body makes no difference. We have awareness, we are still we, we have that forever something, that essence of we:

Soul! Never mind no bodies…

THE DEVASTATING POWER OF ASIF

AH SOO slapped his thigh — a little bit too hard. So he had to yelp out before he could spew out the enlightenment that had descended upon his normally dense self:

"Aiyoh! I've been such a stupid loser all these years! This time I'll make sure. I'm going to be a winner. For the last five years the Promotion Board has been calling me up. And every year I fail to make the grade. Next month I go before them again. This time I must learn from someone who has succeeded. I must find out how that Ramasamy in our Ulu Pandan branch did it. He got promoted last year. What's his secret? I'll get that promotion — even if I have to stand on my head to do it!"

Ramasamy winked at Ah Soo and said he got expert help — from a professional friend. Ah Soo decided to get professional help too.

Ramasamy took him to meet Samson, his friend. Samson happened to be unemployed "pending a job offer to commensurate with my abilities". He also happened to have just set up business as a personal career advisor.

Samson had expressed shock that Ah Soo had not been promoted after such a long time in the same old job. "You obviously need specialist advice to advance your career," the expert said and quoted his reasonable fee. *One hundred dollars only, success guaranteed, which means, if needed, continued advice free for next 10 years till client gets promoted.*

That sounded to Ah Soo a bargain. He accepted. He swore he would do whatever Samson told him — even if he had to go to a Hindu temple to carry the kavadi and walk over fire. He was that desperate.

"My friend, I know your kind," Samson said. "The trouble with you, Ah Soo, is you're too straightforward, too humble, too honest. You must *angkat* (sweet talk) the people you wish to impress. You must be *berani* (bold) enough, not *takut* (afraid) to claim credit for success. You must be ready to *bohong* (lie) a little, backbite a bit. Hey, wake up! It's a dog eat dog world out there. If you don't eat others, others will eat you!"

Ah Soo nodded and kept on nodding. Samson waited. Still

Ah Soo said nothing.

"Yes, I'm ready to accept you as a disciple…" Samson said, opening his palms.

Then he paused. And waited. Ah Soo did not catch on. The born loser remained lost. Ramasamy had to cue him in. He whispered to Ah Soo, who at last caught on and said "Oh yes, I have it right here!" and handed over the fee. And then Samson went on:

"Here's the secret: How to zoom up, how to leave the pack behind, how to score success after success, even in new areas, in things you know *kosong* (nothing) about," Samson went on.

And on and on.

At last he came down to brass tacks, which were all there in a book. He handed Ah Soo the book. "This is going to be the most important book in your life — it will change you beyond recognition!"

The book was, of course, written by Samson himself. And naturally it came with a shining gold cover. And a dramatic title in red:

"The Power of Asif — by Professor Asif Samson."

"First of all, rid yourself of all doubts. Banish all negative thoughts. Promise yourself you'll approach the teachings in this book with absolute faith and trust. Then read the words slowly and with due reverence. Tell yourself you'll give the suggestions in it a chance to work. You'll do everything asked of you. No questions about it. Then, and only then, will it take you where you deserve to go," Samson promised as he escorted Ah Soo to the door with his hundred-dollar book.

AH SOO applied for a week's leave to apply himself to the in-depth study of Samsonism as preached in *The Power of Asif*.

And the book changed all his ideas. It blew his mind. It stood him on his head. He realised that all his life he had been approaching things the wrong way. *The Power of Asif* was right there for the grasping, right there in his mind. All he needed to do was to reach out and grab it. All that it took was the right mental approach — that was it: The secret of success, what the great Samson had learnt early in life.

And so Ah Soo became a convert to the Way of the Great Asif.

It was so simple. One by one, he switched off his negative feelings, thrust aside inhibitions and limitations, real or imagined.

Never again say no, never again moan that you can't do it — never confess don't know how!

And Ah Soo turned on to full power all positive feelings about himself. He started to say yes, he could do it to everything, whether he could or not. On and on went the great self-hypnosis all the way up to his greatest Asif potential.

Yes, he was the centre of everything. The universe revolved around him. No need to care about others. He was Number One. Others were there to be used by him, to be pushed behind. Let the devil take the hindmost!

Ah Soo was now ready to take on the world — starting with that silly Promotion Board. He knew what to say, what to do, how to impress people. It was as if he had become a new man, as if he was now endowed with true power, superiority greater than his superiors. He was greater even than those Board fellows about to question him...

AH SOO did not know it, but his superiors had already decided on his case. They had discussed his record. They knew the man — old Ah Soo, straightforward, humble and honest, never ever trying to *angkat* (sweet talk) his bosses, not forward at all, never claiming credit even when deserved, never telling lies or backbiting others...

They felt it was time they rewarded that good and faithful servant, even though the good points he had shown through his past career were not aggressively plus points.

AND then into the interview room walked the new Ah Soo.

One so full of himself, boastful, opinionated (even about things he clearly knew nothing about), pushy, ready to claim credit, all set to lie and backbite… one thoroughly obnoxious man.

What had happened to old Ah Soo?

The Board members were left wondering.

It was as if he had been utterly transformed.

As if some strange power had taken over the old Ah Soo's soul, here was a weird person who acted as if the universe revolved around him. One who talked as if they owed it to him to promote him. One clearly residing in a fantasy world. As if he had power over everything.

In short, one who did not merit promotion.

In fact, one who deserved to go — into early retirement.

And the conclusion of every Board member there was affirmed by the man's grand finale: Ah Soo's detestable departure line, uttered with such self-delusion of his devastating power as he strutted out with arrogance, toothy grin, cocky wave of hand, and abominable aplomb:

"Gentlemen, it isn't as if you don't know how to decide. I'm sure you'll soon be sending me the good news I richly deserve…"

As if!

THE REVENGE OF THE SISTERS

ANNETTE was found dead in a deep ditch by a dark side road, ugly red blood all over her lovely white face. Hit by a driver who drove off, never found.

And naturally, soon there were sightings of a lady ghost haunting that long hilly stretch.

Annette's twin sister, Sharon, grieved for her. Twins have a close affinity. Whatever happens to one is deeply sensed by the other, more than by other siblings. For a while Sharon went around talking about her inevitable fate. She would die the same way, perhaps in the very same place. She would gladly do that if she could somehow fool that murderous driver into thinking she was Annette's ghost come to lead him to crash into that ditch. That would be a fitting revenge for the sisters.

Friends shook her out of that. They gave her strong support. After she mourned her loss for months, she seemed to have picked up the pieces, and got on with her life, that of a busy college lecturer.

It was now the eve of the second anniversary of Annette's tragic death.

Simon and Kok, her fellow lecturers, both by nature not exactly the modest kind, were arguing about something when she joined them. Simon explained, "Our friend has challenged me to keep vigil tonight at the haunted road — you know, where Annette was hit by the car? His bet is I'll be scared to drive up that road alone, park my car at the top, and then walk down from that dead-end stretch back to the main road…"

"Simon does the walk tonight; and tomorrow it's my turn," Kok cut in. "I can tell you I'll have no problem, not with guts like mine. Our friend here is handicapped: He's a Christian and believes in souls. I don't believe in anything, especially not spirits. The one who chickens out or runs off or starts seeing a ghost — that guy pays up a hundred bucks."

Kok was still bragging after Simon left. "Will you come with me to enjoy the fun? Or meet us there? Around 11 tonight? Walk up from the main road junction till you see us — more likely, just me. I expect Simon will chicken out or run off screaming! Do come, Sharon… I'll wait for you."

"Maybe, Boaster Kok. Can't confirm now."

That was Kok's nickname, given by students and endorsed by faculty.

Sharon planned to go there anyway. It was Annette's anniversary. Sharon felt drawn by her sister's spirit to go to the hill — and that deep ditch.

Was there any truth to that Annette ghost story? Poor Annette! She still missed her. Yes, her spirit must be lonely. None of her close family had gone to join her after her sudden passing — except for those boring oldies, bad-tempered Uncle Roddy and long-winded Grandaunt Wendy. God, how she wished she and Annette could be together as before!

IT WAS a clear moonlit night and there was not a soul in sight as Kok and Simon approached that thinly populated hill. They drove there in their own cars as far as the main road junction. At that junction where the hill road turned off, Kok stepped out to wait for Simon while the latter drove to the top for his descent on foot.

Kok got impatient. Sharon looked like she was not coming after all. The hill road was long and winding. So he started off alone on his uphill climb on foot.

Along the long way up, he thought he heard weird sounds of cars screeching and banging and voices crying out, but he told himself all that was in his imagination.

Spirits? No, he did not believe in them — there was no such things!

After some more time he spotted Simon. Walking down towards him — briskly, but in no panic. No ghost-propelled hurry.

The man had not come upon any ghost, whether figment of imagination or conjured up by religious belief! Kok felt let down.

In fact as Simon drew close, Kok could hear him whistling away.

Aha! A church hymn — a prayer disguised as a tune! The man was actually scared but was putting on a bold front.

"No ghost!" Simon yelled out as he drew near.

"Don't say that too soon. Annette may be near by, waiting for the right moment to come for you!" Kok yelled back, hoping against hope that some animal or shadow would appear to scare the wits out of the fellow.

Simon drew near. He was laughing away. "Sorry, my friend. No spirit. No Annette. Nothing close to ghost…" And then his voice trailed off. His eyes were now fixed on something behind Kok.

Kok turned around. He saw it too.

In the pale and shadowy moonlight, barely five metres away — a ghost-like apparition! Still and unmoving. Staring at them.

Annette? So much like Sharon — and yet so different! Pale, eyes turned up till pupil-less, hair dishevelled. Face and blouse smudged with red slime!

Simon whimpered in fear. He spun a right-about turn and raced back uphill. And no doubt he did not stop till he reached his car and locked himself in it.

Kok stood his ground. His cool and logical mind worked out what all that was about.

That was Sharon. It must be Sharon.

Simon did not know Sharon was coming. Kok did. The girl had exceeded his expectations: Here she was, playing her part so well that she had scared the guts out of Simon!

"Okay, Sharon!" Kok called out to her. "That was a great show. You did way better than I expected. Simon's gone. You can go and change now. Clean off that tomato ketchup or whatever."

The apparition simply stood there.

"Y-you… you're not Annette, are you?" Kok found his voice suddenly becoming a stupid croak, asking a stupid question.

Slowly the figure shook her head.

"Thank God!" Kok said despite himself.

Still that pale face and wispy figure looked eerie — not of this world.

"You're Sharon?" Kok's voice was now a hoarse whisper — and unsure. He needed positive confirmation.

The apparition nodded. Kok heaved a sigh of relief.

"You're not a ghost?" Kok croaked out that silly question despite himself.

This time the apparition merely smiled — a ghost of a smile.

Yes, it's Sharon putting on a great ghost act!

Kok pulled himself together and walked a hesitant walk towards her. A cloud now cast a shade over the moon. And Sharon disappeared from view. At least, Kok could not find her.

Had she gone into the bushes to change?

Kok waited. After a while he called out to her.

No reply.

Perhaps the girl had gone back downhill and driven home?

Kok waited for a bit more. Then he gave up. He hurried down the hill and went home.

The next day he arrived at the campus ready to regale everyone with what happened to that coward Simon — and the award-winner role Sharon played in it.

"Sharon did Annette at the hill last night…" he began his story.

They nodded but cut him short. They too were full of Sharon — and Annette. They spoke excitedly:

"So, you heard too? The terrible news just reported on radio! About that terrible smash-up last night. Sharon was killed near her car just a little way up that hill. She must have been standing next to her car when the other car drove up and smashed right into her and her car. Both cars disappeared out of sight into the deep ditch, where her sister Annette was killed! This time the driver died too, somehow very horribly disfigured and twisted up inside his own car. They found both bodies early this morning. They said Sharon still looked beautiful with a strange smile though she had blood all over her face and her white blouse, just like Annette. The man looked terrified and a total disaster. Some people say it was the same driver, the one who killed Annette! Sharon's close friends here claim Sharon used herself as bait — to get that driver. It was the revenge of the sisters…"

THEY say Boaster Kok is a changed man. He never boasted again.

And neither did he do his promised walk up the hill that night — nor ever after.

And he has become a believer in souls…

Yen For Lie

BETWEEN fantasy and reality there is but a thin line.

Some time or other, we all experience that crossover, transition from real world to unreal world — most only briefly hovering over the border, some going further than that, a few of us making full-body entry and doing even frequent crossovers.

Yen was one of those given to crossovers.

She went through soul-swirling episodes in her adolescent years. She would become different people, migrate to different worlds, switch to and fro from one experience to a totally different one, with little awareness of crossover.

Her parents had to take her to the doctors about her fantasies, especially when she began to enter nightmarish dreamworlds that were real to her.

With help from professionals and support groups, she achieved fair balance. She became better, but there remained danger zones.

She could not take alcohol. Intoxication could blur or erase that thin line not just immediately but sometimes over a long stretch.

And occasionally, with letting go of consciousness in her sleep, that thin line could go blotto — and she with it. She would enter into dream happenings with such vividness that she could not tell whether she was asleep or awake.

Still, that was only at rare times, and when alone in the privacy of her bedroom, so it was not too bad. So she thought…

On balance she had substantially gained control. She was now reasonably poised, able to walk that borderline, to tell reality from fantasy.

So she thought.

YEN fell in love. Madly. With an embracing yen for her Lie that possessed her.

Even for the normal and perfectly poised, love can trigger chaos of heart. For Yen it brought back her potential bomb. So long as her romance with Lie went smoothly, everything went steadily.

Yen and Lie went steady, becoming constant companions. Which was wonderful so long as Lie was true to her…

But Lie was too handsome, and also too weak, for his own (and her) good. He could not say no. And there were so many girls around, attracted to him, all saying yes. Jealousy reared up its proverbial ugly head.

The first explosion happened when Yen caught sight of Lie with a young girl, a stranger to her, on a sidewalk. He was saying goodbye to her. The girl reached out and took hold of his hand. She held on to it longer than necessary for a goodbye handshake. A woman can gauge such things with precision, what more Yen with her possessive yen.

She was crossing her line!

Yen began to cross hers.

Suddenly in her mind she saw, or thought she saw, more than handshake following on. She saw the flirt throwing her arms around her man, and hugging and kissing him with passion. There, in daylight, right before the world and her, on a public road.

Yen screeched out. Without any regard to the cars whizzing by on the busy road, she rushed across to them, triggering a sudden traffic snarl with fearful screeching of brakes. The girl disentangled herself at once, within a split second well and truly unsnarled, looking startled but innocent, as though nothing more had happened than a handshake.

Yen continued to snarl.

The girl took off in fright.

"What's the matter with you?" Lie asked, his face registering true shock.

"What's the matter with me? You can ask that? After she so shamelessly hugged you like that?"

"She what? She did what?"

Yen stared at Lie. She could see he was taken aback.

Genuine?

She looked at the surrounding onlookers. *They looked taken aback. That was genuine!*

That clinch did not happen?

That thin line? It was back with her — and she had just crossed it again?

There followed other occasions — more instances of close encounters between Lie and other girls.

Real?

Or illusion?

She did not know. She could not know. She could only guess. She guessed her thing could be happening to her all over again. She had to get a hold on herself.

She must stay in control, keep within the real world!

Yes, Lie was getting riled. She must not let that fantasy jinx of hers seduce her on!

But more such times happened.

At first with effort she could snap out of it — even tell the difference. Then it became harder…

Each time, real or unreal? Which side of the line was she on?

With greater determination she was able to suppress crossover, stop reacting vehemently to those clinches, whether real or not.

But she could tell. Lie was getting weary of her jealousy. He was becoming cool to her, even though she stopped losing her cool… She just could not hide that instinctive wariness whenever any pretty female came near her Lie.

Yes, her wariness was pushing him away; or his weariness was pulling him away. And so he was now really casting his eyes elsewhere? He was really cooling off?

Imagination?

And then it happened for real.

Lie said, "Look, Yen, it's not working out. Let's call it quits…"

Good God! Lie actually came out with that?

Her eyes turned red. She was genuinely sorry. "No, Lie! It will work. I'll make it work, I promise. Let's give it a bit more time," she pleaded and wailed so loudly and piteously, Lie, never strong, took his weak way out. He settled for that — giving it more time. For now. And so for a while Yen saw no more clinches. No more crossovers for her.

But was Lie true?

One night Lie said he had to attend some business meeting. That night an anonymous caller phoned to tip her off. Her beloved Lie had lied. Right now he was smooching with the jealous caller's two-timing girlfriend in a well-known lovers' lane stretch along East Coast Parkway.

No way that call was fantasy! She could check that out on her message recorder if she wanted…

She did. The call was real.

Hurry there right away, catch them in clinch!

Yen sped to the spot told to her.

She caught Lie, as told, in the arms of Anita.

No fantasy this time: It was real.

Yen jumped at them, tore them apart, lashed out at Anita, her open hand landing on the girl's face with such force she fell to the ground.

Lie stood there, his eyes flashing surprise, then anger, and then — hate!

For a moment Yen wilted. That face of hatred was real. She wished it was fantasy.

Couldn't it all not be only that — fantasy? No real clinch? No real slap? No real face of hatred?

She waited to hear Lie scolding her for imagining things as he had done before. But this time Lie did not scold her. He did not say one word. He gathered the wounded Anita in his arms and left with her. Yen, abandoned, found herself alone in lovers' lane.

Hey! Surely all that was fantasy?

No!

The truth hit her.

SHE found herself back home. Alone. Sobbing — into her pillow. And Lie's pillow, full of the smell of Lie — all she had left of Lie.

That clinch was real. That slap too. And that face of hatred! No doubt about that…

She suddenly needed to drink.

Something to take her across the border into a friendlier world?

Why not? What had she left in this unkind world?

The drink did not help. She felt worse. She had more drinks. She went into a daze of drinking, on into days of drinking. She crossed over with no idea of passage of space nor passage of time. In and out, and back in again.

And in that unreal world, Lie would fight her. Lie would go. Lie would come back again, all sweetness and love…

And over and over, endless episodes of quarrels with Lie and fights with other girls, some ravishing, some ugly as sin, with Lie alternating between extremes, from wrath of fury to passion of desire…

And then her mind advanced to things more deadly. Like slipping poison into the women's drinks, stabbing them, shooting them, chopping them up… and Lie would sometimes be there, real or not. Sometimes angry, sometimes sad, sometimes romantic as in old times before those floosies came along, sometimes just laughing away and enjoying himself as she slashed and shot and slaughtered his endless stream of girlfriends.

Real?

Imagined?

At times happenings would come to her clear as day. *No fantasy at all — absolutely!*

Like when from her window she saw Lie going into the house of her next-door neighbour Rose, a bunch of flowers in his hand. As God's truth, that was God's truth. She was sober then. She could even see they were roses. *Real red roses — for Rose!*

That young thing always had a crush on him. She had kept that in check so long as Yen and Lie were an item, but now that the world knew Lie was single again, that Rose must have started making advances to seduce him. Otherwise why would he be making his way into her house? And with red roses!

Definitely, definitely so — no fantasy!

Yen saw herself going into her kitchen. She saw herself opening the kitchen drawer, taking out her sharp chopper. Now entering Rose's house by the back door that she knew was never latched. Going up to the bedroom. Catching the pair red-handed, shameless as sin, in each other's embrace. Rushing at them with her chopper. Chopping Rose from behind, where she lay on top of him. Chopping the stunned Lie. Over and over, even after both stood up. Till both lay on the floor, twitching in pools of blood, that liquid still shame-lessly copulating even while coagulating.

And still, she saw herself in her frenzy of chopping, land-ing endless blows on those dead meat bodies, again and again, down to their hard hearts of stone, that deserved to be hacked to pieces — as they had done to her own.

Then she got up unsteadily, her own body bloodied down to her feet and slippers, leaving a trail of red smudges all the way back to her home. Where, still in dream-like state, she sang happily as she washed and cleaned herself.

And then she went to bed.

She woke up in the morning, quite excited yet quite easy at heart.

That was some fantastic fantasy!

That flirt Rose deserved to be chopped up.

And so did that liar Lie, that betrayer of hearts!

That was a fantasy to end all fantasies!

A commotion outside drew her to her window. There were police cars and an ambulance down there, right next door.

She saw two bodies, covered with blood-stained cloth, being carried out.

That was no fantasy.

SHE heard the knock at her door. And voices demanding loudly, "Open up at once. We're the police!"

That too was no fantasy…

How My Master Captured The Monster

ON THE wings of dawn I flew from home swifter than bird or wind. Towards the Pearl of the Orient, gateway to the mystic East: Hong Kong.

There I sought my Master — he with the magic of the ages, a binder of myriad spells. I, a humble chronicler of astounding achievements, came in search of yet another story of derring-do from one ever daring to do.

"Master," I asked after due kowtowing and grovelling, "What be this latest mind-blowing tidings I dost hear of thee — thy capturing of that Western monster world-renowned, but of shape and appearance hitherto uncaptured since time immemorial?"

In reply, thus spake the sapient one from the Orient (after he firmly beseeched me to cut the cackle on those thee's and thou's, "unseemly as geeky gobbledygook in today's world of cyber-speak"):

FROM the east, in that twilight zone of dusk (said the Master), my eyes beheld the monster. She rose majestically from out of the sea. Emerald green and scarily scaly. Without a doubt, a descendant of Oriental dragons, awesome and inscrutable as a mandarin.

I should know. As you know, I am a seer and champion well-accredited and descended from a long line of dragon-slayers (each generation's licence renewed by royal appointment) right from the reign of that first Emperor of the Chin Dynasty, Chin Shih Huang Di.

At the time of the sighting, there was not another soul around. (That was perfectly understandable, it being that exalted evening of the revered Football Cup Final shown live on British telly.) So I had a problem. A lack of collaborating witness. As I had no faith in newfangled devices, I had brought along no camera in my journey to the West in search of the beast.

How then was this humble Chinese, there as a mere back-packer tourist, to substantiate that he had indeed sighted that legendary monster that had eluded the benighted natives of this land since the beginning of time?

State-of-the-art oriental mysticism came to my rescue.

One of my revered ancestors, the illustrious Sun Tze (he of *The Art of War* renown) had faced this very problem — and found the answer. He had been assigned by the Yellow Emperor to keep vigil for a dragon and report the sighting thereof, complete with proof. Failing which his head, venerable though it was, would be chopped off. And that was in the BC era (before cameras).

My ancestor sighted his monster. And he did not lose his head. Neither then, nor later. He not only accomplished his assignment, he was also able to bequeath to his descendants a secret scroll that described the technique — how he made his irrefutable recording of the event, unassisted by gadgetry.

That technique I now proceeded to implement to the letter.

I began with the 26 postures of the classic Tai Chi Chuan exercise to put my mind and body in the required state of utter tranquillity. Then I tensed and pressurised the matter of my brain till its temperature fell below zero and one part of my mind became a deep-freeze with sufficient capacity to store, microsecond by microsecond, "as is", the ever-changing image of that resplendent dragon as she wriggled and wiggled through her sexy gyrations.

(Those mind-boggling gyrations incidentally were precisely what convinced me as to her gender.)

Thus captured, the entire happening was now preserved in my head (with no expiry date, barring decapitation) ready for instant thought transference to any other mind willing and able to link up mind-Internet-wise with mine through a process of cerebral IT practised in the Orient for ages — cold, micro-hard technology long before the likes of Bill Gates.

The actual transmission procedure is too tedious to describe here but it includes simultaneous self-hypnosis while both parties sit still and cross-legged on a Tientsin carpet (though Wilton might do nicely too). Verily, it is that easy any simpleton with an open mind and an abundance of gigabytes in it should have no problem accepting that incontrovertible proof transferred from my head to his.

That includes any panel of scientists with sufficiently high IQ, provided that despite the complex convolutions of their cerebrum architecture, they have remained sufficiently simple of soul to encompass belief in the apparently incredible.

And, of course, they must also possess that said prolificity of unutilised bytes to adequately download and ingest a story of such monstrous dimensions.

And that, believe it or not, was how my Master captured the Loch Ness Monster.

Unforgettable
Vignettes

A COMING HOME FOR OLD DAD

CHRIS, an only child, now 30-plus, still single, left home a long time ago after a fierce quarrel with Dad over a girl he loved.

Dad was diehard old-fashioned. Dad would never change, never concede to him.

Chris never changed from that hard judgment, never conceded that, given time, Dad might concede.

Both fierce quarrel and beloved girlfriend became history. But Chris did not contact home. And when he felt he should phone home, he kept on putting it off to a tomorrow that never came — for years.

Now, more than ever, Chris had reason not to call…

No longer headstrong after many ups and downs, and matured by agonising experiences, Chris was a different person. For better or for worse. A person who began to feel the old urge — to go home; all the more now, as Ma had died and the old man was all alone.

Chris knew this could be the last chance for reunion with family — old Dad, the only family Chris had left.

But would there be acceptance? Would old Dad be forgiving after such a prolonged staying away?

So, what eventually happened? Chris told me, an understanding friend all through his crises of change:

I finally wrote to Dad. I said I was sorry. Yes, that stormy quarrel over Suzie was stupid. My rude comments about his ideas on suitable girlfriends for a young man — they were stupid. (I had called him "an old stick-in-the-mud"!) As it turned out, he was right — all the way. Suzie was "a frivolous girl and likely to prove a slut", just as he had summed her up.

And all my other girlfriends after Suzie too — each and

every one was a letdown somehow or other, unlike my men friends who were true friends...

I asked if I could come home. I gave him my phone number.

He replied by mail. He said many things. He explained that he had lost his voice to throat cancer, so we could only talk by letter. And with a flourish that was typical of him, he wrote, "Old Dad forgives you. After all, aren't you always my son?"

"Yes, do come home, Christopher. I love you, dear boy!" he concluded his letter, his words quavering with inky trembles of an old man's emotion.

Those last words in particular moved me to tears. He never called me by any name other than that full name, "Christopher". Nobody calls me by that name now. My heart went warm — and then it also went cold.

Would old Dad really accept me back as I was, the changed person I had become, warts and all? But perhaps he had mellowed and broadened his views with the years? I had to feel that out first.

How?

I wrote to ask him what if I had with me someone I could not leave behind? This friend was not one some people would welcome into their home — someone who needed understanding and help. Could I bring my friend home?

Old Dad replied, "Yes, bring him home. And if it's a girl, yes, you may bring her home too. This time I will accept your choice of girlfriend."

The old man did not ask for details. Had he really changed that much?

I hoped — but still I had my anxieties. Could he be that far changed? I had to probe further...

I wrote again, asking would it still be all right to bring my friend home if he or she had a sexual problem? For example, what if it was AIDS?

There was no immediate reply. Then old Dad's letter came.

His reply was brief, but straight to the point: "He can come. Even if your friend is a girl and she has such a terrible problem, and she is your girlfriend, she can come." The first three words were firm. Was it my imagination or were the last three words a shade more faint?

I was so proud of my old dad. I felt more confident. Now at last, I could reveal the whole truth to him?

Could I?

Doubt lingered and I ding-donged between hope and despair. I had to clear that cloud, the next step in the step-by-step way I was approaching my old dad. So I came right out with it:

"What if my friend is someone who has changed his sex? A boy who has undergone an operation, and is now a girl?"

For one whole week there was silence. Then old Dad replied. In his firm handwriting, suddenly angular as before, a familiar script with his old rigidity, he wrote an adamant "No, not on your life! How can you ask me to accept someone like that under my roof?"

And he went on about the sinfulness of going against nature. He warned me about having friends like that. He even went back to talking about sluts…

I wept.

And I decided not to go home.

No matter how much I yearned to go home, how much I now truly loved my old dad…

Better to suffer alone in my loneliness. Better not to impose an unbearable suffering on him: My old dad is just not able to change that much.

SO MY friend Chris made a decision: The door was closed to that yearned-for coming home to the old man!

History was ready to repeat itself.

Chris wept: *The deja vu of it all. That feeling after that long-ago fierce storm with Dad now resurged in almost identical words:*

Dad was diehard old-fashioned. Dad would never change, he would never concede. And once more Chris would not have changed from that hard judgment, not conceded that, given time, Dad might concede…

CHRIS needed a friend to go and plead on his behalf, someone to talk candidly with old Dad.

About that intimate subject of sex change…

A friend did.

And I found Chris was wrong.

Old Dad had changed. Old Dad conceded.

And Chris came home.

It was a coming home also for *her* old Dad.

A LETHAL BATTERING

BOON was a brute, a surly has-been whose boxing days were long over — except in his fantasy, or especially when drunk, with his wife conveniently within punching range. No one could understand it. How could he treat that long-suffering but still caring woman so badly? And how could Mabel tolerate him and continue to live with him through all that abuse from him, physical and mental?

Some men are like that.

Some women are like that, too.

"Your husband did this to you?" the doctor at the hospital wanted to know, after examining her swollen ears.

"What? What?" Mabel went. Both ears were so badly hurt this time around, she could not hear a word.

The doctor had to use his jotting pad to ask her. She shook her head.

The doctor shook his too.

A battering like that could be lethal…

237

"Your hearing may return. Or it may not. Come back to see me in a week," he wrote.

Reaching home, Mabel found Boon already into a fresh round of boozing.

"Boon, so soon? Drinking again? You forgot what the doctor told you? With your high blood pressure and heart problem, you could drop dead!" Mabel spoke out louder than usual in her deafness and anxiety.

"You dare shout at me? You shut up!" Boon lashed out with his anger. And he also lashed out with his fist, but missed.

"Still trying to punch me? You know the last hammering you gave me has made me deaf? I can't hear a thing now!" Mabel informed him. But that too fell on deaf ears. He just went on with his drinking.

Mabel gave up talking with him. *What to do? Let him carry on — only watch that he doesn't have a stroke or something!*

She felt exhausted. She lay down on their bed to rest. But she kept her face turned towards Boon who sat at the all-purpose table in their one-room flat. She tried hard to keep her eyes open, in case Boon should need her help.

For better or for worse — Mabel still felt concern for her man. He had not always been bad like this. There had been better times. Boon had not always been bane…

She suddenly found herself uncontrollably sleepy. Her last thought as she dropped off was: *It's okay. I'm a light sleeper. The slightest sound will wake me up…*

IN THE midst of his drinking, Boon suddenly fell off his chair.

He yelped out a cry for help. His bottle and glass dropped to the hard floor with a crash. And as he fell he grabbed the linen covering the table on which they also had their plates and cups and other utensils. Everything came down with a resounding crash — a racket deafening enough to wake up the dead.

But not the deaf.

Boon yelled out with all his might. Mabel snored on.

Boon made to move towards his wife to fist her, shake her, wake her up.

He found he could not move.

Immobile in his hell, he looked helplessly at his sound asleep wife.

"Mabel!" he croaked out one last croak with all his desperate might.

So Boon croaked.

All through that commotion, Mabel, unable to hear a thing through the silence of her battered ears, slept on in heaven-blessed bliss, dreaming the boon of better times…

I SAW

AT FIRST I did not see.

I could not see. I was too full of my own misery.

I could not understand why. Yes, why had all the worst things in the world to happen to me? There were so many other people on earth all blessed with happiness and the good things of life. Why had I to suffer so much? Why had I to endure the worst things that can happen to people?

I WAS a foreign maid come to Singapore to work. And of all foreign maids, I had to come from the worst-off country of all.

Filipino maids were of course the queens among maids — they had it best of all. And of all the other nationalities, my own must be the least favoured by fortune.

We were fleeced by our village go-betweens before we got anywhere near to overseas jobs. Then we were squeezed by those greedy agencies back home. And, finally, when we managed to cross all hurdles and were packed up ready to fly off to our new jobs, our national airline employees got into the act, telling us all seats were gone despite our advance bookings. Until we tipped them — and then magically seats were found!

My situation was worse than most maids from my country. I left parents, husband, and a sickly infant daughter back home to come here to work. Someone just had to make the sacrifice, things were really bad back home.

Fortunately, my employers were kind to me.

I was hired to look after their baby. She was a lovable child. That was good.

And bad, too.

It made me remember all the time another child, my own, left back home.

Was she getting better? Was she learning to crawl? Beginning to speak words like this baby? And did she also cry out for her Ma?

This baby was growing up fast, stronger each day… My own baby was not growing at all, in fact getting weaker by the day. The news from home was always bad — and then it became worse…

My employers took their baby to church to pray for her. I went too — and I prayed in their church with them. And later my employer took me with her little baby to my Buddhist temple here to pray for my own baby.

But even as I burnt my joss sticks, I could not help crying bitterly in my heart: *Heaven, why are you so unfair, this little one so well, my own little one so ill!*

When I got home, I got the news, not unexpected, but still devastating. My baby had died.

I did not go home. What was there to go home to? I was left with nothing.

Heaven does not care. Some have all the good things, some all the bad…

I cried a mother's tears for my child. I could do that only at night. When my work was done…

And I spent many nights just gazing at the angelic face of my employers' baby breathing out her gentle baby snore. A child in a sleep from which she would wake up. And her face became misty in my eyes because of my own tears.

She is so lovable…

Life is so unfair!

But perhaps it was right my child should die.

Perhaps I should be happy for her. She is at peace now. For her to live in my kind of world would have been only to suffer more.

Our religion teaches us life is only a passing through. For the sickly and the poor, it is more merciful to pass through quickly — on to a hopefully happier next life:

Samsara…

Still, how can the pain leave a mother's heart just like that? It hurts, and continues to hurt — often suddenly and unexpectedly, not just in the secret quiet of my nights.

AT THAT crowded first birthday party given by my employers' family, I was all right till they started singing:

"Happy birthday to you!"

I felt my heart suddenly bursting.

I had to run to the back of the kitchen to hide that loneliness of a grief I could not share with anyone — a grief that would be seen as a bad luck curse if I showed my weeping face on the happy occasion.

They could not find me.

I heard a guest, who must have seen me slipping away, telling another guest, "So lazy, running off to the back when there's work to be done — she should be helping to serve cake to everyone!"

"Maybe suddenly homesick, you know? She's got a right to feel homesick, right?" the other person was more sympathetic.

"What right has she to feel anything? She's a maid, right? And there's work to be done, right? Aiyoh! Can't she be home-sick later, on her own time! We pay them good money to come and enjoy, or what?"

Yes, my baby is happier wherever she is — surely no other world can be so heartless as this one in which we have to suf-fer as we work.

BUT Heaven began to show me many things. Newspaper reports and friends' stories enlightened me, showed me the hidden truth — the worse things that can happen. The anxi-ety and anguish often masked beneath an exterior of seeming tranquillity. The hidden villainies of some employers towards their maids. The secret misdeeds of some maids. Tensions. Conflicts. Unreasonable demands. Seductions and infidelities. Abuses of the helpless and the handicapped. Inhuman vio-lence. Family disintegrations. Suicides. Murder.

Wealth and good luck do not always bring peace and happiness.
Desire, good or bad, often only brings on more desire.
It is true: Negation of desire — that is the beginning of peace.

AND so I confronted the conflict looming within me.

I felt the future crisis building up inside me. That premo-nition began to weigh me down, heavier with each passing day.

At first I could not see what it was, for always there seemed to be joy…

But it was a joy that would transform into deep sorrow, a cloud of darkness always coming to shade off my sun of joy.

I knew it was an illicit mother's love, that gathering storm within me: An evil that could burst before long to create pan-demonium. A spirit that had to be exorcised before it took full shape and possessed me.

Yes, I found myself growing more and more attached to

that bright and healthy baby passed on into my arms — arms that had left my own dark and sickly baby back home in my poor country.

And so once again, I hardened my heart.

And once again, I had to leave my baby behind…

I decided to quit, try to find myself another job, get away from a baby I was growing to love like she was my own, a thing of beauty and joy. Joy not mine to have…

I did not see before. But now no longer blind, I saw.

It was time to go from this household, perhaps even to go home, even if to nothing…

Yes, that was what I had to do.

As sure as my name is Saw.

Happy or not, that was my path. The *karma* that was me.

I, Saw.

Repaying An Evil

TENG, chairman of the selection panel, looked at the list they handed him. As a short list it was not really short — six candidates to be interviewed for one vacancy.

One name hit him, made him explode a candid "huh!" of smiling pleasure — and launched him into flashback mode.

His mind went back to an aloof man, an unfeeling boss — and irritating incidents and frequent frustration. The man exasperated him. In fact, he was one reason why Teng began to seek pastures new, exploring them whether greener or not.

Lim was a hard working and committed soul but, as a boss, he was a nit-picking nut who knew little about motivating a team as a leader. He would give you a job, and then harass you, reminding you or "expediting" you endlessly. And readily find fault — and then nag, nag, nag… and, after any less then shining performance, he would harp on that, harp, harp, harp... ad nauseam. His methods might work with those needing such goading, but for those who did not, it was exasperating.

Furthermore the man was notoriously niggardly in his ratings of his subordinates. These suffered in consequence, for their performance reports would be compared against the glowing tributes others got from their bosses.

Year after year Teng saw others of his vintage, and even those of a greener generation moving up while he remained stagnant. He knew who was responsible.

Finally Teng had it out frankly with Lim, "You're not fair to your team."

Lim's reply was, "I don't care if other bosses choose to overlook faults in their staff appraisals. I can't do that. I sympathise with you but I take pride in giving my honest opinion. I have my principles and my pride, you know?"

Teng too had his principles and his pride. He quit.

He was not the only one to pack up and leave. Others left after him.

Teng found a job in a new field of work and had to prove himself anew in it. They say people fight best with their backs to the wall. Teng did just that. So he went up and up — and became chief of the human resource department in his company, one of the country's largest.

Lim, in the meantime, stopped moving up. He was honest and focused in his work, but his flaw had been found out. His bosses rated him low on teamwork and motivating staff. So he stagnated — until they could fairly ask him to go on early retirement.

And that was how, after many years, their paths crossed again.

Enter Lim, job seeker, for interview by Teng, job dispenser.

LIM walked in with a confident step. His jaw dropped when he saw and recognised Teng. He turned pale, stood at the door, transfixed for a moment, confidence suddenly eroded.

That was Teng there? And sitting in the centre chair?

"You?" unprepared, Lim exclaimed.

"Yes, me," prepared, Teng confirmed.

Teng spoke softly, but he could not (or deliberately did not) suppress the quiet high in his voice. He was enjoying it. He let it sink in. The irony of the situation! That unsympathetic ex-boss of his was now sitting before him, seeking his okay to get a job. Handing him his moment: His chance to repay the evil.

Surely heaven-sent retribution!

Teng sadistically did not to utter a single word more through that interview. He left it to his colleagues to question Lim.

Lim was left on tenterhooks wondering when Teng would open his mouth and let him have it. The suspense almost killed him.

Still he did start off well, with his prepared spiel, his submission that he was diligent and dedicated — his past civil service testimonials bore sufficient witness to that.

And then he decided to change his tack. He spoke frankly about past wrong approaches, his failure to appreciate his staff… in a subdued voice he confessed that he had not done as well in his last job as he could have done if he had been better at motivating his team.

He looked at Teng. Teng steadfastly refused to make eye contact. And he stayed silent.

He could see how Lim agonised over his non-reaction. He could read what went on in the man's head: *Surely Teng's silence meant only one thing — bad news!*

Lim left feeling dejected — and rejected.

After the final candidate left, the panel debated on their impressions. It narrowed down to Lim and another candidate, as good, only slightly less experienced.

One of Teng's panel colleagues summed up his views: "Our need is for an honest and hard working man. The opening does not need a team leader. A solo operator is okay — teamwork skills and staff relations may not be that crucial. Both candidates are good. But on balance, Lim looks a bit better to me…" But he looked at his chairman and meekly stipulated that he remained ready to be convinced otherwise.

Teng revealed that he had worked with Lim and knew the man well.

The other panelists capitulated, ready to go along with him.

Teng knew the decision was in his hands.

He knew Lim was suitable for their job. Yes, possibly more than the other choice.

Yet here was his golden opportunity. Teng could do it now. The axe was in his hands and he could swing it whichever way he wanted.

Teng made his choice:

Repay the evil — his way.

IT WASN'T just about being objective.

Or being noble.

Repaying an evil with an evil would have let the man off his conscience too lightly…

Sunny Smile

SUNNY was born with that strange look on a newborn baby's face — lips upturned in a permanent smile. The soothsayers said it was a propitious thing. The naysayers said it was a weird thing, not a smile. And they bluntly labelled it a birth defect.

The doctors who examined the baby speculated that the flaw was due to his facial muscles. They came out with some long name for it, hard to pronounce except by professional tongues agile at twisting around convoluted words concocted from defunct languages. (When experts are confronted with something they know nothing about, they sometimes do that, give the thing a ponderous name derived from dead lingo, thus demonstrating that at least they got that first part fixed.) A surgical correction might be possible, the doctors said, but it would be costly and there would be risks.

Sunny's parents could not afford to pay anyway, so they went with the soothsayers, chose to be soothed by those who would call it a blessing.

"God is good. A smiling angel has been born to us, a child of joy sent to bring good luck to everyone."

Their son was born on December 12, so they bought the number 1212 in the 4-digit draw — and after 12 months religiously pursuing their luck, their faith was rewarded. They did not hit anything like the jackpot, but at least they did win $1,200, which was enough to them to prove the point that the child would bring them luck, even if it might take a while.

Sunny grew up a child who involuntarily spread goodwill like largesse, his ever-smiling face bestowing positive effects on the world around him. He turned into a happy spirit who brought to everyone the lighter side of everything, so that even in vexatious situations his appearance would at once show to all how to stay unquashed.

So he had a headstart when he grew up. He got work easily. He did well selling things. His smile immediately sold people on whatever he was selling.

Soon people chose him to lead them in clubs and community associations.

And inevitably people came along who posed to him, "Sunny, what about going into politics?"

He smiled — and that was it: His name was put up by his

friends in the associations.

At public hustings, in handshaking walkabouts around the housing estates, and in interviews with the media, people saw how he kept smiling, no matter what stressful questions he was asked. (His smile came through clearer than his answers.) And so they voted him in.

Actually he had no qualifications to speak of, no experience of real value to help him decide on public issues, no management know-how at all. Which was indeed why earlier the ruling party had, after due assessment, passed him over. On his part he was not on the same wavelength with them anyway — he found their reasoning on the tougher issues of state too complicated for his simple grasp.

The opposition coalition also noticed him. They, too, had approached him. They spoke glorious words about themselves, and they saw that he smiled non-stop. *A sardonic smile?* They spoke angry words about the ruling party, and they saw that he was smiling at their words there too. *A cynical smile?*

When one of them asked him whether he would join them, he did not answer. That was because he could not decide. But they saw the smile on his face, and they read it as *a scornful smile*. So the opposition classified him as hostile, and left him.

His friends put him up as an independent. He won, beating both the ruling and the opposition candidates who split the votes and handed him victory on a platter.

As an independent he could speak his mind, and he occasionally did — with what mind he had. His opinions did not do much for him, but TV viewers liked his face, smiling as he spoke, smiling even when caught by the camera in the background. That counted a lot since many people do not usually listen as much to what is said than how it is said, what with the excess volume of words to contend with nowadays. And anyway people usually hear what they want to hear and a smiling face can say just about anything to them. Or even nothing at all, for that matter.

So Sunny shone in the House, speaking rarely, and when he did without much content to speak of — his smile doing all the talking for him.

Then came a time when the governing party lost its majority through illnesses and defections. Issues now came up that divided the House finely and it suddenly became clear that Sunny's vote had become the deciding voice.

All parties began to court him. He did not commit himself. (Actually he was just bewildered.) So he smiled and said nothing. And he cast his vote this way or that as the spirit moved him, speaking only safely meagre words of rationale, siding now with the angels and now with the devils — and ultimately incurring the wrath of both. But his smiling face in the media ensured that the people still backed him. In fact there was even talk that he could be the next Prime Minister…

Both sides of the House began to realise the fact: *That smiling man was unreliable — indeed he was a menace to democracy!*

Something had to be done.

Something was done.

One night he was bashed up so badly by assailants, unknown and unfound. He landed in hospital. His face was a mess. The surgeons who operated on him, did a great job reconstructing his face. And they threw in a bonus: They corrected that flaw that had for years fixed his lips in a perpetual smile…

The spotlight focused on him. At first there was a flood of public sympathy for him and anger against all the parties. Any or all of them could have hired the unknown attackers. Sunny became a hero of the people as they raged against the parties — and waited in suspense to see what had become of that wonderful smiling face.

The bandages were finally removed. And the media showed the new face of Sunny.

The smile was gone. For good — or bad.

In its place was a blank look. And when the man smiled, it came out a grimace that was nowhere near the old Sunny smile. Those lips looked mournful, weird, even hideous. A definite put-off. They conveyed a hint: The kiss of death.

The spin doctors of the parties went to town to turn the tide against Sunny. They gave that face the widest possible exposure. They oozed false sympathy, digging up the man's old speeches, such as there were, and quoted them without commentary — letting them speak their nothingness for themselves.

And they brought in their own smilers to take over — people with more sunny smiles.

Without his smile, the magic of Sunny was gone. Before long the people forgot him.

Sunny retired from politics. There was no future for him there, nor indeed in any other field where smiling and cheerfulness were essential to selling. He knocked on many doors but they took one look at him and closed them. They did not like his sepulchral look of perpetual gloom.

After a long search he found the one business he could go into with his fixed funereal face.

He joined a funeral parlour. Which proved a sunny point: Whatever your mug, never say die!

THE MAN WHO NEEDED A PASSPORT

THE traveller was well-dressed. And he had money. But he seemed to have lost his memory.

He had come into Friendly Suzie's with that lost look on his face. He sat himself down on the bar stool next to us. We didn't know why. We certainly wouldn't have sat down next to ourselves. Jason and I had just come off our fishing trip and we looked scruffy — and disreputable, not our usual reasonably groomed selves.

"Hi, I'm Lee, he's Jason," I introduced ourselves, smiling a hopefully non-evil smirk, trying to sound suave, or at least a normal guy. He looked preoccupied and distressed.

He responded, "I'm sorry… I can't introduce myself. I don't remember who I am."

Jason was curious — and helpful. "Look inside your pockets," he suggested. Of course, there must be something on him that could jog his memory.

The man felt about his body. He found his wallet. In it was a stack of calling cards — with his name and other information. That was when we (and everyone else around us) also noticed he had a lot of money on him.

A credit card on him established that his name was Ho Fook. His own name card showed that he was a Hong Konger, an import-and-export trader from Kowloon. The other name cards he found worked like magic on him: He immediately started to recall more.

Yes! He was in Singapore on his way to the US.

That reminded him to check for his passport. "I've lost it! My passport's gone!" he hollered out in dismay. He must have dropped his passport after he arrived here, he declared. Where, he could not recall. Then he remembered he had fallen down a staircase somewhere and bumped his head on something hard and after that everything went woozy.

"Hey, friend, it's no problem, really! Just go along to the British High Commission tomorrow and report to them and they'll give you some replacement travel paper," Jason assured him.

"Not that easy, my friend," Ho mumbled.

He did not tell us why immediately. A few drinks later (at his expense, of course, as he was grateful for our friendship, and we were also practised in the art of slow-motion response when the bill was presented for each round), he blurted out his problem when we repeated our High Comm solution for the fourth or fifth time.

Naturally, before he enlightened us, he berated us in that inimitable Hong Konger style necessary before revealing any bit of information: *"Mat, nei kam soh, ah?"* (How come you're so stupid?")

The fact was his Hong Kong passport was not one of those issued by Her Majesty's obedient servants. And his exclusive supplier in Hong Kong did not have a branch operation here in Singapore.

"You can help me?" he asked us candidly.

We could not, and said so.

By now he had become quite uninhibited. He swivelled around on his bar stool and extended his appeal to all and sundry at Friendly Suzie's.

Nobody responded, even when he waved his wad of US dollars in the air, emphasising, "I need a passport... I can pay!"

Well, perhaps not quite nobody. I noticed a seedy-looking character looking at him, sizing him up. And as our loaded friend was leaving, that character sidled up to him and whispered something in his ear. Ho nodded vigorously and the two left together.

We thought that was the last we would see of Ho. But days later he was back at Friendly Suzie's.

He recognised us, joined us at the bar, bought us more drinks, and told us his tale of woe: Yes, the last time there was someone who said he could get a British passport made out for him. He had even given the guy a deposit, earnest money, "to show how earnest I was", as he put it. But the guy had failed to keep his appointment. He made some inquiries and found out the poor fellow had been arrested — and that must have been before he could get a passport done for him. So now he was back to square one, looking for a passport-supplier so that he could get on the road to the States.

He said he had come back because he made contact here

the last time. Suzie's was known to have a few entrepreneurs engaged in unusual occupations among the bar's regular clientail. Yes, Suzie's attracted a mixed lot — that was what made the joint interesting to Jason and myself, both of us writers.

Again, after he had loosened up drink-wise, he again made his overt call for what should normally be a covert service. I did not expect that public advertisement, but perhaps the guy was really desperate. Then, again, maybe he knew what he was doing, since that was how he got his passport done (or almost done) before. Again, as only to be expected, no one answered his call there and then.

This time he was more understanding. He loudly announced his name and the hotel in which he was staying, asking to be contacted there in case anyone could help him with his problem. Still no response — at least none overtly.

We thought that was the last we would see of that generous guy, in a way a pity as he came loaded in more ways than one: He also had lots of money to splurge on drinks for all.

But a month later, believe it or not, we came across the same guy again. This time it was in a different bar. We entered as he was in the midst of his passport-call routine.

He caught sight of us, and looked clearly embarrassed.

"Doing it again?" Jason put to him. "Why? No results yet?"

He looked at Jason, and then at me.

He must have read my eyes: I knew.

"On the contrary, he had results — and that's precisely why he's doing it again," I said.

In our clean shirts we looked okay guys this time. He decided to come clean with us. "Works every time," he told us softly.

Then he put a finger near to his lips and pleaded with his eyes. I knew what he was going to say even before he whispered his undercover secret:

"C.I.D."

WE LIVE
AND LEARN

THE THIN FENCE

HENRY sat silent as his fellow guests at the dinner, all Singaporeans, waxed indignant at the latest news: The opposite take by the Malaysia media on the international court decision on Malaysia's stop-work application.

The Law of the Sea Tribunal had rejected Malaysia's stop-work request. The court allowed the reclamation works in the seas off Singapore's Tekong and Tuas to continue pending its final findings, but it ordered a panel set up for joint environmental study and required both countries to exchange information and consult each other.

Media reports on both sides promptly claimed victory.

"Singapore media correctly claimed victory as no stop-work was ordered. The study panel, information exchange and consultation order were no problem, not any issue at all. Malaysia lost on the key issue, yet their media claimed victory as though the study panel and so forth were hardly the issue." Several diners made that point.

"Why the need to crow?" Henry asked quietly.

"Yes, they always seem to feel that need," someone took the question as rhetorical and concurred.

"I don't mean them," Henry clarified, "I mean us, the crowing on our side."

"But that's what's happening on every issue between the two countries, isn't it? Both sides have an opposite take — and everything gets blown to near confrontation level. The supply and price of water, railway land, port rivalry, border entry procedures… you name it, some people in the two countries will always join issue on it!" another guest, a mite more fair, came in with a sigh.

"Yet we have such long links — links that remain to the present, family blood relationships, and racial, religious, cultural, and economic bonds. We do have strong ties at common people level that can never be broken. There is only a thin fence separating us," Henry said.

Seizing the silence that followed, Henry told a personal story in what seemed a change of subject:

I have a neighbour John (Henry said) whose garden shares a common chain-link fence with mine.

Before John's long term tenant suddenly left for good, the fellow planted three mango saplings, all just a foot away from the boundary line. I protested to him. I warned that the saplings would grow into huge trees — and their roots, trunks, branches and leaves would trespass over the line. The roots would crack my building aprons which are close to that boundary line, and they might even compromise my building foundation.

John's tenant ignored my warnings.

After he left, I wrote to John.

Perhaps John was too busy getting his property into shape to put on the rental market. He did not respond. It could be he felt the problem was not urgent and could be tackled later. The saplings were still little more than saplings.

So when John came to check his vacant house, I went over. I urged him to cut the mango trees early as they seemed to be growing fast.

John, clearly preoccupied with other matters, said he would think it over.

Days passed and apparently he was still thinking it over. (Actually, as I found out later, he was busy overseas.)

Then I spotted him again. I told him my contract gardener would be coming along for his monthly work on my grounds soon and I could ask him to take on the additional job too. That would save him trouble and would be cheaper than finding a contractor specifically to root out and dispose of the three trees.

John said he would ponder on it.

I waited. The trees grew. John kept on his pondering.

(Actually, he was busy at work in and out of the country.)

I managed to contact John again. This time I offered to have my contractor go over to his side of the fence to remove the trees — at my expense. I simply asked for his permission, urging an early reply as my contractor would be coming along soon.

In a brief note, John gave his permission. (I thought my offer had swung the deal, but actually it did not. He had not yet got a contractor. What I offered was convenient. And I was the one waxing impatient to have the trees cut.)

Before the due day for my contractor to work on my garden, I saw some contract men working on tidying up John's grounds — clearing off everything except the three saplings!

In a fit of misunderstanding and vexation, I contacted John and asked him why he had not asked his workers to remove the trees since he had already got them to attend to the rest of his grounds? I must have sounded aggressive.

He replied at length. He pointed out he had been travelling. His contractor, appointed recently, at first said he could not start work at once but later found that he could — and so he proceeded. John was upset at my unfair insinuations. He ended telling me flatly he had decided not to allow my contractor to cut the saplings.

I reflected on his words — and mine.

I wrote him to thank him for the courtesy he showed me by writing his detailed explanation. I had indeed been unfairly aggressive in my reaction.

"We should not be quarrelling like this. On my part, I feel like a fool. It looks like the three saplings have made saps of the two of us — at least, for sure, one of us! And let me hasten to identify, that's me of course!" I apologised.

I assured him that I was not writing in that vein in the hope of persuading him to re-think his position and revert to allowing my contractor to cut down the trees. I still believed that it would be less expensive, less hazardous and easier to remove the saplings at this stage than later, but I would no longer press the issue.

In other words I admitted he had won and I had lost my battle for early removal of the trees.

End of story?

Not quite.

The next day, I found John's contractor at work in his garden removing the three trees, obviously instructed to do so.

HENRY, his story done with, looked at the faces of his listeners. *Had his point sunk in?*

For a moment it looked as though it had …

Then the illusion went pop!

One of the diners exclaimed, "I get it, Henry! At times it's better to seem to soften — to concede victory. In order to win later! That's a damned clever strategy: Lose a battle to win a war — one step backwards, two steps forward!"

DOING FANTASTIC THINGS WITH FAMILY

THE tycoon was what everyone called a self-made man. He was born poor, came to Singapore an immigrant, and he made himself — a self-made millionaire. He succeeded fantastically. And his children succeeded fantastically too. Each one, on his own steam, was now a star — in the professions, in business, in the arts. When he mentioned all that to me I congratulated him.

His eyes shone, then clouded over. We were close enough and he let me in on the sorrow of his life, "I realise it now — too late. All my life I've been too absorbed in making money. I did not spend much time at all with my children. You know, I can't recall a single big moment spent together with them from when they were tiny. I wish we could have done things together, as family. Some fantastic thing, a high in our lives…"

It's a father thing, something all we fathers do: Dream about doing fantastic things with family.

The bad news is that for many it stays that way — a dream until it becomes impossible fantasy. The good news is that it need not be so; all of us, including the most mundane of us, can do those things — fantastic things with family. But that was not something I realised just like that…

A FEW days after he had gone and climbed up to the very peak of Mount Kinabalu, my eldest son Austin (now an engineer) told the family about his feat. He described the thrill and the torment of the tense final ascent — how cold it was, how his hands bled, how his legs went numb on him, how he had to summon up every last bit of willpower to make it to the top.

I was so proud of him and told him so.

Yet inwardly I felt cheated: Was that not something we could have gone and done as son and father? How I wished he and I could have scaled that snow-covered peak together!

But that was of course a mere pipedream. I was young enough then, but I was no climber. Nowhere near an endurance king. I had never even attempted to climb our modest Bukit Timah Hill. When invited to join my college friends to hike up the modest incline drive to the viewing point on top of Mount Faber, I had pleaded a convenient flu. You could say the best hill I had ever done was Emerald Hill, which, for all the road's quaint beauty, was no big deal.

MY SECOND son John (a chartered accountant) did a parachute jump off a plane. He too told us only after the event. As a sport, that was a rare thing in those days and it took my breath away. To me it was fantastic to the point of mind-boggling! I visualised him making that heart-stopping leap. And I wished I could have done it together with him — dive out of the plane, parachute cord in hand, not to be pulled till we had plummeted down our carefully counted seconds.

To have made that glorious leap with my son would have been fabulous! What father would not have canonised that experience as zenith of life, thereafter to be told over and over again as ecstatic father-and-son deed of derring-do!

To be honest, the closest I got to a scary plunge down a height was a ride down a roller coaster, my first and last — although only a modest fairground contraption that offered the gentlest of undulations. Even then I nearly threw up. Still, nothing stopped me from fantasising about an exhilarating sky-dive with my son.

MY YOUNGEST son Patrick (a medical doctor) also did his fantastic thing — his own range of them. The one moment I wished I could have shared with him was a high point in his musical life as I watched him (and his work) on stage. The occasion was his musical *Poverello*, presented in a public theatre, the first of a few successes. He composed the music and lyrics, directed the play, conducted the musicians, and even sang and played his own music!

To be honest, I never had any musical talent whatsoever — I could not have played a nursery rhyme on a kindergarten flute to save my life! But that did not stop me from imagining my son Pat and I doing a sensational musical together. ·

YES, like my tycoon friend, I too could not conceive having ever done fantastic things with family.

And that remained my sad state of mind for a long while…

Then something happened.

Recently I tracked down a specialist who was able to clean

up my very old (and mouldy) 8-mm home movies and transfer them to compact discs. My wife Sylvia and I watched them again — those fleeting flicks of our early family life, dating back almost five decades. There were children's birthday parties galore, outings to the seaside and the hills and the zoo, processions and pageants, holiday travel to various places. Then the National Day parades we watched together, then parades in which our boys marched as NS-men, then their weddings, then the coming of grandchildren…

Nothing spectacular, only things we went through as one ordinary family. But as all that past came back to us, how we laughed and enjoyed again those times we had!

But they were very ordinary. Like all amateurish home movies, boring to all not family. They kept us enthralled, those preserved moments of family together — they plummeted the depths vertically right down into the core of us…

Sylvia, as mother, knew what all that meant all along.

I, blur like most fathers, knew it only at long last — as I enunciated the fact:

"We have done fantastic things with family!"

Notches On A Ring

IT WAS a ring, and yet not a ring.

It fitted loosely on his index finger, but it was more like a coin with a big hole in it. It had a flat doughnut shape, that religious aide for meditation. There were bumps like notches around its outer rim — 10 tiny ones and one big one. On the big mound was a representation of the Lady of Lourdes. (Lourdes is the famous shrine in France that millions of pilgrims visit annually to pray to Mary, the mother of Jesus Christ.)

Joe brought that ring home from Lourdes and it quickly grew on him. The mounds on it became the rosary beads on which he would silently chant his prayer-meditations as he jogged his daily half-hour circuit along Chancery Lane and Malcolm Road. The ring had cost him less than a dollar, but to him it became a priceless thing, a charm that turned him on as he paced his daily trips of soul.

That ring went with him on other trips, near and far from home — shared experiences of peace and wonder that made it mean even more to him. People with religious faith (Buddhist or Muslim or whatever) will understand this. And even those without commitment to a formal religion but cherish a code of values of their own — they too will understand attachment to such a thing: A symbol to help them stay forever connected to meaningful spiritual journeys of their lives.

The ring was with Joe as he prayed for a dying friend by her bed. It was with him as he went to console that friend's bereaved ones.

It was in his hand to help him hold on through many crises — in moments of need for strength, in times of thanksgiving after miracles. As also in acceptance on occasions of no miracles…

The ring became part of him — part of his flesh and blood. But all along he had a sneaking feeling that perhaps such intimate attachment to a thing should not be without end. To truly mature in spirit, one needs to be able to let go of such bonds of matter — and still to keep an even or even higher soul connection…

Easier said than done.

Joe stayed hooked on those rosary beads on his ring.

WITH the passage of time Joe's praying fingers wore down the metal. And the mounds on it began to shine with a silver sheen even as the Lourdes picture on it became faint.

Then Joe visited a new Marian shrine: Medjugorye in Croatia, today attracting its thousands of pilgrims. And while he was praying there he noticed that the silver shine on his rosary ring turned to gold! (Which was no unique happening — as so many other pilgrims had testified to experiencing that same phenomenon: Their rosaries too turned to gold colour and stayed that colour gold for days.)

Such wondrous affirmation attached Joe even more to his rosary ring.

So you will understand his sense of loss when he lost the ring.

IT HAPPENED when Joe was on his daily jog along Malcolm Road. When he reached home he found his ring gone. It had dropped off his finger. He hurried back along the route. He searched for it for hours. And for days after that.

He prayed to find it. His prayers were not answered. The ring seemed gone for good.

Why had this to happen to him? He could not understand it.

He bought a replacement rosary ring. It was not the same, of course. Shared experiences, joyful or sad, do not transfer to substitutes…

In time Joe got over his loss; he accepted that he would never see his ring again.

THEN a few years on, at a church support group meeting for people with family relationship problems, an old man got up and told his story. He said he had a problem — he was bad-tempered with his family and easily stressed. He was given a rosary ring. He would meditate and pray with it. He found that it helped him to calm down and arrive at answers to his problems. He found peace.

Then he lost his rosary ring. The loss affected him badly. Thrown off-balance, he could no longer soothe out the ruffles on his family fabric. He prayed that he might find his ring — and return to his lost calm.

And he did find a ring. Recently. By the side of a road. It

was not his ring. It was an old ring worn down with constant use, the mounds around it shiny like silver. But he felt it had been sent his way in answer to his prayer — to help him survive. And miraculously it began working on him. He had found new balance, and peace of mind once more!

He passed around the ring for everyone to see. "God knows I can't cope without it!" he said.

Joe recognised it at once. It was his old ring.

He wanted to claim it.

He did not.

The old man needed it more. Joe had noticed how the old man's wrinkled fingers had kept caressing it. *No, it would be cruel to make him let it go…*

Joe could let it go. And he did.

YES, Joe had matured. He had learned to let go again — even when he had already let go anyway. He felt good about his goodness, proud of himself, taken up a notch. He had quietly proven himself a better man than that old man, and perhaps all the rest at the meeting too.

As he left that session, a friend who was there too, whispered to him:

"Actually, that ring was mine! I have been in agony over my declining health. Why had God abandoned me? I needed a sign: An affirmation of God's love. And one day, by God's grace, I was led to find that ring along Malcolm Road, though it was only barely visible in the thick grass. I started praying with it. Through prayer I found consolation — even though my health never improved all that much. And the ring stayed with me for a long while. I kept it on my person everywhere I went. When I lost it not so long ago, I was inconsolable. It was truly hard for me to refrain from claiming it back just now. But I could not do that to that old man, could I? Anyway my sacrifice now makes me feel good — I feel taken up a notch!"

Joe felt taken down one notch — but he still felt good.

PUNY MISSING HANDS

PUNITHA THAMBY, plain and tiny, last-born, "Puny" to her family, loved Ma most, and was most loved in return.

Puny never had any other love, never married, never left Ma — till Ma left her, and this world, at 80. Ma left without a word. She had never spoken a word through her life. Ma had been born deaf and dumb. She had always spoken with eloquent hands — till sadly stricken by stroke. She continued to move with her moving eyes. Till the comma of coma. And then the full stop of demise.

Puny missed Ma terribly. To be forlorn at 40-something with the loss of one's only love in life — could there be anything, any tragedy of life, more devastating?

She missed most their simple connection — the touch of Ma's hands, those age-spotted hands now no more. She had spent all her adult life doing things with Ma and for Ma, following in her wake all her waking day. She loved her more than she did herself.

And now, there was no one to care for. No one to do anything for. Nothing. How does one fill in a nothingness that total? She felt loss of balance, lost with no wish to find any way. Like the night she woke up from a dream of motionless hands and closed eyes to rush to Ma's bed to help her pee or poo. And there was the bed empty — with an emptiness so vast!

She sat on that bed. She pretended she could touch Ma's hand. And she moved one step closer to Ma — to following Ma to her world.

Aunt May Ling, Ma's sister-in-law, came to her rescue. An understanding though also a no-nonsense woman, she made her let out her Ma's flat.

"Puny, you come and stay with me!" she insisted.

But months later Puny still languished in her pining mode. She continued to dream about her Ma, and talk about her. But now it was summing up into one memory: "I miss Ma's hands moving for me, reaching out to me, her old hands touching me…"

Then there was progress. Puny told her aunt, "I remember Ma signed to me that, if she went first, I must not do anything foolish, I must not try to go to her. She promised she would come to me. Does she mean coming in dreams — or in other people...?"

And Auntie was touched when Puny added, "Perhaps she's come to me in you, Auntie."

May Ling held Puny's hands with both hands for that. But only that one time — for she was too no-nonsense for such nonsense. Besides she herself was old and not too well. Puny must not bond — and then miss — another touching of hands.

Thank God, Puny was finding balance. Now she might be open to finding help from others. And finding meaning in others.

May Ling spoke with her friends. They got Puny to join them in visits as volunteers to an old people's Home that they had adopted.

On her first day at the Home Puny's eyes lit up a little to see faces there looking so like Ma's. In particular, there was one Madam Marianah, who also had age spots on her cheeks and her hands — so like Ma's. She was also bedridden just as Ma was towards the end.

Marianah needed someone to care for her. The old woman had no family left. No one came to visit her now.

Soon the old woman was softly calling her "Puny" (the way Ma's voiceless lips used to do!)

And she naturally shortened Marianah's name to "Ma".

The Home was well-staffed and often all that Puny had to

do was just hold Ma's hands — the way she had done for her real Ma, especially towards the end, love juices flowing almost visibly both ways.

Ma's two ward-mates on the adjacent beds also loved Puny. They always had smiles for her. They were more fortunate. They had family coming to see them. Even if only once a month or so, with different faces appearing till, by a kind of duty roster, the cycles recycled. The visitors seldom stayed long. Perhaps because they had to rush back to their own lives, they had important things to do *(like TV serials they could not miss? Or mahjong games?)*. But at least those relatives came — Ma's did not.

Puny noticed that these two old women also had age spots on their cheeks — less than her Ma's, but still enough to make them, in her eyes ,also reflections of her real Ma. She instinctively stopped by their beds. And she touched their hands.

Puny was finding meaning.

Not only with Ma and her two roommates, but also with others in the Home. The good people who ran the Home came to look on her as one of themselves — another ready pair of hands. And they called on her help whenever someone needed comfort and connection. There was no lack of those in such need. And Puny reached out to them as she did with her own Ma. Doing lots of hand holding — her speciality.

She came alive once more — with the joy of living life with meaning. *Yes, so wonderful to be alive!*

Then they told her she would not be alive for long…

She had a tumour. She had disregarded the warning signs, ignored her own health till it was too late. By now, Aunt May Ling had passed on. She was alone.

Puny told the good people who ran the Home. She also told them she wished to continue to come.

They said, "Of course!"

When her own time to go drew near she went and asked if they would accept her, let her spend her last days on one of their beds.

They said, "Of course!"

She began once more to dream of her Ma nightly. And during the day she thought of her Ma every moment as she hobbled about among the beds of the Home. Sometimes she felt as though she had already one foot in that other world with Ma.

She had not told the old folks there about her illness — she felt they had enough burden of their own to bear. She kept her secret to herself to her very last days, and then there was no need for telling. They knew it: *Their little Puny was slipping away.* For now, time and again, she would slip off to visitations to that other-world even as she lived through her last this-world days with her old folks.

The end came.

Seated on Marianah's bed with that old woman, sharing a pushed-up pillow with her, gazing absently at Ma's two other ward-mates, Puny momentarily felt alone: Fear, uncertainty, coldness, life slipping away to God knows where…

She closed her eyes.

Ma sent me here to help these people. I think I have helped them — even if all I did was touch them. Yes, surely that helped them. How I miss your touching hands, Ma! How I wish I have your two hands touching me now!

And then Puny felt it: A flood of touch all over her — not two, a multitude!

Six hands were caressing her. Flowing love and warmth into her.

Six age-spotted hands blessing her with her needed touch of hands — even as Puny slipped away for good.

A Truck Rammed Us Dead

THE speeding truck on the main road came at us, a behemoth with an unexpectedly long trailer in its train. The trailer rammed into the driver's side of our car, as cruising in from our slip-road we coalesced with it. An arrowhead convergence of two straight lines merging into certain collision.

Our small car was sent spinning off the road.

We died.

SYLVIA was driving the two of us home in her Impreza, on our return journey from the motor workshop where I had left my car for a repair job. We were in unfamiliar territory — the busy industrial area of Paya Lebar, a concrete jungle bewildering with its sudden and convoluted diversions for extensive road works. The heavy traffic was shatteringly fast, unforgivingly intolerant of slow coaches. Everyone was apparently late as the dark skies had been pouring and it was still raining, at least kittens and puppies. Visibility was poor, especially to our old eyes with compromised peripheral vision.

Added to all that, we were both hot and bothered and wound up tight. I had stupidly lost my way driving myself to the workshop, and Sylvia had waited for me there for an hour, tense with worry, freaked out by fear that I had met with an accident. We were just not ourselves, unreasonably snapping at each other. There is something metamorphosing about sullenly sitting together in a car, a part of the demented rush and roar of the roads — it pummels the balance of the most sane among people. We were deep in that unreal world of senseless ire and unduly hostile feeling — a kind of road rage!

Distracted by a hurtful remark from me, Sylvia switched her concentration from the main road to look at me — with her car just heading out from the slip road. My eyes were focused in her direction; so I saw what she did not see: The huge truck not about to give way, bearing down straight on insignificant us in our tiny car, *who in hell gives a damn* — unparallel lines about to impact!

"Stop! Stop! Stop!" I leapt out from my unreal world and screamed at her with all my might.

That was the moment I saw that monster vehicle come ramming straight at us, sure to pulverise us! Sylvia could now see it too. But would she too re-enter real world in time?

In that split second, that hair's breadth dividing this world and the next, anything could have happened.

I have given one scenario, one ending of our story: We died.

THAT did not happen.

The truck could have smashed us — but it did not.

Sylvia stepped hard on the brakes — just in time.

Death hurtled past our terrified faces, flashing by our car window, almost touching us, scraping past us, then all gone!

Our throats parched dry, whatever we were quarrelling about simply evaporated.

They did not matter one bit any more — those angry concerns and emotions, the small pictures that had become our focus.

Sometimes we need to experience (or almost experience) the big picture, the eternity perspective.

Sometimes we need a moment removed from mundane things that grate and gall. An escape moment from piffling things that have somehow become portentous...

For a long while we could not speak. Halted dead in our mental tracks, just as we had been halted dead in our physical tracks. Shaken by the almost-catastrophe that had catapulted past us...

We told the story to close friends — and the sobering thoughts Sylvia and I shared after our near-death experience.

They knew exactly what we meant. Both friends with religion (as the word is understood) — and without. They recognised that moment. Some called it an awakening, a God moment come to us.

In life at times we stand in a tight slit between life and death — and a defining and divining moment is given to us.

By whatever name called…

A PROMISE NOT QUITE NOT KEPT

"BUT you promised," she cried. "I'll never trust you again."

Those were the only words in the message Frank could make out. But for the life of him he could not match the crackly voice to anybody, so poor was the recording on his answer-phone tape which, he discovered, had turned mouldy.

It was obviously a woman's voice but who could she be? She sounded overwrought over that promise not kept, whatever that was. There was agony in that "I'll never trust you again".

Frank interrupted preoccupation with another matter that had been heavy on his mind and tried to guess who the caller was. It sounded like it could be one of those sweet young things he had been asked by Human Resource to interview for a junior executive appointment? Elaine? Or Sharon or Juliana or what's her name… Petrina? Had he promised them anything? Surely not. It was not his habit to make promises lightly, hold out anything definite when he did not have the authority to make the decision. But could he have unwittingly given anyone of them that impression?

Certainly he had said the usual pleasantries, like "I like what you have". Or "You should be hearing from us." Or even "You're a promising candidate. Hopefully, you should be getting what you want…" But he could swear he never made any specific promise to any girl…

No, it couldn't be those ladies — they were urban office workers, tough female troopers, used to both interviews as well as rejections.

Could it be one of his office colleagues then? Had he promised anything to any of them? Frank racked his brain.

Yes, he did promise Lily he would support her for that Frisco seminar, a trip which was more perk than true training. But he had kept that his part of the promise, only the MD himself had some other worthy in mind. Lily was naturally disappointed and she did sulk quite a bit but he thought she understood. Could Lily have made that call? Possible… but unlikely, knowing Lily's resilient nature.

Who then? That Mrs Teresa Lim, the management consultant? No doubt he had picked her brain for ideas, motivating her with hopes of a contract for her firm. In the end, the Human Resource GM had overruled his recommendation because he already had another consultancy in mind for that the plum assignment. Teresa could hardly blame him, she herself was present when he spoke up for her to HRGM. No, it couldn't be Teresa. The tone of the recorded message was too emotional to be the thoroughly urbane Teresa, who was as cool as they came.

His mother-in-law — that's it! It must have been her. She was always accusing him of undertaking to do this or that, and not performing. Had she found out anything Heard something slanderous and exaggerated? It would be just like the dragon lady to ring him up and scold him. But he had been careful, especially in the last few days. He had taken pains not to cross her in any matter whatsoever, responding promptly to her smallest whims, bending over backwards to avoid having her on his back for any reason. But, perhaps it wasn't the old lady…

Perhaps it was worse: It was his wife! That must be it. It was Wendy! Frank trembled. God forbid! Somehow she had found out his dark secret: His chance reunion with Gloria at a party three nights ago, after which they had walked and talked at length... Wendy had been away in Penang where she was visiting a sick friend. She must have phoned from there. My God! He could be in for a repeat of that last domestic explosion.

After their blow-up over Gloria a year ago, he had promised Wendy never to see the girl again, faithfully broken up with that pretty secretary of his, immediately had her transferred out of his office, and honestly turned over a new leaf — despite Gloria's heart-breaking sobs and his own sadness of heart...

But maybe it wasn't Wendy after all. How could Wendy have found out? What was there to find out anyway? He had done nothing wrong, at least not as yet! He admitted he entertained ideas, hopes, possible plans even, but as yet, nothing had happened although Gloria's eyes and her slightly-open mouth signalled promise. But he was still in his temptation agony, at that struggling stage — and still faithful to his wife. So far, it was purely impure desire, no impure action. No, he must be over-reacting — it couldn't be Wendy.

Maybe it was worse!

Gloria! Gloria, no longer collected and sensible like she was three nights ago. Gloria, back on heat, seeking renewal of love liaison. Or worse, Gloria now insisting on his divorce from Wendy (which in one weak moment long ago he had nodded his stupid head to). Gloria demanding nothing less than that they be united in marriage!

Damn that blasted tape! He wished he had the rest of the message in the answer-phone...

There was only one way to find out: Go to the horse's mouth, phone Gloria. If it was her, he could try to mollify her, calm her down, put her off, reassure her whatever way he could. And then try to resolve the matter with her when she had cooled down.

If it wasn't her, then it had to be Wendy, and if it was

Wendy, he would still be wise to first blast away any hope in Gloria's heart for a renewal of relationship, make it clear that he would not see her again — and then phone Wendy, acting out the role of a repentant husband.

Gloria was sweetness itself. It was obvious it wasn't her who had left the message. So he made the position clear to her. He broke off with her once more, this time even before anything had bonded. He felt glad, clean, unburdened from his uneasy preoccupation over the past few days…

After that he rang his wife in Penang.

Wendy said "hello", sounding distant and dispirited. And she remained quiet. Frank knew his Wendy. In that mood, she was either really downcast over something (and that could be her friend's illness), or it was the calm before that storm hanging ready to burst over his head. He could not take any chance on that.

He had to act fast. He had to pre-empt her before she exploded. He abjectly confessed his sin.

He told her he had broken his promise not to see Gloria again. He admitted he had been tempted, even that he had nearly succumbed. He promised to sin no more, despite having failed to keep his promise not to see Gloria and therefore no longer deserving his wife's trust. He hoped he was able to sound as genuine as indeed he was.

Wendy remained silent for a while. Had she heard about his evening with Gloria, perhaps from one of her friends who had spied on them as they walked off together, maybe even embellished what she saw, as gossipers tended to do? And so Wendy had made that phone call to him?

Was she moved at all by his voluntary confession? Or was she angry beyond words, in no mood to forgive him? Frank was left hanging in doubt and agony.

Then, out of the silence, he heard Wendy crying at the other end. Which was a good sign.

Wendy was moved. She forgave him, she said. She was

proud of him. Then she gave him the news that her friend was dead, which was why she was so sad. The funeral would take place the next day. She would be home the day after.

"I love you, Frank," she said. "I never doubted you would be faithful to your promise. I trust you!"

"Thank God!" Frank said from his heart.

But he needed to settle the unresolved question in his mind. "Did you phone me earlier today?"

"No"

So the vexing question remained unresolved.

But not for long.

Soon after he put down the receiver, the phone rang. It was a woman. She demanded to know why he had not returned her call after she had asked him to do so on his answering machine. Her voice was emotional and high-strung. And familiar.

The caller dispensed with all further courtesies. She called him names: "You bastard! You two-timing swine!" She screeched out that she would never trust him again. She swore at him for his infidelity to herself as his faithful mistress, berating him for not keeping his promise to stay away from "that slut, Vanessa".

Vanessa? What slut, Vanessa? Frank was puzzled. And speechless.

"Why no answer? Have you become dumb, Shawn?"

Shawn? Who's Shawn?

Frank got it. He stammered in reply: "Lady, I-I'm not... this, this isn't Shawn. There's no Shawn at this number..."

There was an embarrassed silence from the other end. Then a small voice apologised, "I must have dialled the wrong number!"

"THEN again, perhaps not quite," Frank said to himself, grateful for tender mercies from God, even if channelled through unknown quarters.

GOBBLEDYGOOK

THE waiting room at the Police Human Resource Office was packed with hopefuls. And these were only the short list — the possibles sieved from the many applicants for trainee detective vacancies. They were waiting for their interview numbers to be called out on the loudspeakers.

The cushioned seats were comfortable and there were magazines and free coffee and cold drinks. Intriguing posters and notices filled a whole wall. There was even a telephone for those who did not bring their own handphones and wished to make calls.

Simon, just arrived, looked around at the faces around him. Some looked bored — perhaps they had been waiting a long while. One of these grumbled, "They have no proper schedule for interviews. I've been here some time, gone through three magazines, downed two cups of coffee, and still they've not called my number. And some who came later than me have been interviewed and gone off!"

Simon hoped he would not have to wait that long. He looked around. He duly went through the notices and posters, big and small, pinned on the huge soft-board on the wall in front of the rows of seats.

Some were direct and dramatic — about the Force, about serving the Republic in the Home Team, about the mission of preventing crime. Some were information sheets with statistics about various offences and offenders. But a good number were mysterious, or even puzzling. Some used acronyms, abbreviations, code numbers, and technical terms — these must be for police people initiated into the mumbo-jumbo.

Simon found some of those postings tantalising. He had a natural curiosity about mysterious messages. He stood in front of one of them trying to figure out what the gobbledygook on it was about. The contents were like something in alien language even though written in Romanised form. They made no sense. They challenged him to make sense of them.

The words, if they were words at all, went:

"FIOUYNACREHPICEDSIHT

LAID17666526

DNAKSAROFNIOSNETXE13

ROFYLRAE

WEIVRETNI"

"Somebody's word processor went wonky there," one fellow-candidate commented with a laugh.

"Or the computer got hit by a virus!" went another.

"No, that's probably for eye-testing of candidates," yet another hazarded his guess.

Some others stared at the thing for a while, sipping on coffee, then shrugged and went on to read other notices, or for more coffee.

Simon watched as someone with a big forehead and big glasses stared at the gobbledygook for a long time and copied them down and sat down to puzzle them out. The man suddenly sat bolt upright, and drew out his handphone and dialled — and then smiled broadly. And soon after that he was called in.

And he came out soon with an even broader smile and left the office.

"The password to the interview room is in that notice!" Simon concluded with inner excitement. He too copied down the letters. He studied them intently.

He zeroed in on the first set of numbers. The eight digits gave him his first clue. It must be a phone number. That itself led him to the second clue. Since phone numbers started with a "6" the number could be in reverse. He reversed it and immediately recognised the Police Manpower exchange number. Working from there he started reversing the letters and separating them out to make sensible words.

That was how he decoded the message on the notice. It was the secret password, an open secret:

"If you can decipher this dial 6-256-6671 and ask for extension 31 for early interview."

He followed the instruction. He dialled. He was told to go right in when the next candidate came out.

He went in. The panel said it was a hard choice for them: All the short-listed candidates seemed equally good. So they had to come up with a device, some test, something quite simple — to gauge the base-level problem-solving skill of the would-be trainee detective.

Simon was selected.

CLIMB TO HIGHER GROUND

DEREK stepped out into his garden. His hilltop bungalow stood high over neighbouring properties. But he had no time for the view. He drew his morning regimen of four deep breaths. The air felt good. He remembered where he had felt better: The cool, crisp air of Mount Kinabalu.

He wished he could fly there now, take a holiday, relax in that environment of cool nature.

Wishful thinking! What with one thing after another coming up non-stop in the office, that was an idle dream. That dawn air in his garden was the most he was going to get.

His eyes surveyed the clouds floating by and the rustling trees and the skyscrapers in the distance. The view was okay, better than from most other people's houses in Singapore, but nothing like the fantastic scenery from that Akinabalu mountain top. He sighed — who doesn't get jaded with the same old things, the same old view, the same old life?

Muriel joined him. She reminded him to go and see Gerald.

"He hasn't long to live, you know?" she said, frowning an old frown he had not seen for a while. To get her off his back he grunted okay, okay, he would go that evening.

Yes, he would have to visit the poor guy. He did not relish going, but he was under obligation to Gerald, even though, unlike Gerald, he was not much good at comforting the sick and that sort of thing. In fact, on principle he never visited the sick, nor buried the dead, for that matter.

But that trip to the hospice had to be done, had to be got over with, whatever important things he had to do or think about, decisions involving millions, or at least tens of thousands.

Gerald had helped Muriel through her crisis three years ago — and now the man was dying.

Gerald was one year his senior at school but, probably because he was nowhere near Derek's level of IQ (not many were), career-wise Gerald had not done as well. They saw little of each other after their school days, until that day when suddenly Gerald came back into his life, and with a vengeance — in the role of his wife's saviour!

That was the time Muriel first started to go about wearing that frown of hers. She had become depressed (possibly even suicidal, as Gerald had "diagnosed" though he was no psychiatrist). And all that over a whole lot of ridiculously trivial things — so silly to him, but apparently not to his wife!

She had dialled SOS, the Samaritans of Singapore. Gerald was the volunteer on duty.

He calmed her down, held her hand (over the phone, and later in counselling sessions). In due course, with her agreement, he contacted Derek. That Gerald had turned into a most kind-hearted and perceptive fellow as a do-gooder and church worker. And Gerald convinced him that, however crazy her reasons, Muriel was definitely in crisis.

Gerald got him to play his part — and together they saved Muriel, helped her come out of that self-created (but still surely, absolutely unnecessary!) crisis. A crisis that could have become his as well, for the silly woman had confided to

Gerald that she was actually considering divorce! Imagine that? Divorce over no earth-shaking issues — only piffling things like his not spending time with her, forgetting their wedding anniversary or her birthday (one or the other), not listening attentively enough to her on-and-on talk about the children and relatives and such-like? Good grief!

Gerald insisted he and Muriel should go on a holiday, their first in years. Derek remembered his words: "Get out of your low plain. Go to a mountain resort. There are times when you have to leave everything behind. Climb to higher ground!"

On Gerald's recommendation, they had gone to Kinabalu, the mountain the native Kadazans called Akinabalu, the home of the gods.

That time together ("your bonding time", as Gerald had promised) worked wonders for Muriel. And Kinabalu became the key opening her to peace of mind.

And in a way Kinabalu was a key for him too, though not as lasting. It did something for him for a while, as he had to admit. The invigorating air, the clouds of heaven above and below and often immediately around too, the natural friendliness of the Kadazan people — all that bestowed a magic respite, peace away from the frenetic world down below.

It was truly a sojourn to the home of the gods...

They returned to the world, both recharged.

In time though, recharge power weakened for Derek — and the key no longer opened any door.

THAT day, like all office days for Derek, passed all too quickly. But unlike all days, everybody seemed soft-spoken, considerate, sympathetic. He guessed why. May, his secretary, must have let out that he was grieving over a dying friend at a hospice, which was of course an exaggeration.

Grieving was not something he did.

But he took full advantage of the situation, played his role of a grouchy, wounded animal, got things from his colleagues they might not have conceded him in other circumstances. He knew he was being manipulative... but surely the essence of management is the art of using people...

His colleagues put in extra time helping him deal with his calls and in-mail. May told him that and said he might wish to thank them. He grunted. He was not one to waste time on thanks. They were just doing their shared office work, weren't they? Thanks has no place in jobs. That's the way the world goes, man!

That evening he went on his uncomfortable mission to comfort a dying man. He was shocked when he set eyes on Gerald. So damned depressing! The fellow was so emaciated, so horribly yellow, a ghost of his former fat self — yes, soon to be a ghost, period.

"Never mind," Derek promised himself at once, "I won't stay a moment longer than necessary."

Gerald was lying down in bed, but when he recognised his visitor he pushed himself up, sat up for him.

"Hi, Derek!" he greeted him first, his voice surprisingly cheerful. Then the mask fell — he coughed and was in agony and had to suck in oxygen from the face-cup by his bedside.

"Don't strain yourself, Gerald." He put his hand on Gerald's, and almost drew it back at once, for the thing was cold and revolting! He was touching a skeleton, there was no flesh, only skin and bone.

"Oxygen is God's wonderful gift," Gerald said with a smile as he breathed easier. "We take it so for granted, we don't even thank God for it. Till when we can't get it." The poor guy should know; his lungs were practically all gone, eaten away by cancer.

Derek thought of his morning breaths of air out on his hilltop garden. That air was good, something to be thankful for. Yes, elsewhere it might be better, but what he could get in anywhere was still good. Kinabalu did not seem that important any more...

Gerald was now looking out of his window. There was nothing much to see. Derek saw only a huge, ugly rooftop, and above that, a dull sky with one nondescript cloud in it. A depressing, thoroughly boring view!

Gerald remained silent. Feeling sorry for himself? That was understandable. Who would not, in his place?

Then, with a sigh, the man spoke: "What a lovely view, Derek!"

Derek looked at him in disbelief. But on Gerald's face there was only unfeigned admiration. The guy was not putting it on! Derek had to take another look. Yes, there was something beautiful, enchanting in a sombre way, about that lonely cloud sailing by in the darkening sky.

"God gives us such a beautiful world. It's such a pity we don't open our eyes to see it!" Gerald said, his soft voice now entering the less-travelled road in his friend's heart.

Derek thought about the view from his hilltop place. That was good. Only lately he had stopped really noticing it. But he knew he would see it tomorrow.

A nurse came in to fuss over Gerald, tidy up his bedside things. She smiled, and he smiled.

"People are so good, so considerate. Yes, people are kind, Derek, aren't they? You too feel good the moment you think of their goodness," he said, his eyes glowing.

Despite himself, Derek felt that warmth getting infectious…

Derek thought of his colleagues back at his office. Yes, they were good. He felt good about having them. But he had made use of their goodness. He did not feel good about himself.

He was staying longer than he had intended.

He realised why.

He was getting more than he came to give; yes, getting more than what he had to give. This dying man was still getting more out of life, even what little he had left of it. And the man was giving him wisdom he never had, higher IQ regardless…

For a while they remained silent.

Seamlessly, without prompting, Derek had begun to sort things in his mind — what mattered, what did not…

He reached out and held Gerald's hand. No shrinking away this time. Gerald's hand was as cold and bony as before, but now it felt like a true human hand — real hand, essential hand, against the unnatural flabbiness of his own puffy palm.

Gerald spoke his last words for Derek — last words from someone for whom Derek now felt nothing but respect. Words to become engraved, like on stone, in his heart, new wisdom for his new self:

"Don't you worry, God will guide you! Things do get better, we only need to find our way — the right way to look at things."

Gerald died that night.

And Derek remembered what his friend had urged on another occasion: "Get out of your low plain. Go to a mountain resort. There are times when you have to leave everything behind. Climb to higher ground!"

He took Muriel to Akinabalu.

They found themselves again.

In the years that followed, Derek and Muriel would again and again take time off to do just that:

Climb to higher ground, other high places, other homes of the gods — leaving the plains, the low ground of mundane anxieties to colleagues, whose stalwart support Derek now cherished as treasure…